**"I'm sorry," Gray whi** **face but not moving in for more.**

"For not being what you need. For not figuring it all out sooner."

"Gray..." Sage's whisper floated away on the wind before he could hear intention in the tone.

"I'm sorry for loving you so selfishly, and for accepting your love, for letting you love me..." Maybe the stiff scotch had loosened his tongue. It hadn't rattled his brain.

Sage's hands flew up to Gray's as he started to let go of her. She held his hands against her, staring up at him. "You didn't let me love you, Gray. You had absolutely no say in that matter. The choice was mine. You don't get to take that away from me," she said as he stared down at her.

Standing there, so close, with the rest of their bodies not touching, those seconds were everything. And not enough.

"Loving you then...helped grow me into the woman I am now." She was staring at his lips. Didn't want to look away.

Gray wasn't moving. Just stood there, staring at her, his expression still holding pain. A lot of it. And she leaned forward. Doing what a woman did.

She put her lips to his, to kiss the pain away.

After that...was a blur.

Dear Reader,

Welcome to *Her Christmas Wish*! I love it here and have a feeling you will, too! Many years ago, there was this exclusive resort on a cliff overlooking the ocean outside of San Diego. The resort had a long private drive down to the ocean, where there were cottages on the beach for the rich and famous to rent without fear of paparazzi or being approached. The resort eventually closed and the cottages went into disrepair.

But they've been rescued! A new owner has bought the cottages on Ocean Breeze and is offering them for individual resale. The drive down to the beach is still private. The two-mile stretch of beach is situated between two cliffs and is a great place for the resident dogs to run free and play with each other. And their owners are all becoming friends. There's so much going on in their lives!

These people have become family to me, and they're eager to bring you into the fold. First up is a second-chance love story that ends well! There's a set of twins with cottages on the beach, a writer, a couple of lawyers, at least one veterinarian, a pediatrician, a dancer and so many more people waiting to share their lives with us. So, please, come in, relax and become a valued part of Ocean Breeze.

*Tara Taylor Quinn*

# HER CHRISTMAS WISH

## TARA TAYLOR QUINN

Harlequin
SPECIAL EDITION

**Harlequin®**
**SPECIAL EDITION™**

Recycling programs
for this product may
not exist in your area.

ISBN-13: 978-1-335-40211-0

Her Christmas Wish

Copyright © 2024 by TTQ Books LLC

For questions and comments about the quality of this book, please contact us at CustomerService@Harlequin.com.

TM and ® are trademarks of Harlequin Enterprises ULC.

Harlequin Enterprises ULC
22 Adelaide St. West, 41st Floor
Toronto, Ontario M5H 4E3, Canada
www.Harlequin.com

**Printed in Lithuania**

MIX
Paper | Supporting
responsible forestry
FSC® C021394

**Books by Tara Taylor Quinn**

**Harlequin Special Edition**

***The Cottages on Ocean Breeze***

*Her Christmas Wish*

***Furever Yours***

*Love Off the Leash*

***Sierra's Web***

*A Family-First Christmas*
*Old Dogs, New Truths*
*Their Secret Twins*
*Her Best Friend's Baby*
*Reluctant Roommates*
*His Lost and Found Family*

To my family at Harlequin, the ones I've known for thirty years and the ones I have yet to meet. The work you do, the talents you share and the long hours you put in help so many people find warmth, relaxation, happiness and hope. Together, we keep love alive in hearts and minds every single day.

# Chapter One

The smile left Sage's face. Wiped away by the serious, and slightly worried, expression her twin brother was wearing.

He'd been smiling, too. Laughing out loud, even, as he'd walked over to her porch from the beach just a couple of feet away. The concerned look in his eyes was clearly for her.

Which would have been understandable if she had anything troubling on her plate. Scott could read her better than most.

As she could him.

Filling with terror, she sat up, her gaze swinging out at the beach to make sure that Leigh, her whole life, was still there. Laughing infectiously. Throwing her entire pudgy four-year-old body into the game of catch she was playing with Scott's corgi, Morgan.

It was a game doctors had never thought the little girl would be able to play after her premature birth. Leigh's chances hadn't been good.

"Iris is good with her," Scott said, sitting on the edge of the second high-backed rocker on Sage's newly built wooden porch. His gaze followed hers out to the foursome just yards away.

Tall where Sage was short, her brother leaned forward, his elbows on his knees as he watched the longtime Ocean Breeze resident—a well-known professional photographer—playing with Leigh and Morgan, and her own canine companion and sole housemate, Angel. A miniature collie.

He was stalling…

"What's wrong?"

Glancing over at her, his blue eyes identical to her own, Scott almost as quickly glanced away.

Sage set down the applications she'd been going over. As the newest partner in Bryon and Bryon, the corporate law firm with which she'd been employed since passing the California State Bar ten years before, one of her duties was hiring new associates.

It was a task she was taking as seriously as she took everything in life.

Watching her twin, another shard of fear shot through her. "Tell me, Scott. Is it your health? Something go horribly wrong on a case?" As lead prosecutor for the county, there were any number of things that could have popped up in that arena.

All of them manageable.

Her brother was straight up. No way he'd be involved in anything illegal.

Scott looked at her again. "It's not me," he said. "Well, not directly. I kind of made an offer, but I need your okay first."

The hard grip on her stomach softened a little. "You've got it, whatever it is," she told him. "What are you buying?"

A surfboard was her immediate, albeit silent, answer to herself. A wannabe star surfer from the time he could walk, her brother bought boards. The best. Determined to master the sport. But never did.

He was too tall. Too lanky. And just not a good enough surfer to make the boards wise investments. Which wasn't why he'd be coming to her. He knew she worried about the damned thing flying up and conking him on the back of the head.

"I'm not buying anything," he said. "I offered my spare bedroom to an old friend in grave need..."

Sage threw up a hand, shaking her head. "Then offer it," she said, cutting him off. "You don't need me to tell you that. Or need my permission..."

Her own soliloquy broke off midstream as an early October breeze off the ocean rustled Scott's thick blond hair, and he didn't immediately reach up to run his fingers through it. Something he'd been doing as long as she could remember. As though being out of place drew attention to the unconventionally longish strands.

Unconventionally long for a county prosecutor—and for their father's son, when they'd been younger. Not at all long compared to California standards.

"Who is it?" she asked, after studying him silently. But she knew.

Understanding floated over her first. Then started down, slowly flowing around her, but not touching anywhere she could feel.

As though she was being prepared from afar.

"He has to stay local, sis. He's innocent and is fighting to get his life back. To open a new clinic. Affordable vet care is too hard to come by these days and animals are suffering because of it. Owners are either opting not to get regular care for their pets, or just plain can't afford to do so. He's changed hotels numerous times. The press, and clients who'd trusted and felt betrayed, continue to hound him. He has nowhere else to go."

He wasn't telling her anything she didn't already know. She was a corporate attorney. The news of the local chain of veterinary clinics being shuttered after an employee veterinarian was caught writing hundreds of fraudulent prescriptions for people over a period of years was fodder for gossip all over the firm. Not because Grayson Bartholomew and GB Animal Clinics were clients. They very purposefully, she was sure, were not. But because attorneys all had to ask what they'd do if a client was found in a similar situation.

It was human nature to be shocked. To talk about it. To theorize.

Scott hadn't just told her anything she didn't know. But he also hadn't told her who he was talking about.

He hadn't needed to.

Her and Grayson's broken engagement had been the one major disappointment Sage had inadvertently given her and Scott's millionaire, very strict, powerful father.

Taking a deep breath at the thought of a powerful man gone too young, reminding herself that she was her father's daughter, Sage found a pretty decent smile for her brother. Mostly by glancing out at Leigh and letting her adopted miracle completely fill her focus. "I'm fine if Gray stays with you, Scott. It's been ten years. And I've got the life I always wanted."

When she was sure she could trust herself to put oomph from inside her to the words coming out of her, she turned the smile on her brother. "When's he moving in?"

Scott didn't return her smile. He studied her instead. Intensely. And then, still watching, said, "As soon as I call him and tell him it's okay."

Her heart flipped and then flopped. A perfectly normal reaction considering she hadn't seen the man in a decade.

Residue from the past.

Muscle memory from a time when she'd thought her heart, her ability to trust in love, had been irreparably broken.

"He knows I live here?" Her twin had sworn to her that the few times he and Gray met up at various functions, neither of them ever mentioned her.

Didn't mean the man couldn't have done a search on property records.

"He does now."

Scott's look was forthright.

"You told him."

Her brother nodded. "Right after I blurted the only offer that made logical sense—that he come to stay on Ocean Breeze. He knows I live in a renovated cottage on a private beach with a gated entrance at the only, very steep, road in."

"Everyone who's lived in Rockcliff more than a minute knows about the cottages on Ocean Breeze," she said laconically. "And since Gray grew up in town…"

She was forestalling the information that was trying to hit her brain. And then it was there. "Gray knows you're asking me."

"Yep."

That one word shaped her right up. Stiffened her spine. And, as she glanced at Leigh, her confidence and intent. "Then by all means, call him. Let him know he's welcome. I don't blame him for choosing lifestyle over family. On the contrary, I appreciate the fact that he came clean before the wedding. Granted, it would have been nice if he'd figured things out before all the invitations had been sent out. Or, before he asked me to marry him. But still, he could have waited until after we were married, then have cleaned up in the divorce and saved himself years of hard work to earn the kind of life he craves…"

She shut up before Scott figured out she was rambling, rather than giving a viable, thought-out argument. As a good lawyer would do.

Her brother didn't stand, as she wished he would. Instead, he sat with her.

Pressure built up inside, creating butterflies in her stomach and itching under her skin. Causing her to reach out a hand, laying her fingers on the back of his tanned skin, and say, "Seriously, Scott, call him. I've been following the case. He's a good man and doesn't deserve what's happening to him. Not on any level. It's a good thing, you're helping him."

The words came forth, giving her brother part of the truth mixing with the rest of the equally accurate tumult that had been brewing inside her since the news of GB Animal Clinics' legal woes hit the airwaves.

All of which slid to dark recesses when Leigh's excited pitch hit her. "Mama, look!"

The four-year-old, curly-haired blonde, ball in hand, reared back her right hand and threw with what looked like a world of might. So much so she stumbled and almost fell.

The ball, which hadn't been released until her palm was facing downward, hit the ground and rolled a couple of feet in front of her. At which time, Morgan and Angel raced each other to reach the prize first.

"Good job, sweetie!" All the joy within Sage tumbled out at the words.

"Angew got it!" Leigh squealed then, clapping her hands together and bending over with glee as she giggled. "Did you see that, Mama?"

Without waiting for a response, the little girl was off stumbling across the sand as quickly as her feet would take her and grabbed the ball again.

"It's Morgan's turn now!" she called out to Iris, rolling her *r*'s in the babyish talk that caught at Sage's emotional strings every single time.

With her heart overflowing, Sage was able to look her brother straight in the eye and say, "I've got what I've always wanted right here." She glanced out at Leigh, at the cottage behind her and at him. "My own family and a home filled with love. Call him. I'll be fine."

And in that moment, she fully believed she would be.

Grayson wanted to move into a cottage bedroom on Ocean Breeze about as badly as he wanted to live his recurring nightmare of waking up naked in court.

Temporarily bunking at the home of the attorney who at one time had been his best buddy in the world had seemed like a dream come true when Scott had first made the offer. Gray had never, for one second, considered that Scott would do such a thing unless there was no chance of Sage ever visiting him there, even for a second. Gray's failed relationship with the man's twin sister had effectively diminished their friendship.

Something that had been slowly building again, as years passed, first with chance meetings, then with the surf lessons like the ones that had drawn the two of them together as teenagers. Gray being a better than decent surfer, and Scott just…not. But determined to keep trying.

They'd been meeting up for beers every now and then, too, over the past couple of years. Sharing travel and women stories. The latter mostly embellished, of course. One-upping each other.

Bragging about work accomplishments.

Real ones.

All possible with the unspoken caveat that Sage's name was never mentioned, nor was any reference to her existence ever made. Period.

Including that day, when the two men had met for lunch and Scott had offered Gray a place to hide out. Gray had already had his luxury SUV loaded with hanging clothes and the couple of suitcases he'd figured he'd need for an extended stay on the beach, had been about ready to lock up his lovely cliffside home and speed by what paparazzi were after him that day, when Scott had called to tell him to hold off heading to Ocean Breeze. He'd had a confession to make first.

When Gray had found out that Sage also owned one of renovated cottages in the row—what used to be, fifty years ago, part of a luxury resort—he'd told Scott not to bother. He'd continue to move from hotel to hotel, until the rabid social-media hounds got bored with trying to go viral with footage of him.

After his ex-associate's case went to trial and the press moved on to other hot news, putting an end to one faction of the months-long nightmare.

Scott's response had been almost a challenge to Gray's ability to be around Sage. Telling him he was certain Sage had moved on so completely that having Gray in the vicinity wouldn't create an issue. Which was why he'd given the invitation without even thinking about Sage's reaction. But if it was going to be a problem with Gray...

Of course, he'd had to insist that it would not be.

And was fairly certain he was right. Just...seeing her again, with eggs splattered all over his face, his great life he'd left her to have in a shambles. Not quite the way he'd ever envisioned the moment.

But as he pulled up to the gated entrance, typed in the code Scott had given him and headed down the steep road to Ocean Breeze, the small beach neighborhood he'd only seen from a distance, he had to nod. Scott had been right. The chance to get some peace—and have private beach access—was just what he needed.

He'd just avoid the part of the beach where Sage lived. Staying away from her shouldn't be a problem. In ten years' time, they'd never sought each other out.

Not even when her overbearing, way too strict father had followed his submissive wife to the grave thirteen years after she'd died of lung disease. Scott had called Gray the night after the funeral. Asking him if he wanted to meet for a beer. The man had talked about the rigidity with which he'd grown up, the hard times, but the way he'd loved the man, too, as he'd slowly sipped a couple of beers. But he'd never mentioned his twin. Not in the stories from childhood, nor from the funeral.

And as hungry as Gray had been for word that she was coping, he hadn't asked. At one time, he'd have been privy to every single emotion and word Sage had to share.

But he wasn't the guy she'd needed.

And by that same token, she hadn't been the woman for him, either.

No matter how much he'd tried to give himself time, to convince himself otherwise.

They'd fit so perfectly in so many ways. Outside the bedroom, too, which had been quite a stunner for him. Both career-driven, getting doctorate degrees, wanting Rockcliff to be their permanent address, in a luxury home with an ocean view...

Both caring that their work benefited others, not just themselves.

Even just chilling in front of a movie...he'd enjoyed life more when she'd been around.

Until he hadn't.

They'd wanted so many of the same things. And she'd wanted more. Things he didn't want at all. The pressure had been too much.

He'd kept hoping that she'd see him, understand that while she'd had every opportunity growing up, he'd had none yet. He needed the chance to explore those opportunities and make them all possible for himself. He wanted her to love him enough to change her life's dream just a little bit.

Or love him enough not to need more.

He'd wanted her in his life so badly, he'd held on to the possibility until the very last minute…

That last moment had come and gone. Long ago.

Parking in the slot next to Scott's snazzy red sports car, Gray grabbed his two bags from the trunk and rolled them up to the cottage's back door.

He'd worked too hard for too long to give up on the life he'd built. The life he'd always wanted. And if hanging on—while he figured out how to rise up out of the ashes in the most expedient and cost-efficient way—meant he had to share a private drive with Sage Martin, then that was what he'd do.

He'd already faced the hardest challenge of his life.

With great success.

He'd moved on without her.

And somewhere along the way, he'd gotten over her, too.

## Chapter Two

Finding Scott's place empty, Gray took a second to look around, and then moved his stuff into the clearly unoccupied bedroom before texting Scott to let him know he'd arrived.

He'd stopped for a case of beer on his way, and helped himself to one as he headed out the back door to the porch Scott had had built, separating the cottage from the sand, to get a long, healthy breath of ocean air.

The balmy, seventy-degree October air did not disappoint. If not for the dress attire he still wore, he'd have headed straight down to the water.

Better, anyway, that he wait to find out which cottage down the way belonged to Sage before venturing out.

Scott had assured him, during his initial sales pitch, that the cottages were all far enough apart to provide good privacy. They would have been since they'd been built to house the rich and famous in a more private setting than the resort's hotel could offer. His friend hadn't embellished that point a bit. Looking to both sides, he took in beach as far as he could see. Saw some people, but could make out only the most basic features.

Far enough away to give him back a small sense of personal space. Of freedom from hell.

A collie caught his attention to the right. She had a straight stance and kept perfect pace at the heel of the man who was heading down to the water. Gray watched as the two reached wet sand together. And then the girl was running and diving into a wave, as though she'd been born a dolphin. He watched, amazed, grinning.

And nodded when man and collie came out of the water together, to do it all over again.

With one hand in his pocket, he raised his full bottle to his mouth. Took a long sip. Scott had been right. Ocean Breeze was going to be good for him.

His text app pinged. Scott. Saying he was talking to Iris and would be right up.

*Iris.* A woman Gray was eager to meet. The gorgeous, platonic friend of the playfully womanizing confirmed bachelor Scott had become.

Gray had waited for months for Scott to admit he'd slept with the woman. But after three years of Scott and Iris being *just friends*, Gray was finally convinced his friend had no sexual interest in the woman, an anomaly given his flirtatious nature. Scott appreciated the female form even more than Gray did, if such a feat was possible.

Texting back, he told his friend to take his time. Thought about sitting back in one of the redwood porch chairs, but changed his mind. Standing tall, taking in long breaths of salty air, felt good. More right than anything had in too many months.

He noticed people come and go from various cottages, more like stick figures in the distance. He didn't let himself wonder if any of them were Sage. Didn't try to pick out her petite perfect form, or her long, wavy blond hair. Had no way of knowing if she was still as spritely as she'd been when he'd known her.

He saw Scott, though, coming up the beach. The man's six-foot-three-inch height gave him away to Gray.

And was part of the reason the prosecutor, no matter how hard he tried, was likely never going to be a proficient surfer.

A woman walked with him. Not Sage. Inches taller than Sage. She'd once told him that her brother's towering over her by a foot was a result of selective fetal growth restriction. Scott's placenta had "hogged the womb," she'd said with a grin.

Gray had had a womb all to himself, but at five-eleven he'd still ended up several inches shorter than his friend.

Two dogs ran up behind the pair. A miniature collie and Morgan, Scott's corgi—Gray's patient since her birth.

The miniature collie...would make the taller woman Iris. Gray nodded. Thought about going for a couple of beers, to have them ready when the two approached.

He turned, ready to do just that, when a little person came darting out across the sand—he assumed from one of the cottages.

A girl, judging by the long blond curls and pink frilly shorts and shirt. She must have called out to them, as the two stopped instantly and, as one, turned toward the child.

Expecting to see Scott falter, to step back and let his friend handle the child, Gray was shocked when Scott offered a hand to the little girl, and watched as the woman he presumed to be Iris did the same on the child's other side.

Mouth open, Gray watched as the threesome continued toward him.

Did Iris have a child?

Tipping back another sip of beer, Gray smiled. There was one mystery solved.

Scott didn't date women with children. And he didn't sleep with women he didn't date.

Still grinning, feeling lighter than he had in a while, Gray watched the trio, with the dogs darting around them. Picturing himself out on the beach, getting to know some of the many dog owners Scott had told him inhabited Ocean Breeze, Gray turned, thinking he'd change after all. Then another person appeared in the picture. Coming from what looked like a porch four cottages down. That far in the distance, he could see the building, but couldn't tell much about the place— except that it had a small green area between it and the beach.

One of the places with a small lawn that Scott had mentioned when he'd first bought his place.

Gray didn't pay much attention at first, when the person, in light-colored shorts and a short-sleeved shirt, approached the party. Scott had mentioned the unofficial dog owners club that fraternized regularly after work on the beach. Except that the blonde, a woman, who'd just joined, didn't seem to have a dog.

She started walking—next to Scott—and Gray's smile flattened. His entire being…flattened. Breathing flesh that didn't think. Or feel.

And didn't retreat.

He'd said he was on the porch drinking a beer. And he would be. Calm. Casual.

He'd have run into her sometime. At least from a distance.

Might as well get it over with.

He'd have liked more time, but he'd have liked a lot of things he didn't get in life. He didn't dwell on what he couldn't change. He moved on. And worked damned hard to gain a lot more of what he wanted than he'd lost.

Telling himself he was fine, ready, he took an extra-long sip of beer. To solidify the reassurance. The choice to be okay.

And saw the little girl drop hands with Iris and Scott, to run to Sage, throwing her arms up.

Grabbing up the little body, Sage settled her on one hip—in a hold that could only be deemed familiar. A regular occurrence.

His heart skipped. As if caught in glue, he stood, watched as Iris and Scott stopped and turned to the woman and child. Of all things, he noted the stillness of the dogs standing with them.

Sage waved and turned. Heading back toward the cottage with grass from which she'd come.

With the child.

And he knew.

The Iris mystery wasn't at all solved.

The child hadn't been hers.

Sage had moved on, too.

Had gotten what she'd wanted more than a life with him. She had a daughter.

Sage, his Sage, had become a mother, and Scott hadn't said a word.

Gray had had no idea.

Bound in a moment he couldn't escape, he watched her all the way to the cottage. And stared at the cheery-looking building even after Sage had taken her little girl inside.

Scott never talked about his sister, but being an uncle… that was something a guy might share…

Sage was a mother.

Gray was happy for her.

Genuinely happy.

For her.

But try as he might, he couldn't escape the disappointment crashing through him. Had he really thought, when enough time had passed and she still hadn't had the child she'd thought she'd had to have to be complete, that she'd someday settle for him?

Had he been willing to accept being settled for?

He was shocked. At himself, at the child, a vision of Sage as a mother, the knowledge that she'd become what he knew he didn't ever want to be—a parent. Gray couldn't just stand there.

Turning, he left his beer on the kitchen counter, got out to his SUV, and was partway up the drive before he stopped long enough to text Scott and let him know he'd be back in a bit.

That was all. He'd be back. Didn't say where he was going. Or why.

He didn't know where.

And the why? He couldn't explain his change of plans. Didn't completely understand them.

He just couldn't pretend that things were okay.

That he was.

Because they weren't.

And he wasn't.


Ten years without Grayson Bartholomew being mentioned in her personal life—and in a blink, he was on the premises.

Not in her actual cottage, but close enough.

Too close.

She hadn't seen him. Hadn't even glanced toward her brother's cottage.

But she'd known he was there. Could feel his presence like fingers walking up her spine.

And back down again.

Horrible.

And…something out-of-the-real-world good.

Which was worse than horrible. It was disastrous.

She could not, absolutely never, allow herself to fall back into her own sexual weakness for the man. The first time she'd done so had knocked her to her knees.

Maybe almost killed her.

She wouldn't have been on the beach at all. She'd taken Leigh inside the second she'd heard Scott say that Gray had texted that he was there.

At the time the text had come through they—the brother and sister duo—had been explaining to Iris—their closest mutual friend on the beach—just who Scott's temporary roommate was to the Martin twins. As opposed to who he was in the news, which Iris had already known. A friend from high school. One Scott had been in touch with on and off over the years. No mention that the man had once been more than a friend to Sage.

As soon as Sage had heard her brother read the text aloud, she'd gathered her daughter and had taken her in. But Leigh, watching the dogs out the back window, had seen them heading up the beach with Scott and Iris and, crying "I wanna walk with Uncle Scott," had run out.

She knew not to leave the house, ever.

Unless Uncle Scott and Morgan were on the beach. And then she had to get her mother's permission first.

Sage had gotten them safely back in the house with the five-foot-high lock latched on the beach-side door, something she'd had installed when she'd first moved in. She'd refrained from disciplining Leigh about waiting until Sage replied before running out. She needed time to calm herself down first, to make certain that she didn't let any of her own angst shower upon her little girl.

At bedtime, they'd had a brief talk about waiting until Sage said okay before Leigh followed through on her announced intentions.

And then they'd read a story. They'd cuddled.

And the four-year-old bundle of energy had fallen asleep with her head on Sage's shoulder.

Sage had tried to work after that. Couldn't get into the applications she'd been going over. None of them excited her.

Which was probably her answer.

But before she turned away a possibly stellar applicant, she needed to get outside her own drama and take one more look.

Just to be sure.

At the office. In the morning.

Sitting at the desk in her home office, she opened a contract that she'd be presenting to a client the next afternoon.

She had a lot invested, emotionally and mentally, in the client and the project. She figured it would get her mind out of the past and back into her own space. Except that she'd been over the contract for a final time that afternoon. There was nothing there to grab her.

Already on her computer, she clicked to the internet. Figured she'd look at how the market had closed for the day. Something she did every night before bed.

And had her attention immediately caught by a headline on her home screen news feed.

GB Animal Clinics had permanently closed.

The news was a couple of weeks old. No reason to be showing up that night.

A sign to her?

More like a product of the artificial intelligence that tracked previous searches.

Because, yeah, she'd looked up Grayson Bartholomew's business when the news of illegal drug trafficking had first hit the headlines.

Months before.

And had kind of been following bits and pieces.

Because of talk around the office.

She'd never let herself read fully.

Couldn't take a chance that some inner, younger part of her would turn traitor on the mature, happy woman she'd become and latch on to his woes.

Want to help him.

Or worse, feel for him.

But hearing her twin read a text, telling her that Gray was right there on the beach, that very minute, in her brother's house...

She felt.

Too much.

Had to sort it all out.

And so, she did what she'd learned to do to survive all those years ago. She went into her head. Tackled life cerebrally.

She opened a news source she'd vetted enough times to trust its reporting. Typed in her search parameters. And beginning with articles from five months in the past, Sage started reading.

# *Chapter Three*

Gray stayed in his room until after Scott left for work that next morning. The only way he knew to deal with life was to take what he had and make good come out of it. What he didn't do, ever, was cry on others' shoulders.

Seeing Sage with that little girl, living the life she'd been certain she'd been meant to live…had been one of the tough moments. And he hadn't yet found the good that would come out of it.

Somewhere in the middle of the night, just before he'd dozed off, he'd figured out that the good had already come. For her. He'd freed her to be happy.

And for him, too. If he'd married her, he'd have given his all to make the marriage work, to keep her happy. Even, perhaps, fathering a child with her. Giving up the life he knew he'd be good at for one that he didn't see himself living.

Trapping himself beneath a weight he knew would suffocate him, one breath at a time. He was dedicated to contributing to society. To giving to others.

Even to sharing life with someone. As an equal.

The idea of being responsible for another human being… of having someone dependent upon *him*, of being the direct overseer, even partly, of the shaping of a young life…gave him the cold sweats every single time.

And yet…there was that buried part of him that had figured that if neither he nor Sage were married when they were in their forties, maybe they could be each other's backup plan.

It had been his way of coping. He'd realized that as he'd driven around the night before, revisiting spots where he'd made memories with Sage. Spots he'd avoided ever since.

Like the hidden alcove formed by cliff rock on the San Diego beach where he'd kissed her for the first time.

He'd needed some time to say goodbye. To accept the closure he'd thought he'd gained years before. And he needed to be certain he was done grieving a pipe dream he hadn't fully recognized he'd held on to before he faced Scott Martin again.

He didn't have much time since he was staying in Martin's home. He couldn't avoid the prosecutor's scrutiny for long. No way he wanted the freakishly astute man to conclude that Gray still had feelings for Sage.

He didn't.

Not in the light of day.

And if the previous night's sojourn had been as successful as he was thinking it was, he'd just let go of any veiled yearnings attached to the past as well.

With his path more clearly in front of him, Gray was finalizing his decision of which of the Realtors he'd interviewed to hire when he got a text from Scott. Asking if he could give Sage Gray's cell number.

And while Gray was tense all over again, thinking about why she'd need it, he texted back granting permission. With him moving in four doors down from her, albeit very temporarily, on a shared private beach, he'd look ridiculous withholding the number.

As though he couldn't bear to be personally contacted by his ex-fiancée.

He could bear it. But wasn't at all fond of the idea.

Why did Sage need his number? What could she possibly want from him?

And then—when Scott replied with Sage's number so Gray would recognize it when he saw it—it hit him. He was dealing with two extremely bright lawyers. Twins on the same wavelength.

Taking care of business.

If anything, Sage would want to lay out the terms by which the two of them would coexist on the beach without actually spending time in each other's company. He opened the text that came through from the number Scott had just texted to him.

Business to discuss. If interested, please respond accordingly.

He hadn't talked to her in more than ten years. But he was staying with her twin brother, with whom she was obviously still close since she lived just doors away from him. And she'd given him *please respond accordingly*?

Yep. She must be setting up guidelines that would keep them both at peace under the potentially uncomfortable situation.

Open to discuss.

His response was sent in seconds.

As was her return message.

I have an opening this morning at ten. Can you be at my office then?

A second text immediately after gave him her address. That made sense. How could he know if he could make it unless she let him know how far he'd have to travel? He glanced at his watch.

Ten. It was already a little past nine.

Less than an hour? She was setting up a business appointment with such little warning to the other party? He hadn't even showered yet. He headed that way as he typed.

And then stopped typing when another message from her popped up.

I rescheduled another matter.

Which made him not an I'll-squeeze-you-in-if-you-can-make-it-but-otherwise-forget-it proposition but a priority?

Looking back at his screen, he read what he'd already typed, added the period at the end and hit Send.

I'll be there.

He'll be here.

*Oh, God.*

Pacing her office, worrying that her navy skirt was too slimline, the tailored cream blouse too…she didn't know what, her thick fourteen-karat-gold hoop earrings too bold. Sage stopped at the small mirror over the small table at one end of her maroon leather couch. Up close, she got half of her head at once. Moved around to check the whole thing.

Blond hair could be a bit less…thick and wavy. Should have cut it short.

Lipstick needed to be reapplied.

Or not.

Why would she want to draw attention to her lips? She

marched back over to her desk, grabbed a tissue and wiped the color off.

And chewed her lower lip as she went back over to check the damage.

She had use of the private bath just outside her office door. Shared it with just two other partners who were both out of their offices at the moment.

The mirror she was using wasn't meant for assessing looks. It was a piece of art, surrounded by stones and jewels, all natural. Something she'd picked up years before at an outdoor fair because she'd liked the colors. And the idea that if she could see into the center of anything, she could figure out a way to understand it.

Thinking of law issues, of course.

Not past mistakes.

Her lips looked…naked. Kissed.

Licking them, she went for her lipstick. Saw the clock on her computer screen. 9:45. She had another fifteen minutes to wait.

Glanced at the files she'd amassed the night before.

The plethora of notes she'd jotted.

She should use the quarter hour to go over it all again. Allow the possibility that other things might yet occur to her.

Instead, with her stomach knotting, she grabbed the keys to her office door, locked it behind her, pushed the elevator button and waited for the door to open.

Leigh's private day care, hosted by the elite high-rise building that rented the top floor to Sage's firm, was on the third floor.

And had parent viewing windows, so she could see her daughter in class but wouldn't be seen.

The elevator dinged.

The door opened.

And Grayson Bartholomew stepped out.

Fully suited, including red power tie.

Fifteen minutes early.

Forcing Sage to take a step back to give him room to exit.

Not at all how she'd planned their first meeting in over ten years to play out.

Of course she looked gorgeous. Gray had expected that.

But the instant and fully inappropriate physical reaction he had to that petite, perfectly shaped, womanly frame was a surprise.

Highly unwelcome.

And thankfully unnoticed. He'd buttoned the jacket of the suit coat he generally only wore to weddings and funerals as soon as he'd exited his car.

Not for privacy, but for an equally pathetic reason.

He'd wanted to appear successful, wealthy and untouchable.

Commanding respect.

Or, at least, appearing more important than he'd ever been back when she'd known him.

She'd taken a step back the second the door had opened and she'd seen him there. Had turned as though to head down the hall. "You're early," she said, leaving him a view of a backside he knew almost better than his own. If you considered the number of times his gaze had feasted on hers naked and compared it to the times he'd actually seen his own butt in the nude.

"There was less traffic than I expected—I hit every green light and I didn't want to leave you waiting." He gave her far more than a minimal "yes" response, which would have been all that was necessary under the circumstances.

As though they were still the couple who told each other

more than they ever relayed to anyone else. In more detail, at any rate.

Good to note. Something he'd pay attention to in any future dealings. Make sure it didn't happen again.

He could have taken an extra step, walked beside her, but Gray chose to follow wherever she led down the hall. Giving himself a chance to regroup before another chance to be face-to-face presented itself.

He hadn't been prepared. Hadn't thought for one second that she'd be at the elevator to meet him. He'd thought he'd get a lay of the land, the firm's layout. Hadn't known he'd be shown to a private elevator that accessed the executive suite portion of the top floor. But as he walked through a quiet hall, and passed a corridor, he could see the glass wall that separated them from the rest of the thriving firm.

A flash of Sage's face as he'd first seen it when the elevator door opened hit him. And he realized what he'd been too shocked to take in the first time around.

She hadn't been expecting to see him, either.

As evidenced by her *you're early.* She hadn't been there to meet him. She'd been on her way somewhere else.

And hadn't been pleased by the interruption to her plan.

The thought gave him a hint of a jaunt to his step.

They were on equal, uneven footing.

He could work with that.

She couldn't work with him. Shouldn't have reached out. She'd made a huge mistake.

It seemed to be a habit with her, an unhealthy pattern, where Grayson Bartholomew was concerned.

And the lipstick, dammit. She still had it in her hand with her keys. Had thought, maybe, if Leigh was just coming in from the playroom, she could slip in a quick hug and kiss…

She was going to have to move the lipstick to her left hand to use the keys in her right to unlock the door.

Or risk dropping the tube at Grayson's feet.

She'd been planning to show him, with complete professionalism, how far she'd come without him. By having him in her new partner office, yes.

But also by being able to offer him some expertise in an area where he had great need. All without any sign at all that seeing him again was having any effect on her.

Instead, she was going to fumble with lipstick? While she wasn't wearing any? With a meeting between them just minutes away, as though she'd been on her way to put some on for him?

He had to go.

Before she made more of a fool of herself.

She'd look like a complete idiot if she told him she'd changed her mind. He was there, on less than an hour's notice, at her behest.

And she hadn't arranged any kind of escape call.

Hadn't even thought of the prearranged plan to have a friend call in case she needed an excuse to leave an uncomfortable date. Not since college.

Really?

She was a grown, very successful woman. A respected partner in a well-known law firm. A responsible, dedicated mother.

She was going to let one lone man unnerve her?

Honesty was her policy. In both her business and personal life.

She couldn't tell the man she'd changed her mind because he was setting her back a decade.

Likewise, if she suddenly remembered some other commitment, he'd know she was chickening out.

They'd been walking for many seconds without any conversation at all. Her door was just ahead.

Think! Do something!

"This is it," she said, shocked at how normal her voice sounded. Stared at her door for a split second, frozen, made immobile by indecision. What was she going to do?

Her gaze focused. Saw the gilded sign on her door bearing her name.

Brought her hands together at the doorknob. Slid her lipstick into her left hand as her key slid into the lock.

Turned the key, reached for the knob.

And dropped the tube of lipstick on Grayson Bartholomew's expensive, shiny black leather shoe.

# *Chapter Four*

She hadn't been waiting for him.

She'd been going to meet someone…?

The lipstick.

Another man.

Sage had a lover somewhere in the building and had been going for a quick tryst before meeting up with the ex-lover who'd walked out on her right before their wedding.

The potential facts laid out before him as though in huge letters on a movie screen as he followed Sage into her impressively windowed, decent-size office.

Her high-heeled pumps making no sound on the plush beige carpet.

She had a view of the ocean in the far distance.

And a lover in the building.

Which was a good thing, it occurred to him as he sat in the leather armchair she offered in the conversation seating at the opposite end of the room from her desk. A current lover was just the stake he needed in the heart of whatever nonsense had struck him the night before.

Seeing her on the beach.

With that cute little kid on her hip.

Her daughter's father…

Where was the guy?

Did he work in the building? Had the lipstick been for him?

She offered Gray a bottle of water and at his "I'm good, thank you," proceeded over to her desk.

The farthest spot in the room from him.

She picked up a folder.

Was she planning to address him from there? While standing behind her desk?

Like he was a recalcitrant schoolkid in class?

He turned his focus on the view in the distance. The ocean.

Whatever she needed him to sign, agreeing to keep his distance from her, he'd sign. Probably some form of unofficial restraining order, that would become official somehow if he disavowed it in any way.

If he couldn't be near her, it meant that she couldn't be near him, either. Or she'd give him just cause to disobey the order. He might not be a hotshot lawyer, but he held a doctorate degree just like she did. He knew things.

And could figure out others.

He watched the city move in the nearer distance down below. The birds flying against an azure-blue sky. She hadn't started her spiel yet.

He kept his hands relaxed on his thighs. Intending to show her that he had no skin to lose where she was concerned.

She was sharp. If he allowed her to call the shots, following her lead, she'd get it.

Quickly, he hoped. He was a little unclear just how much time he could give himself before he started to show some obvious tension.

By politely asking her to get on with it so he could get the hell out of there.

He smelled her perfume before he heard her approach. Glanced her way long enough to see her settle on the couch, but focused on the paperwork she'd set down on the table.

Not one folder.

Several.

A yellow pad, blank, lay across the top of her skirted knees.

What the hell?

Were they going to negotiate, line by line, what they could and couldn't do over the time he was on Ocean Breeze?

He leaned forward, his hands planted firmly on the chair arms. Ready to stand and let her know he'd find another place to stay.

"I think I have a pretty good understanding of what you're facing here." The voice, so not anything he'd ever heard from Sage, had him settling back in his chair as his gaze lifted straight to her eyes.

They were looking right at him.

But not as though she was seeing him—the guy he'd been to her.

She was treating him like a stranger.

Her tone had been kind. And completely, 100 percent impersonal.

Not at all confrontational.

Or…

Had she just said *he*? What *he* was facing?

Not them?

Was she trying to tell him that she knew he'd been thrown for a loop, seeing her again, but that she was completely unaffected?

Because of lipstick man?

As he continued to stare at her, she started talking again. Laying bare the atrocities that had imploded his life and consumed most every one of his waking thoughts over the past months. Stripping him, fact by fact, until he felt completely bare, raw, sitting there, alone with her, in her office.

He'd never, ever have pinned her as a cruel person.

But she'd done him one favor, at least.

He might be allegorically naked, but he no longer had even a hint of a hard-on.


The morning was one disaster after another. Not following the plan in any way.

Floundering in her huge fail, trying to stay afloat, she just continued to do what she knew—lawyering.

And making matters worse.

She was supposed to have offered coffee, which she'd planned to have already brewed, but she'd had a case of nerves, he'd come early and seeing him in that suit…seeing him in person…she'd lost all ability to think straight.

To remember the plan.

Instead of a kind *hello*, a polite *it's nice to see you*, issued with a nonchalance that would show that the past didn't matter to her—that she was long over it—she'd walked in silence and dropped her lipstick on his shoe.

In her office, hoping that the atmosphere would set her straight, she'd stood behind her desk having a hint of a panic attack.

Had forced herself to take deep, calming breaths while the silence strangled her.

Finished with her initial summary, she looked at the man she intended to help and saw…

A man she'd once loved so deeply—and been so devastated by—she'd sworn off getting that close to a partner ever again.

"What I need next is for you to fill in the details that weren't in the news. Files. Contracts. Employee statutes. Access to account records…" Her voice faltered as his frown grew from confused to…something more.

He shook his head. "What are you doing?"

"I'm trying to help. I'm a corporate attorney. A damned good one. This is my area of expertise…"

The man swung a suited arm like a model at a car fair, showing her the expanse of his chest, as he said, "This is far above my pay grade. My assets are frozen."

He glanced pointedly at the table filled with files, which she'd told him were all from his case. The reading she'd done the night before. Which had included the frozen asset information.

And then looked up at her. Did he think she was some kind of lovesick girl who'd had to glom on to the suitor who'd said he loved her but then rejected her?

Gritting her teeth for a second, she held his gaze. Took a deep breath. "I apologize for my abruptness." The words came out, feeling…okay. "I've purposely stayed away from news of your case," she admitted then. "But when Scott told me why you'd be staying with him, I spent the evening familiarizing myself with the details."

"To make sure your brother wasn't harboring a criminal?"

She shook her head. Frowned. His response had been… personal. "Of course not. Scott's a stellar attorney. He doesn't need my expertise. You do."

*There.* If he wanted to be personal, she could put it right out there. "Your assets are frozen, your attorney can't represent you, personally, because he has to represent the corporation, GB Animal Clinics. You've been completely exonerated, but your business is permanently shuttered. Your image has taken a huge hit. And at some point, your personal finances are going to start showing some pain." Other than that last assumption, the rest was textbook.

With a bit of a shrug, accompanied by that nod of his head that she used to love, he said, "I'm aware."

He hadn't accepted her help. Or thanked her for the offer, even.

She wasn't going to beg. Had been recalcitrant about getting involved at all. Just… "With you staying close…and us, our past… I just thought it best if our association was a business one." She blurted the truth she'd meant to utter to no one.

Because it acknowledged that she had a problem with him joining their small private neighborhood. Even briefly.

Which made it look like she wasn't completely over him.

Opening her mouth to assert her claim, since she'd opened the door and had to get it slammed shut immediately, her words were cut off when Gray said, "Maybe you should hear the details that aren't in the news before you solidify your offer."

She stared. He was accepting her plan? At least preliminarily? Giving them a way to coexist without the past seeping all over them? "That's fair," she told him.

And then thought of his initial statement. The expanse of chest that had been revealed as he'd motioned around her office. "And I'm offering to take on the case pro bono," she told him, quickly continuing. "The firm's bylaws state that every partner must take on a certain percentage of pro-bono work—part of a give back to the community mandate—and I'm under the gun here to choose a project."

*Project.* What the hell? She saw his eyes harden as she said the word.

"I apologize," she told him with heartfelt sincerity, looking him straight in the eye. "It's a term used internally to designate all non-money-generating work we do. We have a general project board, and we each have project lists. For instance, the most pressing project on my list right now is to hire a new associate…"

She heard the rambling. Let it attempt to save her.

Or him.

She wasn't really clear which. Just knew that she'd blundered and had to make it right. Gray grew up in an apartment complex that the city had called the projects. Had been born to a single mother who'd dropped out of high school to have him. And who'd eventually left him with his aging grandmother when she was killed in a car accident.

Sage's words had faded. Her gaze locked with Gray's as he nodded. "It's okay, Sage," he told her.

And her body flooded with a warm, almost liquid, sensation that felt like an old friend. *Sage.* First time she'd heard her name in that way that melted her in a long, long time.

"I'm not eighteen and have nothing to prove anymore." His gaze left hers to fall down toward the files on the coffee table between them. "Not to myself, anyway."

"And not to a lot of others," she said, glancing at the top file. "You have a slew of clients—pet owners—who vouch for you. Those testimonies—used in a way that I vet fully, every step of the way, to make certain that there isn't even a hint of anything that could come back to bite you in a legal sense—can help you to rebuild your image. But first, we need to get a new corporation registered, draw up bylaws and practice procedures, with a solid, legally binding vetting process that allows you to hire and fire at the least infraction—for you, to ease your mind and any mistrust this experience might have caused you to have, but also for your customers. We'll put out a statement regarding the vetting process for each employee on your staff..."

His smile stopped her. She stared.

He shook his head. "Sorry," he said. "Vetting. Veterinarians..."

Reminded her of a glasses joke she'd heard while representing a firm of ophthalmologists…and she smiled, too. Glad to see that Gray still had his sense of humor.

Through his own turmoil.

But in her presence, too.

Vetting. Veterinarians. As plebeian as it was, it had made them both smile.

For the first time since she'd heard her twin mention Grayson Bartholomew's name on her porch, she had hope that she was going to get through the unexpected, and wholly unwelcome, reunion just fine.

# Chapter Five

He'd thought he was stripped bare.

Grayson buttoned a second button on his suit jacket as he bolstered himself to expose intimate details he'd given to no one. Something Sage Martin would figure out on her first time through his financials.

"My project for today is choosing a Realtor to sell my house." He started in easy. Sitting back, one hand resting lightly on the chair, the other up under his chin, as though he had nothing more pressing on him than the pondering of a happy, contented man.

Something he'd been right up until the world he'd created—the life he'd left Sage to build—had imploded.

The irony wasn't lost on him.

He'd left her to have a different life. Made it happen. Was thriving. And when it exploded around him, she was there to pick up the pieces?

He still hadn't wrapped his mind around the fact that she was actually sitting there offering to help. Rather than slapping him with a stay-away order.

Gray felt like he was in some kind of twilight zone as he played along until he got his mind back into gear and seriously considered how he was going to handle the situation.

Sage's open-mouthed stare wasn't helping the effort any. "Did you say you were selling your house?"

He nodded. Didn't see the need for any further embellishment on that one.

"But... I thought you were just staying with Scott because you needed a place to go where people weren't always at your door and windows, leaving things on your car...trying to get an interview...or go viral on social media..."

"I am."

"But..." Her frown, the small shake of her head, reminded him of the time he'd told her that he'd sold his favorite surfboard to buy her a pair of earrings. She'd loved the earrings. Hadn't known. But had missed his surfboard. Asked him where it was.

"Things are things, Sage." He repeated a rendition of what he'd told her then. "I crave nice ones. The best. But I don't grow emotional attachments to individual items. I'll find another house."

He wanted to believe that. Would get there.

The house on the cliff above the ocean. For the first time in his life, he'd...grown attached. To an inanimate object.

Her face flattened. Disapprovingly? With a flashback to how she'd never understood his lack of attachment in the past?

He'd bet the Realtor's fee that it wasn't because she was remembering the earrings. He'd never seen them again after he'd told her where his surfboard went.

"I own the house free and clear. I'm out of money. I have to sell."

The alarm on her face couldn't be faked. And didn't make him feel one whit better. "Out of money?" she asked, as though she couldn't imagine the horror.

He could, of course. But the lack of funds wasn't big on his scale of woes. Bills were pretty scarce now that he had nothing to pay for but utilities, phone, food and gas. Insurances were paid until the end of the year. Thankfully, he had no living beings dependent upon him.

He'd intended to let silence stretch as long as she needed, to give her time to assess, to reevaluate her desire to help him. But couldn't sit there much longer, watching her watch him.

It was like being under a damned microscope. She didn't know him at all anymore, of course, but how much of what she'd known still existed? Giving her information he wasn't freely offering?

"You have no money at all?"

He shrugged.

"Your three-month cushion is gone?"

She remembered that? Something he'd mentioned maybe once? He didn't even recall telling her about his habit of keeping liquid cash to pay three months' worth of bills.

"No." It was money that wasn't there. Couldn't be touched. A lesson repeated to him over and over from the grandmother who'd been cranky with pain, too old to be saddled with a healthy, active wannabe surfer boy, but who'd loved him wholeheartedly.

Thinking of the old woman who'd died the year before he met Sage seemed to put Gray on a clearer track. Reminded him who he was—not who they'd been...

When Sage shook her head, her hair fell around her shoulders. They seemed to sink beneath the weight. Weren't as straight as they had been. Like his news had taken the air out of her wings.

"I'm guessing now that you know I'm broke, you aren't as impressed by the good work I did all these years..." The words were beneath him. Unfair. Cruel.

She'd given him her whole heart when he'd been a pauper. Had never once even hinted at any kind of prenuptial agreement, even though she had a sizable trust from her mother.

But that deflated look…as though he'd disappointed her… got his dander up.

"That was unfair." She held his gaze, mostly because he made himself withstand the punishment.

"I know. Truth of the matter is I'm not all that eager to tell you what you're going to find when you go over the accounts."

"There better not be anything illegal hidden there." She sounded more like a parent warning a child than an attorney talking to a client.

"There isn't."

Sitting back, she took up her pen, poised over the legal pad that she'd angled, ready for writing, and settled more firmly on her lap.

Gray ran a hand over his face, sat back, dropped both hands on the chair arms again, really relaxed that time, as he gave up the fight.

"I didn't think big enough," he told her. Appreciated the way she focused, listening, and yet, when he paused after the dramatic opening statement, waited for him to collect his thoughts and go on.

"When I incorporated GB Animal Clinics—I opened a series of bank accounts."

Her nod didn't seem so much encouraging as it was an acceptance of the practice.

"One of the accounts, and only one, was in my name only. I'm the only signer on it. The firm's lawyer and, later, an accountant, had access to all the others. And as we grew, each clinic had its own spending account with the senior veterinarian a signer on that account."

So far, so good. She'd jotted a couple of things. Was still seemingly focused and on the job. But then, he hadn't gotten to the foolish part yet.

Rather, he had, but he hadn't yet exposed his very large, very immature, mistake.

"I opened the account when I hired the accountant who oversaw all of GB Animal Clinics' payroll, among other things. I have always been on salary, just like everyone else, with any proceeds being fed back into the business. As we became more successful, and at the advice of said accountant, I eventually set up a bonus plan for all clinic employees, on a tiered percentage rate. I was top tier, by five percent. The other senior veterinarians were five percent ahead of the veterinarians that worked for them and so forth down the line."

He was stalling. If she'd figured that out, she had the grace not to say so.

"My bonus, which grew into a substantial amount, was also deposited directly into the account with only my name on it."

Her pen held in midair, Sage said, "You're about to tell me that you didn't invest the money or put it in some kind of money market account. You just left it there."

She always had been sharp. "Yes." He said it straight-out. And then, not looking away, added, "Most of it. I invested a small amount. A sum I felt safe losing. It's what I've been living off for the past five months."

Sage didn't grimace or shake her head. She didn't send him a pitying glance. Instead, she wrote something and then said, "I need all the account information. My first challenge is going to be to get that one account unfrozen. It's legally your money. We can prove it's your money. We just need to get the judge to listen to reason…"

Gray stared at her. Just stared. She made it sound so easy. So doable.

"You're a corporate attorney, just like the two men I've had on my team for years. You have to represent the corporation, not me. That's why I'm selling my house. So that I can hire the best team I can find to represent me, personally."

She nodded. "I know the way the law works, Gray," she said, a slight smile on her lips. And in her voice, too.

Gaining her an extremely inappropriate nudge of appreciation from beneath his jacket. Which was where it stayed. And would stay. Completely undetected.

"I can sign on as your personal lawyer, representing you as you separate from the business you started. And our firm has experts we work with who can handle anything I'm not able to do. Either because it's not my field of expertise, or I end up with some kind of conflict. And I can help you establish a new corporation, to get you working as soon as humanly possible, so that we mitigate client loss."

He got that she wanted to help. And that she'd always lived with the stars shining over her. But… "Have you been listening? There's no money to start a business yet…" He'd already be working if there was any way he could be doing anything other than the volunteering he was doing at a couple of shelters in the city.

Until the case was settled, no other clinic would want his bad publicity. Nor would he ask them to take it on.

"One of our partners' area of expertise is start-up funding," she told him, making another note. Alight, suddenly, as though she'd had a fire smoldering that had just shot into life.

Reminding Gray of something he'd forgotten over the years.

That fire… He'd once been the match that lit up her glow.

And there he was, lighting it up again.

In an entirely different way, of course. Professional not personal.

But still…

For that second, it was nice.

* * *

Filled with adrenaline and determination, with purpose, Sage asked Gray—as soon as he'd turned over access to his accounts—to give her a couple of hours. Telling him that she'd get back with him after she'd had a chance to look things over.

He agreed to keep his phone handy.

He hadn't agreed to accept her help.

She purposely hadn't asked, figuring him for more of a no than a yes at that point.

Because he didn't realize that help really was possible. Or didn't think people would help him unless he had money. The man had always been infuriatingly self-sufficient.

You could tell a whole lot by a man's financials. When Gray was in town, he ordered lunch from a place by the first of the GB Animal Clinics, six and sometimes seven days a week. He ate out at least four of those nights—usually upscale places with well-known chefs.

He had regular bar tabs, once or twice a week, but not high enough to indicate more than a few drinks. And not always at the same places. On the contrary, they were all over San Diego and her northern suburbs, including Rockcliff.

Did he still prefer beer? Scott had always been a beer drinker. Their father had preferred scotch. Only the best, perfectly aged. And Sage...sometimes in the evenings, after Leigh was in bed, she'd pour herself half a shot of the expensive whiskey. Not on the rocks like her father had taken it. She put ice in the glass, and a whole lot of water, too. And sipped slowly. Appreciating every swallow like she used to savor Gray's touch...

His grocery bills were high—which didn't make a lot of sense with all the eating out. Obviously, his expensive tastes carried to the kitchen as well. But could hardly be a cause for concern. The man wasn't even an inch overweight.

Then there was his travel. The guy had been everywhere. Or close to it. Beaches she'd never heard of, mountainous hikes, deep-sea dives. Almost always with luxury hotel bills and what appeared to be first-class flights attached. From the accounts she had in front of her, she couldn't tell if he'd traveled alone. His paying for a companion could account for the high airline fees.

When she found herself looking at food expenses during the times he was gone, to try to determine if he'd paid for more than one meal, she stopped herself.

Ashamed. Disappointed.

And glad for the warning, too. She could do so much but couldn't push it. Like someone who'd once been an over-shopper having to limit exposure to stores.

What she'd been looking for, and had been able to determine, was that not one dime of money from that sole account under the business name, the one with only Gray's signature allowed, had been spent on business.

They had a good argument for getting that one account released to him.

After another hour of research, she had enough evidence in front of her to present Gray with a solid case as to why he should accept her help, on behalf of her firm.

Didn't mean he'd accept.

Gray had had a real thing about anything he considered to be charity flowing in his direction.

To the point of never letting others do a favor for him.

Not that she owed him a favor. On the contrary, she had every justification for shunning the guy.

And it wasn't going to happen. No point in kidding herself about that one.

So she'd come up with a plan. A way to interact with her

brother's temporary guest and keep herself safe from his bizarre ability to rile her up.

Never before, or since, had she met anyone who seemed attached to her inner emotions as Gray had been.

Except for Leigh.

Her four-year-old daughter owned her now.

And that changed everything.

Including Sage's ability to keep any wayward yearnings for Gray at bay. He didn't hold first place in her heart anymore.

Her plan to see him only professionally was merely an insurance policy.

A peace-of-mind gift to herself, to help her sleep easily at night.

With Grayson Bartholomew in bed just four doors down from her.

She'd be fine, either way.

She had Leigh.

But helping Gray have the means to get out of their midst as quickly as possible still seemed like the prudent, right thing to do.

The second time Gray saw the elevator door open on Sage's floor, he was better prepared. Refueled with his sense of self-power. Felt like he was taking back control of his life.

Starting with lunch. Sage had given no prior warning when she'd asked him to appear at her office, and only a vague indicator of a couple of hours before she'd called him back.

He'd spent those ensuing two hours hiring a Realtor, signing all necessary forms, and had been told a For Sale sign would be hung outside his place yet that afternoon. Her call had come just as he'd been about to get himself something to eat.

Figuring she'd been working the entire time, too, he'd brought enough for two.

She could partake, or not. He'd take whatever she didn't want to the dog shelter. There was a group of homeless people who generally hung out there, waiting for him and the bag of nonperishable groceries he always brought for them. A few of the fancy tacos Sage loved to go along with the bag might be a treat.

If they didn't want them, he could feed them to the dogs.

Her door was open when he reached it. He saw her, with that wavy blond hair framing her, sitting behind her large mahogany desk as she typed on a keyboard, her focus clearly on the screen in front of her.

And was hit with an urge to swipe his arm across the desk, clearing off everything in his way, grabbing her up, laying her down on top of it...

"Gray? You don't have to wait out in the hall." She'd stood, was walking toward him. "Come on in."

He'd left his suit coat in the car. His dress pants were loose, but...she was looking at the large brown sealed bag he was carrying.

"You went to El Serrano's?"

Silently thanking the bag for holding all her attention, he held it in front of him as he took a seat back where she'd earlier directed him. And ignored his body—and hers— allowing calm to shrink him back to general appropriateness, as he pulled out the insulated, disposable containers.

"Calle Pollo, chicken marinated and grilled with onions and peppers, street corn salsa, cotija cheese, crema and a side of lettuce," he said as he laid out big, soft paper napkins and thick plastic cutlery beside the container on the couch side of the table.

He looked at the container he was opening for himself as

he finished his response to her rhetorical question with, "Two years of hearing you order them, eating what you couldn't finish…"

And had to stop, realizing, as she'd joined him, that he'd just exposed his own lunch to her gaze. Identical to hers. "They're good," he defended himself. And dug in.

He was hungry and did not allow food to go to waste. Ever.

# *Chapter Six*

In the past they'd shared one of the huge orders of El Serrano's Calle Pollo. Gray had just finished an entire order himself.

So what, he'd gone hungry when he'd eaten with her before? To save the cost of two meals? Never saying a word?

Was he no longer willing to sacrifice his stomach in such
a manner?

Pausing in her laying out of specific plans for him, she
closed the lid over her half-eaten, very delicious lunch and
walked it over to the small refrigerator behind her desk. He
was looking over the figures and charts she'd printed and
presented to him, the example charter, some potential employee handbook models, along with a mock fundraising
agenda and a quick example of what a brief might look like
on a motion to have his GB Animal Clinics bank account
released to him.

"It's all very simplified at the moment," she told him, re-
turning to the table with another two of the same bottles of
water she'd brought the first time she'd approached, offering one to him. "As soon as I have your go-ahead, I'll make
some calls and get to work in earnest."

With his legs spread, his forearms resting on his knees,
he'd been leaning over, sifting through the piles of informa-

tion. And glanced up as she spoke. "You're assuming I'm going to accept your offer."

It wasn't a question. Remaining standing, even though she knew it was a power move—one he'd likely interpret to mean that she thought herself above him—Sage said, "I know it's your most intelligent move at the moment, and you tend to make left-brain decisions."

He frowned, staring up at her. "What in the hell does that mean?"

Ahhh. An obvious loss of calm. The first he'd exhibited during their entire encounter that day. While the sign of a chink in his armor made her smile inside, she managed a fairly nonchalant shrug. "You make intelligent choices, based on fact, not emotion," she told him with confidence. Because she knew she was right.

Like selling his prized surfboard to buy her a pair of earrings.

At first, she'd been bowled over by the gesture. Until she'd realized that, just as the surfboard hadn't meant a great deal to him—hadn't represented a big loss—the earrings wouldn't have been significant to him, either. He'd traded one of his things for a thing for her. And in the end, they were both just things. And replaceable.

He'd apparently lost whatever edge he'd had there for a second as he was once again going through pages. "Since you've already got me figured out, I'm guessing you have someplace where I need to sign?"

Sage licked lips gone suddenly dry. Sat.

"I have a couple of caveats first," she told him, her stomach tripping over the food she'd sent it. Before her nerves wrapped like bands around the organ, shooting it with fire.

He glanced up at her, his eyes almost rolling with an "I'd expected as much" gesture. Or, maybe, "Here it comes."

And then, vacating all information on the table, sat back, holding his water bottle with both hands, where it rested on his belt area.

Just above other things she absolutely could not notice. Not even peripherally.

The fates tempting her? Showing her the dangers? Warning her she was making a huge mistake?

Focusing on a photo of Leigh on a tall, thin table of them along the wall behind him, she said, "This is strictly business. Meaning all interaction between us needs to be here, in my office." She'd been about to say that she never brought business home, but just by nature of her having spent the evening before going through his files, that statement would have opened many cans of worms.

And would have been a lie besides. She worked most nights after Leigh went to bed.

"You want to make certain that we don't...run into each other...on the beach." His tone wasn't at all defensive. And when she looked, his glance seemed sincere.

"Yes."

He nodded. Her stomach settled. And then he said, "Good, because I feel the same way. On Ocean Breeze we both work to stay out of each other's way."

Right. Spot-on.

Exactly what she wanted.

So why did his easy acquiescence, his seeming relief, feel more like a letdown than a victory?

She was good. Damned good. The proof didn't surprise Gray in the least. He'd known Sage was going to be a powerful woman, mastering whatever she set her mind to.

What he couldn't wrap his mind around was her putting her mind to him.

Mostly, as he drove back to Ocean Breeze just before dinnertime that October Wednesday, what consumed his thoughts was all the information she'd given him. The facts about his situation of which he'd been completely unaware. Rights he hadn't known he had.

And skills for which he hadn't tapped his previous corporate attorney. Securities, for instance. Corporate fundraising. He'd hired the firm when he'd been one doctor in one office, just incorporating. As he'd grown, it had all seemed so straightforward to him. His clinics, while highly successful, hadn't been a part of rich society. His locations were middle- to lower-middle class. His clientele, the same. His pricing and services had been designed to serve those who didn't have hundreds of dollars to spend on canine and feline cancer treatments, or state-of-the-art testing that ran into the thousands per test.

He'd never considered himself a business that could and should invest in securities.

However, as he helped himself to a beer from Scott's refrigerator and headed out to the porch, he was intrigued by the thought of future investment potential.

And by an idea that had started to form when he'd been going over Sage's information. When he got up and running again, if he was even half as successful as he had been, he needed to think about franchising. With strict caveats that would protect his brand and give him rights to intercede if he ever felt that policies weren't being followed as they'd been designed.

He'd texted Scott that he was back. He wasn't intending to leave the porch. He'd avail himself of early-morning beach time, when he could surf, and though the Ocean Breeze sandy oasis was surrounded by cliffs on each side, he'd figured that he could still play around a bit. The beach, with more than twenty cottages set on nearly a minimum of an acre apiece, stretched for two miles. As long as he stayed center beach, and didn't ride out too far, he'd be fine.

Equally important, by only using the beach in the morning, he wouldn't incur the risk of running into Sage.

The woman was giving him a quicker lease on a new life than he'd envisioned ever happening. No way he was going to screw that up with some chance encounter because he craved the feel of the ocean on his skin.

The sand beneath his feet.

Those had been the panaceas for his pain after a hard day for his entire life, his sleep aids. But he could thrive just fine without them.

All he had to do was step off the porch to feel the sand. He could see the ocean. Inhale the salty breeze. And oftentimes he went weeks without a trip to the beach.

He could also head to a public beach in San Diego if he had to. They'd sufficed for more than half of his life.

No, the problem wasn't that he couldn't go get in the water in front of him. It was that Sage Martin could.

She had nothing to lose if the stay-away agreement between them was broken.

The woman was savvy as hell. He'd pegged her right for wanting an unofficial restraining order. At home. In her private space. Her personal life.

And she was paying one hell of a price to get it, too.

Sitting there sipping, no longer avoiding sights down the beach—he'd already seen her up close—he had to admit he admired the hell out of the woman as much that night as he ever had...

"You aren't Scott."

The friendly, feminine voice came from—the opposite direction from Sage's place. Gray swung his head around to see the slender, model-gorgeous brunette standing at the rail of Scott's porch, smiling up at him.

"No," he told her, meeting the open brown gaze with a smile of his own. "I'm Gray. Grayson Bartholomew." He said the full name without forethought.

So relaxed, and relieved, so lost in thoughts of Sage Martin, that he'd failed to hold his tongue.

"The vet in the news?" The woman's smile had faded, but the friendliness behind her expression had not. She'd taken one of the three steps up to the porch, bringing lovely, long, tanned thighs into view beneath the short white denim skirt she wore.

"That's the one."

"I didn't know you were a friend of Scott's."

He shrugged. "I didn't know you were, either." They were sizing each other up. He could give as good as he got. And then some. Wasn't sure how hard he wanted to try.

"I'm Harper. I own the place just down that way." She pointed to the right. Which meant he'd driven by her driveway several times in the past two days. Just as Sage had driven by Scott's. With Gray's SUV parked in one of her brother's two spots. One road. Only way in or out.

He nodded. They'd already covered his introduction.

And before he could decide whether or not to offer her a beer, a big flash of brown came around the side of the cottage and up the steps, to sit straight up on the porch, tongue hanging out, staring at the woman.

Harper laughed, an infectious sound that made Gray smile, and said, "I'm sorry. Meet Aggie. She's particularly fond of Morgan, though you wouldn't think so, based on their sizes."

Sitting forward, Scott reached out a hand, calling Aggie with the soft, soothing voice that came naturally to him. And when she came, told the dog to sit.

Aggie, easily one hundred twenty pounds, sat. Lifted a paw for shaking, and Gray accepted the greeting, returned it.

"A Newfoundland," he said then, petting the dog, and, because he couldn't help himself, looking her over for good health, too.

"Yeah, full bred," Harper said, climbing fully up on the porch to sit in the empty chair. "I never saw myself for such a big dog, but she's the most gentle, kind being I've ever known."

A note in her voice gave Gray the impression that perhaps Harper had known a particularly unkind being at some point, but he let it pass. Offered the woman a beer instead.

And spent the next half hour feeling like a normal guy enjoying a few relaxing moments after a good day's work.

As she got up to leave, Harper seemed open to a repeat experience. Gray opened his mouth to offer—she was not only beautiful, but also an accomplished choreographer and dancer—but then he shut his chin without saying anything more than that he'd probably see her around.

He'd enjoyed his time chatting with her.

He'd enjoyed Aggie more.

And didn't want to even consider the idea that seeing Sage Martin again, feeling her presence down the beach, had anything to do with his reactions.

At. All.

# Chapter Seven

Sage had seen them, of course. Even before Leigh had seen Harper's Aggie and had darted up the beach toward the huge gentle dog.

Scott, who'd been on his way home from his nightly exercise with Morgan, had grabbed up Leigh, pretending to eat her neck, making her squeal, and had brought her back to the porch where Sage had been standing.

She'd gone out when Leigh had seen Scott and Morgan through the sliding glass door and had run out to give the corgi a hug.

The little girl had grown up on the beach, seeing her uncle and his dog most evenings. Sage couldn't expect, overnight, to have the child suddenly confined to the cottage. Or even to try to do so.

But when Scott had asked if she had a problem with Grayson bunking in his spare room, she'd pictured him in the cottage.

Not out on the beach.

To his credit, he hadn't stepped off Scott's porch.

There was absolutely no reason why Grayson Bartholomew couldn't relax with a beautiful woman.

And as a human being, Harper was one of the best.

Sage had it all worked out satisfactorily in her mind, ex-

cept for the part where seeing Gray with Harper was ripping at her.

"Are those cookies I smell?" Scott asked, depositing Leigh
on the porch and waiting to follow the little girl back into
the cottage, Morgan beside him.

"Chocate chip!" Leigh said. "Mommy maked them. Even
afore dinner!"

Bringing up the rear of the small procession, Sage smiled,
with a twinge of guilt mixed in. She'd started the cookies
to keep Leigh's attention inside. The little girl loved to help.
And lick the bowl.

Sage hadn't accounted for the minutes after the bowl was
licked and the cookies were cooling. Which was when Leigh
had been staring longingly outside and had seen Scott.

She fed her daughter the "sketti" leftovers she wanted.
And then, while Leigh sat in her booster chair, spooning as
much spaghetti sauce on her lips and chin as she was getting into her mouth, Sage collected and started chopping
the myriad vegetables she'd be combining into a salad for
herself. Some nights just felt like she couldn't stomach anything but pure health food.

She didn't ask Scott if he wanted to stay. He had a houseguest. And she didn't want to know about their dinner plans,
or lack thereof.

Didn't need to hear any of the details of Gray's private life.

Her twin didn't take the hint and leave.

Scott leaned back against the counter, his gaze mostly in
the direction of Morgan, who was on duty around Leigh's
chair, scarfing up anything that dropped. "You have something you want to tell me?" he asked.

She couldn't stand there looking him in the eye. She was
using a very sharp knife. Had to keep her focus on the blade
and the veggies between her fingers. "No."

"Anything you probably should?"

Sometimes the whole twin thing got on her nerves. Scott thinking because they'd shared a womb, they each had the right to butt in when the other had stuff going on. Of course, when the shoe was on the other foot...

And far more crucial to the point, Grayson Bartholomew was staying with him...

"He didn't tell you?"

"If you're referring to Gray, he and I have only ever mentioned your name once since you two broke up. Yesterday, when I told him I had to talk to you before he moved in with me for a bit."

She faltered. Or rather, stopped moving so that she didn't cut herself. "You never mention me?"

"Nope. And, for the record, that's not going to change. He's my friend, but you're my sister. My loyalty is to you. If he needs or wants to know anything about you, he'll have to ask you."

Emotions tangled up inside her. Running amok. And settled when she glanced at her daughter, who was feeding Morgan a long string of spaghetti. She should stop her.

"He knows about Leigh, though, right?"

Scott's shrug, his look of emptiness, was not faked. "No clue. Definitely not from me."

Okay, wow. She'd assumed...

Nodding, reminding herself of Gray's habitual short bobs, she resumed chopping. Took a deep breath to steady herself, dipped into her professional persona as far as she could go, and said, "I've offered to help him get some of his assets unfrozen, and to get him reestablished with a new corporation."

She glanced at her brother as she finished. Saw his jaw drop. And a deep frown slowly form that seemed to consume his entire face.

"You and Gray have been seeing each other?" He finally got the words out. She couldn't tell if he sounded injured, or just plain incredulous. "And you didn't tell me?"

She went with injured.

"No," she said, putting down the knife and turning toward him. "I texted him this morning. Had him come to my office. We made a deal. I'm helping him, pro bono as I'm required to take on at least one pro-bono case per quarter, and—"

"Wait a minute," he interrupted. She stopped talking at the quick shake of her brother's head. "You're already working with the company trying to get Safe Haven boxes outside of all city fire stations and medical clinics..."

"At least one..." she interrupted back, reclaiming the conversation. "Although Gray doesn't know that, and I see no need for him to do so."

Nodding, Scott's gaze was piercing as he watched her, silently. Waiting, she knew. The man was way too good at getting people to tell him things with that look. It was what made him a hugely successful prosecutor known for getting criminals to confess, but at home... "You really need to soften that look a bit," she told him.

Which gained her a raised eyebrow in addition to the rest.

She could have called him on that, too. She thought about it, feeling petulant. And maybe would have if she didn't intend to reserve the right to come at him when she knew something was wrong.

With Leigh and Morgan, he was all the family she had.

"Knowing that he was going to be invading us here, I went online last night to investigate the details of the case. I'm sure you already know that he was clearly an innocent party and has lost everything when he's done nothing but serve his community with a valuable business."

Scott's look softened. "I do."

"And it occurred to me that I could make a win-win deal with him."

Their father had been big on the whole win-win philosophy. They'd grown up with him making such deals with them. He'd get his way on things, but they'd get something they wanted out of the deal, too.

Scott's silence was more of a comfort at that point. He'd quit pushing.

"His problems are right up my alley. It'll be a no-brainer, helping him. And in exchange, all our associations must take place at the office."

"He keeps his distance from you at home."

"And I keep mine from him as well. There will be nothing personal exchanged between the two of us."

When Scott sucked in his lips, for a second there, she'd thought he was going to tell her she was ridiculous for thinking such a thing could work.

Instead, he shrugged and said, "Sounds like a plan," stole a stack of the cucumbers she'd just sliced and, popping one of them into his mouth, clicked his fingers. Morgan's call to attention.

The corgi glanced up at once, looked back at Leigh, then up at Scott a second time and moved to his heel.

Giving Leigh a kiss on the head—avoiding, Sage noticed, the tomato sauce–smeared face—he let himself and Morgan out.

"Somebody's not got a brain, Mommy?" Leigh asked as soon as it was obvious the adult conversation was done.

"What?"

"You said 'no-brainer' to Uncle Scott."

Shocked, smiling and proud of her little attentive human being, Sage came back with, "Do you even know what a brain is?"

"Mmm-hmm." Leigh was playing with her food more than eating it, a sign that she was full, but hadn't turned around, or asked if she could be excused, so Sage let her sit there. "Means the thing in your head that makes you talk."

Putting down the knife again, Sage wiped her hands on a cloth and went over to the table. Lifting the girl up against her, uncaring that Leigh's hands wrapped in her hair, she kissed that messy face. "Yes, ma'am, it does," she said, "and now it's time for your bath."

She'd get back to chopping. And to dealing with the vagaries of life.

At the moment, her daughter was there, needing her attention.

And that was all that mattered.

Gray wasn't surprised to have a text from Sage the next morning. She'd said that she'd have a portfolio of goals with an overview of how they'd be met ready for him. Along with paperwork for him to sign to make their working relationship official.

More like covering the firm's liabilities, he was sure.

And was on board with that.

Sage was also going to get every dime she'd earned once she did her job and got him back on his feet. He didn't want her charity. Even if, by some quirk of his fate, she failed, he'd still find a way to pay her.

Out of his house sale, if nothing else.

He had to request a later appointment than the nine in the morning she'd requested. He had a seven o'clock tooth extraction to perform on a rescue dog from a shelter he used to service with his own pro-bono program.

But made it to her by ten.

"You had a tooth extraction?" Sage asked as he appeared

in her open office door and she waved him in. He'd come over straight from the clinic, was still in blue scrubs— having exchanged the top for a clean one when he'd come out of surgery—and felt decidedly underdressed for her black suit with the red blouse.

All power.

He got the message.

"A two-year-old with a couple of broken teeth that had become infected," he told her, taking the same chair he'd used— twice—the day before.

Feeling way more at home there than he should have done.

And way too aware of Sage's small form, the perfect shape, as she came to join him, closing her office door on the way. Her curves weren't overly bountiful. If anything, they were on the smaller side, but they fit her perfectly.

And he knew from experience that they were perfect in every way.

Having a baby didn't seem to have changed her shape at all.

Thoughts he had no business entertaining.

Harper had left her phone number. As soon as he got out of there, he was going to use it.

She had no interest in anything serious, she'd said, as she finally stepped off Scott's porch. But if he was interested in something casual...

Definitely what the doctor was going to order himself to pursue.

Sage was frowning as she laid a different set of folders on the table and took her seat. "I thought you weren't working," she said.

"I've been volunteering at a couple of animal shelters. Doing well checks, that kind of thing. And have a buddy that I've known for years who lets me rent space at his clinic when I need equipment."

"What about technicians, to aid in the surgery?"

"He volunteers for that. Don't worry. It's all done legally. Just quietly. No one at the shelter knows where I take the dogs, and no one at his clinic knows I'm there. We work strictly after-hours. I get signatures on everything, and sign all prescriptions, etcetera, myself. My license to practice wasn't suspended," he reminded her, in case that hadn't been clear the day before.

She nodded. "I know it wasn't," she told him, glancing down at the folders on the table.

Right, she'd have looked up his state licensing in the process of investigating his situation.

She wasn't picking up the folders. Or looking his way, either.

She ran a couple of fingers through strands of hair at her shoulders instead. Slowly. Repeatedly. Not a nervous habit he remembered from the past.

Interesting.

"If you need to change your mind about things, I'm perfectly fine with that," he told her. He wasn't fine at all.

But he would be.

She owed him nothing.

His statement brought her gaze up to his. But left him even more unsure of what was going on.

She seemed…uncomfortable.

He wasn't getting it. He hadn't asked for, or instigated, any contact between them at all. His being there was all her. So…

"I'm sorry to have to do this…" As she started to speak, his gut dropped. Preparing himself to sit politely through her reneging on her offer—mostly by stiffening every muscle in his body and envisioning his quick escape to and through her door—Gray didn't even blink.

"We might need to change our agreement some," she said. "Due to unforeseen circumstances…"

He sat forward, ready to push off. "That's fine, Sage," he said, clapping his hands together. "It was nice of you to offer, but I completely understand…" He was standing by the time he was done, heading toward the door.

"Grayson Bartholomew, you are not walking out on me. Not again."

# *Chapter Eight*

Gray froze in his tracks.

Not sure he'd even heard her correctly.

"I'm sorry." The words were strong. But sounded sincere enough that he slowly turned. "That was completely out of line. But I would appreciate it if you would hear me out."

"To what end? You made a generous offer. You need to walk it back. I never should have accepted in the first place. We both know you owe me nothing, Sage. Not even, apparently, politeness…"

He stopped then. Knowing that last dig to be beneath him.

Almost on par with hers.

Which made them what? Both pathetic?

"If you'd rather not accept my offer, that's your choice. What I have to say still has to be said."

"Okay." He stood there, waiting. Felt more in control, stronger, more like himself, with his exit strategy halfway complete.

"Could you please come back and sit down?"

Good Lord, what was the woman trying to do to him? Extract every last nerve ending in payment for the humiliation she must have suffered? He'd left her to let hundreds of guests know, with only two days' notice, that there wasn't going to be a wedding. Canceling the caterers, the flowers, the church and minister, the lovely beachfront country club…

As his mental list quickly piled up on itself, Gray had the sense that moving back to the chair would be more prudent. He did so.

"I can't force you to accept my help," she started in a few silent seconds after he'd done as she'd asked and reclaimed his chair. "I would, however, appreciate you giving some strong consideration to agreeing to the working relationship since I've already involved the senior partners in my firm, as well as others whose expertise I might need."

Another surge of guilt hit, along with the list that had been piling up on him a moment ago.

"I'm listening."

"We agreed that while we will have a professional relationship—whose term is yet to be determined—that we will stay completely clear of each other on a personal basis."

He frowned. "Yes." He said the word succinctly, before continuing with, "And I've been very careful not to take any chances…"

A wave of her hand…and the way that appendage landed at her hair again, with those fingers working strands…piqued his curiosity.

In a completely unprofessional manner.

"I've realized that when I made that stipulation, I hadn't taken into consideration some circumstances that have since occurred to me."

She was looking at him. But blinking more than normal. And if he wasn't mistaken, her upper lip was trembling.

Interesting. Growing more so by the second.

"I'm listening," he said again, pushing aside the thought that he owed the woman more than he'd ever be able to repay with money and should be doing whatever he could to put her at ease.

"These…circumstances…are largely out of my control,

and while I'll admit up front that my proposed stipulation change is grossly unfair to you, I must make it, anyway."

That was when it hit him.

She'd seen him with Harper the night before.

And wanted him to keep his trysts—as she'd obviously pegged the uninitiated contact—out of her sight.

The only reason Gray could think of for her to make such a request would be if she still harbored feelings for him.

His body leaped to life...again. Annoyingly so. He wasn't a guy who walked around getting hard. Ever. And had done so three times in little more than twenty-four hours?

Still... Was there some way he and Sage could reconnect?

He'd had the thought through the years, thinking they'd have to wait until they were forty. But if it was strictly physical...

"My change is that there be a one-time session, today, to discuss any potential information that could affect our abilities to keep clear of each other, personally, in the days and weeks to come."

Definitely a slam of the door on a strictly physical possibility.

And...he frowned...on any problem she'd had with Harper visiting with him the night before. Because his having what he'd perceived Sage to have seen as a date...wouldn't have affected their abilities to steer clear of each other.

If anything, his having another woman would make it more awkward for him and Sage to have contact.

The woman would be a definite buffer.

He was confused.

Didn't like being that way.

Tried to read her expression and came up blank.

"I agree to the session," he told her.

And hoped to hell he hadn't just opened another Pandora's box.

* * *

What the hell was with all the drama? Sage cringed as her brain spit back a quick replay of her last five minutes.

And, figuring the buildup for a childish attempt to stall, hating that she'd seemed to need one, blurted, "I have a four-year-old daughter." Without officially starting the session.

"I know."

Her mouth fell open. She closed it. Stared at him. Opened it again to say, "You know."

And got that nod. Short, easy bobs.

His gaze held hers without any visible tension. He hadn't tensed.

She hadn't shocked him.

"You looked me up?" she asked then, the only logical conclusion, since Scott wouldn't have lied to her. Was feeling a flush of…something not terrible at the idea of Gray having been interested enough to… No, wait.

"No." His response interrupted her.

And when he was done, she said, "Harper told you." She was truly fond of the woman. Couldn't hold it against her at all to have talked about Scott's family to one trusted to stay in his home.

Flooded with resentment, with no good cause, she awaited Gray's confirmation. Using the time to get herself in check once and for all.

"No one told me," he insisted, steepling his fingers in front of him, with his elbows on the arms of his chair.

Drawing her attention to the bit of chest hair she could see at the top of the loose-fitting scrub shirt.

"I saw you with her Tuesday night." He saved her any further embarrassment by filling a potentially volatile silence with words. "My first night on the beach. I was on Scott's porch, and she was riding on your hip as you carried her off toward your place…"

He'd seen her with Leigh.

And was completely nonchalant about it. Didn't seem to care one way or another that she had a child.

The family he'd let her believe they'd have together.

Until two days before the wedding when he'd told her he didn't ever want to father her, or any woman's, child…

He'd been watching her.

Had met with her the day before, knowing about Leigh.

Was that why he'd so easily agreed that there'd be no personal contact between them? Because she had a child?

When he'd told her he'd tried to get on board with the idea of having a family, but just couldn't, that the idea of marrying her knowing that a family was coming was keeping him up nights, and not in a good way…

Wow.

She took a breath. And another.

She thought of Leigh. Her heart lit up inside as her brain replayed the little girl's laugh, and her initial fight for life.

Sage's own life righted itself for a moment. Long enough to say, "Okay, then, I hope you understand that she's had the run of the beach from my place to Scott's since she was able to crawl. She might, at some point, appear down by Scott's and I would then need to come get her. I ask only that you be kind and polite if that were to happen."

He grinned. "She gets away from you, huh?"

He was *enjoying* this? Giddy with relief that he'd escaped the life himself?

"She knows her rules and is fantastically good about abiding by them. She just gets ahead of herself sometimes when rules collide. She's allowed to move freely on the four-cottage stretch of beach as long as either Scott or I are present. Sometimes, she misinterprets that word *present*. She knows we're always watching her, keeping her in sight. And she's incredibly fond of dogs. She knows every member of the canine population on Ocean Breeze, calls them by name and thinks they're her family."

"Even Aggie? That girl is a hundred twenty pounds minimum."

"And the sweetest living being on Ocean Breeze." Her lawyer hat was on. Defending herself. Her parenting. "But she knows she's not allowed to run up to or away from Aggie. She's not allowed to be in touching distance, unless a trusted adult is with her. Precisely because of her size. And Aggie's."

She could show him a picture where the two had fallen asleep together, though. On the beach one night, during a bonfire. Harper had been sitting right there, too. Leigh had crawled up into the other woman's lap to pet Aggie. She'd fallen asleep, with her body on Harper and her head on Aggie's thigh.

A sweet memory. Not one she was going to share with a man who'd rather leave her than father her children.

And, the other side of her brain reminded her, not wanting children in no way made Gray a bad guy. On the contrary, the fact that he'd been honest with her—albeit last minute—was honorable. Minus the last-minute part.

For a second there, she wished she could shut that part of her up. But she knew better. A good lawyer always looked at both sides. It was the only way to predict what an opponent could throw at you. And to make sure your client's business was fully prepared and protected at all times.

Likewise, in her personal life, she had to make sure that she and Leigh were emotionally as well as physically safe.

And that meant taking honest looks.

Even if they hurt.

\* \* \*

They'd established that they both knew she had a daughter. He wasn't comfortable with any of the reasonings popping up as to why that fact had been important enough to Sage that she made a point of having a major conversation over it. Like, what, she'd really think that if the kid showed up close to him, he'd be rude to her?

A four-year-old?

He had to be reminded to be kind?

His reluctance to have a family had obviously come off worse than he'd realized.

Watching Sage sit there, fiddling with her hair, Gray wanted the conversation done, and wasn't quite ready to let it go. "Are we still in session?"

She blinked as though, while she'd been looking in his direction, he most certainly had not been her focus. Bringing to mind, once again, that father of her child.

She'd mentioned her and Scott looking after Sage.

Not a dad.

And not a topic he had any justifiable reason to raise…

"We can be, if you have something you need to bring to the table."

Because she'd said it was a one-time thing. He got that. Either then or never. The child's father was off-limits, but, "What's her name?"

"Excuse me?"

"Your daughter. Granted, I know diddly about kids—other than all of those I deal with every day at work when they come in with their parents to have a pet cared for…" The dig was beneath him. But was boldly out there, unretractable, so he went on. "But it makes sense to me that I would appear kinder if I knew what to call her." He stopped. Didn't like the blank look on her face. Had to wipe it off.

And came up with, "If she ever comes down my way... you asked me to be kind..."

Figuring he was in the weirdest, most awkward conversation he'd ever had, Gray was oddly willing to remain sitting there and be in it.

"Her name is Leigh."

No last name. Was it Martin? Like hers? Or did the child have her father's name? Had the guy been around when Sage had carried the child? Had he been there to help her through the birth?

Was he still there and just traveling at the moment?

Whoa. What in the hell was he doing? What was she doing to him?

A father being present for a birth? Not his cup of tea. Or anywhere close to his normal train of thought.

"Leigh what?"

She frowned. "Leigh Marie."

Okay, still not what he'd been asking. And he couldn't come up with a viable explanation for wanting to know the child's last name. Had to get himself off the wrong turn.

"You mind sharing any pointers, just in case she happens down my way, and you aren't immediately on her heels? Do I ignore her unless she calls out to me? If she starts to come up her uncle's steps, do I tell her she can't?"

She stared at him, more like a deer in the headlights than the confident lawyer he knew her to be.

He didn't blame her.

He was halfway being facetious. The whole topic was over-the-top. A kid comes down the beach, of course he'd be kind.

He liked kids. Enjoyed having conversations with them.

He just couldn't bear the weight of the day-to-day being responsible for one. The overall daily shaping of one.

None of which he shared. Wasn't information necessary to their current status.

He awaited Sage's response mainly because he wanted to understand and abide by her wishes.

Or at least understand so that he had the ability to abide by them, even if he didn't want to do so.

Ultimately, at that stage of life's game, she called the shots.

And didn't seem to be coming up with any feasible plan.

Gray sat forward, rubbing his hands together lightly. "Look," he told her. "I'm great at being kind. You could ask any of the thousands of patients I've tended to over the years—they just won't be able to answer in English, of course. But if you saw me around animals, saw how I treat them and how they respond to me, maybe you'd feel more comfortable."

She was still staring. Her chin trembled a bit.

"I swear to you," he continued, feeling like he was on a good roll. "If she, or you, or she and Scott, or the three of you come down the beach, I'll be fine, Sage, I promise. I didn't break things off because I didn't care about you. Or like you. To the contrary. I want the best for you. I always have."

He tried to stop there, but the words just kept coming. "I'm glad you have Leigh. You got what you most needed out of life. I didn't want to be responsible for depriving you of that."

Her lips tilted upward a bit. Not quite a smile but going in that direction.

"I actually like kids." He let go of the thoughts he'd just determined to keep to himself. "They're honest to the core, say what's on their minds and have a very refreshing way of viewing life in the moment. They also say some of the funniest things…"

He stopped as she shook her head.

And figured, when he noticed the moisture that she blinked from her eyes, and his gut wrenched for her, that he'd just lost the hope of a quick launch back into his own world.

# *Chapter Nine*

He liked kids. This man, who'd crushed her heart because he couldn't bear the idea of fathering a child with her, sat there blithely telling her he'd grown a fondness for children?

As though he didn't know...

Of course he liked kids. Blinking, Sage shut down the overload of emotion being dumped on her by being with Gray again. She was better than that.

Just seeing him again...

He looked so good. Was as...warm...as she'd remembered. Still had that tone to his voice, the look in his eye.

Why in the hell couldn't she get beyond the man?

No answer was forthcoming, which was why she had to get her butt in gear, do her best work and get him out of her brother's cottage and back into his own life.

Blissfully apart from her and her small family.

But...he liked kids.

"You'll like Leigh." The words that finally made it out of her mouth were not at all what she'd been about to say. "She's astute beyond her years, and so innocent at the same time." Thinking of her daughter brought genuine joy to her heart. A smile to her lips.

And cleared her vision, too.

"If she makes her way down to you, she'll probably just start jabbering. She won't talk to a stranger, but I'm going to tell her tonight that Uncle Scott has a friend staying with him, so she'll likely make an excuse to check you out."

Gray's brows rose. "Check me out?"

With a chuckle, Sage said, "She has a system for weighing the people in her midst. You won't know it, but she'll come home and tell me what she finds."

Gray sat back, his hands on the chair arms, as they'd been the day before. "Such as?"

Sage shook her head, brimming with humor as she met Gray's gaze. "I never know. One time it was *he stinks.* I thought she meant the father who'd brought a new child into her day care was a bad guy. Turned out he had on some cologne that she didn't like. Another time she told me a lady had crossed eyes. She meant that the lady looked like she was in a bad mood—you know, cross. She has a friend who bubbles up a lot. And no, she didn't mean burps. Kaylee starts laughing with her mouth closed and then opens it…and she laughs a lot."

Gray's expression sharpened, and she realized that she'd been going on as though they were friends. Not very temporary professional associates.

"I'm sorry," she quickly inserted. "You didn't need to hear all of that." Never, in all her years in practice, had she ever lost sight of her professionalism in such an overt way. Even when her own associates asked about Leigh. Which was why it wasn't good to mix business with conflicts of interest. Once she got him going, if he chose to remain with her firm as a paying client, she'd be turning him over to one of their other lawyers.

"No need to apologize."

His kindness, the personal look in his eye, as though they were two people who were friends, shook her up again. "It was unprofessional." She could hardly tell him she didn't usually do that. Though she wanted him to know that her professionalism was never, ever an issue, she didn't want to give him any sense that he was messing with her equilibrium. So she finished with, "You stiffened, and that look in your eye…"

He was still looking at her. Like he knew her. "Your voice…it's the first time I've seen the real you in more than ten years." He stopped. And when she said nothing, added, "It was nice."

It *was* nice.

She couldn't share that thought. Or let it become something. Wasn't sure she could trust herself, not at the moment. And, out of desperation, she said, "So, you like kids. Does that mean you've finally come to the realization that having them wouldn't be the kiss of death?"

The question was bald, bold and wholly inappropriate. She sat up straight behind it, taking him on.

She had to know. Not because she expected a change of heart. If the man wanted kids and a family, as gorgeous and kind as he was, he'd have them.

She'd been rude because it was the only way to ensure her defenses.

"No." He didn't blink, didn't even have the decency to look away as he delivered the succinct, one-word answer.

Almost as though he knew.

And wanted to ensure that the walls she'd put up against him remained firmly intact.

The "session" ended as abruptly as it had begun. Sage had asked him if he had anything that needed to be said, any requests or requirements. He'd repeated the "no" he'd just issued on the other topic.

And the business meeting began. He signed a ton of papers. Met a couple of attorneys who would be advising Sage where appropriate and was told that either of them would be happy to represent his new firm once he was ready to hire a corporate attorney.

After they left, Sage gave him a portfolio filled with everything he'd signed and walked him to the door.

"I want to make one thing clear," she started, and Gray braced himself.

But didn't back away. Maybe he should have. Enough was enough. He needed to hand her back the paperwork and walk away. In any other situation, with any other person, he was certain he would have.

Which meant that he should have done it with her, too.

Instead, as he took a couple more steps with her, he waited out Sage's silence, curious to hear what else was bothering her. What other concerns she had about him.

Because for a woman who was over him, fine with having him around and fully happy with her life, his presence sure did seem to be bothering her.

Which wouldn't please him in any way if hers wasn't also bothering him.

Stopping with her hand on the doorknob, she turned to him. Looked him straight in the eye. "The pro-bono work I'm doing is strictly because I want to do it. Because I think you're a good man who got a raw deal and I can help. The other partners, saying they'd be happy to represent you… they were obviously impressed with you during our meeting. Their offers were sincere, and in no way tied to what I'm doing." She pointed to his portfolio. "This isn't an attempt to earn your business later."

He'd been falling for her all over again right up until that last part.

"You trying to tell me you don't want me to accept their

offers? You don't want to be in any way associated with me long-term?"

Eyes wide, she said, "No!"

The one word he'd given her. Twice in a row.

He felt the impact.

Tapped the portfolio against the palm of his free hand. Smiled. And was about to thank her when she added, "I couldn't represent you, regardless," she said. "A firm mandate. To ensure that pro bono doesn't turn into attorneys doing seemingly free work with a behind-the-scenes quid pro quo in effect."

He needed to let it go. Let them both off the hook and get the hell out of there. Take a shower. Put on something besides scrubs. Instead, he held her gaze. "So you'd be okay with me accepting one of their offers?"

She blinked. Took a deep breath. "Yes, of course I would."

He could tell she'd meant it. And that she'd just lied, too.

Which had Gray smiling all the way to his SUV.

The woman wasn't as completely over him as she wanted to be.

He had no thoughts whatsoever of getting back together with her. They both knew it wouldn't work. But it felt good to know that he'd meant even half as much to her as she'd meant to him.

That he wasn't the only one feeling a sharp pang of regret as a result of their unexpected reunion.

Turned out at least one old adage was true.

Apparently, misery did like company.

He'd asked two questions as one. *You trying to tell me you don't want me to accept their offers?* And *You don't want to be in any way associated with me long-term?*

Which he'd then segued into, *So you'd be okay with me accepting one of their offers?*

All three of them ran through her mind the rest of the afternoon, plagued her on and off on the drive home, interrupted by Leigh's back seat sing-along. Sage had one of the little girl's favorite albums of educational kid songs cued up through her phone.

And when her mind would free her enough, she even sang along with a couple of them. Smiling at her daughter through the rearview mirror when she was stopped at a light.

But then, as she concentrated on driving, sensations from the day intruded, bringing her back to the conversation with Gray.

She'd never been in a situation where she didn't agree with herself. Where parts of her were warring inside her to the point of total cacophony. Temptation, she got. Could fight. It was a part of life. Wanting what you knew you shouldn't have.

Or heart against head. She'd been there, too. More than once.

But the stuff with Gray…it was head against head. Her mind saw it both ways.

And her heart felt pain and joy both ways, too.

She didn't get it.

How could she be in such conflict with herself?

Any way she looked at it, any time she asked herself, she truly wanted Gray to be able to continue with her firm if he wanted to. She wanted him to be successful to the point of needing and affording a corporate attorney.

She also wanted to know that he was being well taken care of.

And she so desperately needed to know that he would soon be completely and permanently out of her life.

She was pulling onto Ocean Breeze when the reason for her conundrum hit her. She was over Grayson Bartholomew, which was why she'd truly wanted her brother to offer to help the man in his time of need.

He wasn't a bad guy. She'd never have been so deeply in love with him if he had been. And because she was over him, the hurt inflicted by the inability of their lives to fit together was past. A part of her past. A memory.

The current problem had to do with the fact that she'd never let go of how badly she'd been hurt. Unbeknownst to her, she'd been living the life of the victim—even while she'd taken control, taken charge and had built the life she'd wanted more than any other.

It wasn't the pain itself that was getting in her way. It was the fact that she'd been hurt. That her life's plans had been so abruptly and painfully interrupted.

It was hard to believe, with all that she'd accomplished, all that she'd built. But in that one area, she hadn't moved on.

Leigh was still happily busting out tunes as Sage pulled into their driveway. And, glancing back at the little girl, Sage smiled, feeling as though she was back in control. She knew the problem.

So could find the solution.

"As soon as Mommy gets changed, you want to walk up the beach and meet a nice man who's staying with Uncle Scott for a while?" she asked her daughter. Gray might not be home. And if not, they'd try again another time.

The point was they'd try.

"Can I play with Morgan?" Leigh asked, her still-babyish features pulled into a frown.

"If she's out, of course you can."

"Yeah!" Leah chimed, her little feet kicking back and forth as she reached to unlatch the buckle across her chest, and then the trickier one at her waist. No matter how long it took, Sage wasn't supposed to help. She'd been given the mandate quite clearly shortly after the little girl's fourth birthday and respected Leigh's need to take charge of her own destiny in the areas where a four-year-old could do so.

And reminded herself of that when, twenty minutes later, barefoot and in a black-and-white-flowered sundress, Sage headed out to the beach. She wanted Leigh to hold her hand.

Needed her to.

The next minutes weren't going to be a cakewalk. But in the end, the result would be like a birthday celebration. A rebirth.

A new birth.

For herself.

"No!" Leigh said, not in a scream, but quite emphatically, pulling both of her hands into her chest. "You told me, here to there, I don't have to."

She'd set those boundaries, yes, but...

"You held Uncle Scott's and Miss Iris's hands the other night."

"I know," the little girl said, as though she was tired of being told something she already knew.

Focused fully on the child, Sage wondered what she'd done. Had she somehow transmitted her uneasiness to Leigh? "Are you mad at Mommy?"

With her arms crossed against her chest, Leigh stood there. "No."

"Then why don't you want to hold my hand?"

"Because I want to do this!" Leigh yelled out with a laugh and turned a somersault in the sand.

Her heart giving a jump, her insides filling with light, Sage said, "A somersault! Oh my goodness, Leigh Marie! Did you learn that today?"

With sand dropping from ringlet curls, Leigh jumped up

and danced back and forth between her two feet. "I been learning at school, and today I gotted it!" At that, she bent and turned another circle feet over head in the sand. And then reached for Sage's hand.

"I did it good, huh, Mommy?" the little girl asked, as she half danced next to Sage, pulling on her arm with each hop, as they made their way slowly down the beach.

"You did great!" Her own joy bubbled over—as it generally did where Leigh was concerned, and Sage felt better than she had since Scott had first dropped his bombshell two days before.

She was living her best life.

And was back up on top of it.

# *Chapter Ten*

Gray spent Thursday night at a small private gathering of veterinarians. All doctors who'd worked for GB Animal Clinics. As part of Sage's revitalization plan, he had to determine whether he was going to start out solo, as he had the first time, or if he wanted to include other practices along with his own—as he'd ended up.

While his gut instinct was telling him to go it alone—he'd been burned once, it could happen again—he knew that sometimes his gut reacted in accordance to conditioning from his childhood, more than from the life he'd built.

With, of course, that one exception. The doctor on his staff who'd chosen to deal illegal drugs on the side.

He didn't want to let one ex-friend and golfing buddy—current criminal—shape his future.

But he couldn't help but to do so.

He left what turned out to be a late-night affair undecided. And with a lot to think about.

Not a bad thing, if it kept him focused on the future and away from mental wanderings wrapped around Sage Martin that were going nowhere. Friday was equally consumed with tasks his interim lawyer had given him. Looking for one or more places he could rent in the short term to get himself back up and running.

She'd already drafted a letter to his personal client list—and a second to the entire GB Animal Clinics client list—both of which he'd signed the day before. The mass mailings, both snail and email, would be going out that day. Before the weekend, she'd told him in her office on Thursday afternoon.

And Friday night, he had a meeting with his Realtor. Apparently, there was a bidding war going on for his house. He'd priced it to sell. The bids had risen above asking price.

He'd considered all of them. And accepted the one that offered cash on the spot—no long wait for financing and closing. It was also the highest offer. And had come in first.

No chance of any improprieties or claims of unfairness.

An inspection could be done as early as the next day, Monday at the latest, and after that, the title work could take as little as a week.

Could be longer. But in any event, he'd at least have some working cash sooner rather than later. A circumstance he'd provided himself without Sage's legal advice, intervention or even knowledge. Why that mattered, he couldn't explain in any good detail to himself, but he felt good about it just the same.

He woke up Saturday morning with a sense of satisfaction he hadn't known since the news of his colleague's illegal drug dealing had hit. Got up just after dawn and, pulling on his swim trunks, hit the beach. The water would be cold.

And just what he needed to get an invigorating start on the first weekend of his restarted life. Most importantly, he'd have the beach to himself.

Wouldn't have to worry about a little four-year-old running up to see "Uncle Scott's friend."

The thought slowed him some as he walked quietly through the large cottage to let himself out the back door without disturbing Scott or Morgan. Shamed him a little even as, in the quiet, with nothing to do but be alone with his thoughts, he couldn't escape the fact that he'd purposely stayed out late both Thursday and Friday nights so that he'd run no chance of coming face-to-face with the child.

And since he'd spent the past ten years dealing with children, all of them pet owners, in his practice, and enjoyed conversing with them, there could only be one reason why he'd be shying away from interacting with—or even seeing up close—Scott's niece.

Because she was Sage's daughter.

He made it to the door, a bit warm as the realization washed over him with full consciousness, complete acknowledgment rather than being brushed aside to deal with later. Had the lock undone and knob turned when he heard the thump telling him that Scott's corgi had just jumped down from the end of the king-size bed where she slept.

He'd heard a similar sound one other morning, when Scott had had an early meeting before court.

Figuring, as a good houseguest, he had no other choice but to take Morgan out to do her business, since he was the one who woke her, Gray headed on out—with his unexpected companion. Kind of glad for the company.

As soon as the dog had relieved herself, she trotted happily beside Gray down to the water. Sat, and looked up at him.

Telling him she'd wait, he knew. Scott had shared that he had her well trained. But Gray figured it was more than that. If Scott was ever in trouble in the water, the dog wasn't going to just sit there. She'd do whatever she could to rescue him.

Taking his first few steps into the water with that thought, he turned and looked back at Morgan. And an idea struck. Diving into the wave coming at him, he welcomed the shock of cold, and the start of a new plan, together as one.

He could thank the residents of Ocean Breeze for their

welcome into their private domain by offering a water service course to their dogs—any who wanted to partake.

He'd been working with service dog programs since
college—way before he'd become a licensed veterinarian.
And being born and raised on the California coast...water
rescue had been his first discipline. As plans gelled, his arms
reached farther. Harder. His legs kicked a strong, steady beat.
And when he'd gone far enough, reaching his sweet spot, he
lay supine, smiling when he caught a wave and rode it in.

Was still smiling as he stood in the waist-high water...
until he glanced at the beach where Morgan would be waiting for him, to see empty sand.

What the hell!

Racing out of the water, shoving at the waves with thighs
that would not be denied, he glanced up and down the deserted beach, quickly, once, and then, reaching shore, turned
and studied the water. Completely focused. If a wave had
caught Scott's companion...

He knew how to spot minute signs of life in the water. Partially to keep himself safe from water predators. He scoured
frantically for any sign that Morgan had been washed away
and was trying to make it to shore.

Scott wouldn't have just taken the dog back to the house.
Not without letting Gray know. Not when she'd been on a
sit and wait command—spoken or not.

Precious seconds passed as he searched the waves, and
then, while his gut clenched, fearing the worst—that he'd
been responsible for his friend's companion and hadn't prevented disaster—he jerked to the right when he heard the
sound of a dog barking frantically.

Morgan's bark. Once. And then nothing.

The girl was down the beach, soaking wet, and...she had

a life vest in her mouth. One she'd dropped to alert him, and then picked back up again.

The thing was almost as big as she was.

Feeling almost as exuberant as the dog appeared with her ears back and flying toward him as fast as she could with her goods, Gray jogged toward her, thrilled to see her healthy and safe, but flooding with a huge dose of relief, too.

At work, doing his job, he never doubted that he was worthy to be responsible for other lives. Veterinary parameters he knew. He'd been able to study until he could test perfectly on all of it. And then left the rest up to fate, confident in his knowledge.

But in his personal life, when things like waves could come up and sweep away a dog that had spent her entire life on the beach...

The idea of spending every day of his life having to be aware enough to offset unseen dangers...knowing that a dependent could perish if he didn't foresee them. The idea of having to spend every second watching so he didn't risk missing what he didn't know to watch for...

He wasn't made that way.

And figured fate had just given him that reminder.

In case his long-buried, resurfacing emotions from the past reminded him too much of why he'd asked Sage Martin to marry him, and not enough about the reason he'd broken her heart and walked away.

Sage was up before Leigh on Saturday morning. She purposely rose early in order to provide herself with half an hour of quiet time, to drink a cup of tea and reflect on...nothing.

She just wanted the tea.

Two nights in a row of walking down the beach with her daughter, trying to take the bull by the horns and get rid of the past once and for all by not avoiding it. Two nights in a row that Gray had been absent from her brother's porch, the beach and even his cottage.

Sitting at the kitchen table, staring out the sliding glass door toward the beach, she sipped. Not reflecting.

The night before she'd actually stooped so low as to make an excuse to walk home via Ocean Breeze, the street that ran behind their cottages, the paved lane from which their parking places protruded.

Scott's car had been absent. She'd known he'd been home earlier to tend to Morgan and had an evening function. A fancy dinner celebrating a judge's retirement, to which many attorneys, both prosecutorial and defense, had been invited.

The letdown she'd felt had been due to the second empty parking spot at Scott's cottage.

But still, no need for reflection. The unresolved emotions inside her were merely due to the closure she'd set out to get Thursday night. And had yet to obtain.

She'd let go of Grayson a decade ago. And had hung on to the gaping hole of loss.

Once she'd seen the distinction, she'd understood how to remedy the situation.

And that had been irritatingly absent...

Stiffening, Sage sat up straighter, her fingers clenched against the handle of her mug, as she saw Morgan run up the beach.

Alone?

Scott generally slept in a bit on Saturdays...

When Morgan dove into the water, Sage left her cup on the table and raced to the door. By the time she had it unlocked, the corgi was back out of the water, dragging something with her.

A life vest that had been washing up to shore. Sage had

seen it bobbing on the water earlier. Had figured it for having fallen off a boat. Like many of the other items that eventually washed up on their beach. Set in between high and miles-long rock faces as they were, those things trying to wash to shore bobbed against mountainous rock until they finally found solace in Ocean Breeze sand.

And Morgan often dove for them.

But never alone...

With her hand frozen on the still-closed door's pull handle, Sage watched the clearly safe dog run up the beach.

And saw the man she ran toward. With a strong surge of inappropriate warmth, she recognized him. Quite personally. That thick, dark bed of chest hair in between his nipples...the way it trickled to a single line as it ran down to his belly button...

The scar just above his right hip...

A surfing thing, he'd said, blowing her off when she'd tried to pry further. But he'd welcomed her tongue offering its own consolation down the scar's length.

Many times.

"Mommy?"

Spinning, Sage saw Leigh, in pajama shorts and top, rubbing her eyes as she came through the living room to the kitchen. Leigh's little nose scrunched as she looked up at Sage. "Why you standing there?" she asked, and came to push in front of Leigh to stare out.

"It's Morgan!" the little girl cried, and with both hands on the glass, pushed the still-unlocked door open enough for herself to fit through and slid out.

"Morgan!" she cried out, dancing on the top step of the porch.

Sage had to go out, in spite of the cutoff sweat shorts and spaghetti strap top she'd worn to bed being her only attire.

"Leigh, come on back in here, we aren't dressed," she said, just as the little girl turned around to talk over her.

"Can I go see her, Mommy? Pwease? It's pwite to say good morning!" The little girl repeated something Sage had told her a time or two when they'd arrived at day care and a little boy that Leigh didn't like had said hello to her.

"No!" Sage said as the little girl started down the steps.

Dying of humiliation at the thought of what was coming, Sage was relieved—and surprised—when Leigh turned back around and looked up at her.

Perhaps her tone in that *no* had been overly harsh.

"We aren't dressed yet, sweetie," she said then, offering her hand out to walk Leigh back inside. "Remember, we have to be dressed to go outside, even on the beach between our house and Uncle Scott's house."

Leigh immediately climbed back up to the porch. Reached the top and looked up at Sage, her expression a study in seriousness.

"Morgan's not dressed," she pointed out. Then turned her back and went inside.

With a grin, and a last look down the beach—relieved to see that Gray and Morgan had disappeared, hopefully into Scott's cottage—Sage followed her daughter into the cottage.

Score one for lack of closure.

She'd get it next time.


Gray had barely come from the shower, had been stepping into clean scrubs for his morning stint at a Rockcliff pet shelter, when his phone sounded an incoming text message.

Incoming from Sage. He'd set the single clunk sound as a ringtone specific to her. Unobtrusive, innocuous…he'd know it was her, but the sound wouldn't draw undue attention or interrupt anything else he might have going on.

But he grabbed it up like the house was on fire.

He'd seen her on her porch. When he'd heard the undeniable child voice call out for Morgan. The little one had been there, too, pretty much obscured behind the stair-rail post.

But Sage...the spaghetti straps, mostly bare thighs...

Tapping quickly to open the text, he read:

Congratulations. Let me know if you need any help getting it closed.

Remembering, only then, that he'd texted her the night before to let her know about the house sale—a necessary action considering she was completely up on his financial situation at the moment.

Dropping his phone in his shirt pocket without a response, Gray grabbed his keys, nodded at Scott, who was having coffee in the kitchen, exited the cottage as quickly as possible.

And Ocean Breeze, too.

# *Chapter Eleven*

Sage dressed with care on Saturday. Herself and her daughter.

Calling on her one day a week to be allowed to choose Leigh's clothes on her own, she laid out a unicorn-covered smock, with a small ruffle around the bottom edge, and purple shorts to match. It was her current favorite of Leigh's clothes. A gift from Iris's collie, Angel, the previous Christmas.

"But, Mommy, this is my bestest," the little girl said as she wiggled into the shorts. And then pulled the top on, sliding her hands into sleeves with the tornado force she was, and ran off to the coloring she'd been doing—unaware, uncaring or both, that the shirt was on backward.

Sage let it go while she pulled on a white denim skort, midthigh length, with the necessary Lycra attached undershort in case she had to climb or crawl to rescue or play with her daughter.

Topping the skort with a formfitting, short-sleeved black blouse, she slid into her favorite pair of two-inch wedged black flip-flops with the silver-and-pearl-studded bling, and went out to convince Leigh to turn her shirt around.

And then, with a determined demeanor and a spirit filled with purpose, she suggested that the two of them walk up to Uncle Scott's house to meet his friend. She was done playing childish games. Enacting scenarios where she and Leigh could just casually run into Gray, get the introductions done and the awkwardness over.

Leigh was the key.

The closure.

She had no reason to carry the loss from the past any longer. She had the future she'd most wanted. The future she'd chosen.

Was truly happy.

The problem was bridging her current world to her past pain, in order to make herself one again.

That was the closure. Welcoming Grayson Bartholomew into her new life, rather than shunning him. A person shunned pain. Loss.

She'd forgiven Gray. The fact that she'd opted to help him—truly wanted to help him—get his life back was proof of that to her.

She just hadn't completely let go of the pain he'd caused her.

"What's Uncle Scott's friend's name again?" Leigh asked as she skipped beside Sage on the beach, sending grains of white sand atop both of their feet and ankles.

"His name is Grayson Bartholomew, but you can call him Mr. B."

"How come the mister? That's only at school and when you work."

On the beach, Leigh called most people *aunt* or *uncle* before their first names. But only because their neighborhood was such a unique place on earth.

"What about Lindy's mother?" Sage asked, in her flow with the little girl. As long as she paid attention, she was usually able to keep up, and a lot of times stay a step or two ahead. "Lindy's your best friend and you call her mother Mrs. Miller."

Leigh stopped to pick up a shell. Carefully put it in her pocket, and then started hopping toward Scott's cottage.

"Is Mr. Buzzing Bee Uncle Scott's best friend?" the little girl asked a few yards later.

"It's just B, Leigh. Like the alphabet letter. Bartholomew is a long word and it starts with B so that's why I told you to call him Mr. B."

The child looked up at her, those blue eyes filled with incredible, joy-sustaining life. "I like Buzzing Bee, anyway," she said.

And didn't return to the best friend question.

For which Sage was grateful. Sometimes distraction worked. Sometimes not.

Gray texted Sage as he walked to his SUV outside the second shelter he volunteered at on Saturday.

How soon will I have a first draft of company bylaws and regulations, specifically pertaining to the multiple clinic model and multiple veterinarians?

She could be working. She'd said she sometimes worked on Saturdays.

In its current state, his whole life consisted of work.

And he'd had a great conversation with two other veterinarians from San Diego, who'd been visiting the shelter he'd just left. Doctors he didn't know, who knew all about him, and when he'd said he was in the process of working with a corporate firm to reestablish himself, they'd both expressed interest in joining him.

Not at all put out by his reputation.

On the contrary, they'd been impressed by what he'd managed to accomplish, by the business practices that had largely become public knowledge as, piece by piece, his life had been laid bare.

They'd chosen to believe that he'd had nothing to do with the illegal drug dealing going on at GB Animal Clinics.

And yet, when he'd gone to speak with established clinics—hoping to find work for himself in the interim between his clinics being part of large-scale criminal charges being brought, and the case actually being adjudicated—he'd heard an entirely different story. By and large, established, successful practices hadn't wanted to be associated with him.

With the news hounds and viral social media posts, there were a lot of people who believed he was guilty by association.

GB Animal Clinics was his corporation. Therefore, he had to have known what was going on inside at least one of the sites.

Gray was in his car, debating about what to do with the rest of his day—deciding on piling his back end with moving boxes and tape, and heading to his house to begin the onerous task of packing—when the clonk sounded again.

Deciding not to wait until he got to the store, he drove another block and pulled over instead.

I'm not working today. Will you be back at Scott's in time for a cookout on the beach?

He read. He sat. He stared.

And read again.

*No.* He spoke the mental answer in total silence.

What did that mean, *I'm not working will you be back in time for a cookout?*

That she wanted personal time with him?

Wanted to know if she could have a cookout with her brother—and he assumed others since it was on the beach—without worrying that he'd invade her space?

If she wasn't working, the question had been personal. Not part of the strictly business mandate between them. But couldn't really be part of the one established exception—that he be nice to her kid if he ran into the little one on the beach.

Bothered by how much weight the text was carrying into his day, he typed:

No.

Stared at his phone some more.

Considered his quiet, remote, locked-up and sold home.

The hours of packing with only darkness outside. Mirroring the darkness that had fallen over his world.

Hit Delete.

Typed again.

Is this an invitation?

And hit Send.

Sage was busy calling other Ocean Breeze residents, arranging salads and veggies and other goodies to complement the meats that she and Scott would be providing, when Gray's text came back.

With a quick call to her brother, she had Scott take over the Gray-being-there portion of the impromptu gathering she'd talked Scott into hosting.

Under the guise of introducing Gray to everyone in the neighborhood. Canine and human.

Leaving it up to Gray to determine whether or not he wanted to make his profession known to them. He'd come to them as a haven from the mongrels who were trying to keep drama going by insisting that he had to have something to do with the drug dealing at his properties. He was the owner. The buck stopped with him.

In the smallest part of herself, she knew the truth. She'd

suggested the gathering to get herself out of that past and into the present.

To heal herself.

Impromptu meeting attempts hadn't worked.

Storming up the beach looking like a hundred bucks hadn't worked.

She had to find a way to ensure that Gray would be present.

A party in his honor ought to do it.

As the morning and early afternoon had worn on, and acceptances poured in one after another, she'd begun to consider her idea inspired.

Gray deserved the enthusiastic welcome their neighbors were offering him.

And she could get the bridge gapped from past to present without ever having to speak with him one-on-one at all.

A party. With lots of people. All wanting to meet him. Say hello. Welcome him.

Most of them dog owners, which would give Gray a lot to talk about with them.

And she could be a fly perched...somewhere.

Watching Leigh—currently the only child on the beach of cottages owned by successful single professionals.

Other than arranging the food and time, getting the burgers out of her freezer to thaw, reminding Scott to take out the brats he had in the freezer—leftover from a Fourth of July gathering—she wasn't doing much. Everyone knew to bring a chair.

They'd set up in the middle of the beach—which ended up being in front of Sage's cottage—and Scott would wheel out her grill.

Needing to keep Leigh occupied, she put the little girl in the car and drove up to town for buns. And stopped at a store that sold discounted goods for a couple of new outdoor fun toys to occupy Leigh once they were down on the beach.

Knowing full well she wouldn't need them.

Ocean Breeze residents, both canine and otherwise, adored Leigh. It was like they'd all adopted her—their vicarious child—and she moved among them with a confidence that filled Sage's heart.

Still, just in case, she didn't want her four-year-old to have an age-appropriate meltdown the first time Gray met her.

The closure would be more complete, and quick, if it was perfect the first time out.

She was just pulling back into her space on Ocean Breeze when her text sounded.

Scott says you're organizing food. What can I bring?

She read it twice. Looked at Gray's contact information twice and smiled. A not altogether wholesome expression.

Generally speaking, the guest of honor was told not to bring anything.

But it was Gray.

He was going to attend.

And was playing nice.

She was safe.

Was getting her closure.

The weeks ahead looked brighter.

So she typed:

The broccoli salad your grandma taught you to make. The one with the dried cranberries in it.

And hit Send.

Darkness had fallen. Gray stood at the edge of the small gathering—residents from thirteen of the fifteen occupied cottages on Ocean Breeze. The other two had had previous commitments. He'd already met the residents from one of the two—Harper and Aggie. And there were still several more cottages yet to be renovated and sold. Or sold and renovated, he'd been told. In case he was interested in joining them.

That last had been offered by Dale, a bearded writer, whose constant companion, Juice, was the quiet but strong man's service dog.

He'd been so busy meeting neighbors—at least ostensibly—that he'd managed to be out of speaking distance of Sage's daughter, Leigh, ever since he'd arrived. He'd caught sight of her, of course, many times, but had always had his attention drawn back into one or another of the conversations going on around him.

Talking to everyone, most particularly Dale, he'd been germinating his impromptu morning plan to perhaps start a service dog water rescue course on the beach. And as he stood there, with a brief moment in the shadows, holding his mostly full bottle of beer, he contemplated just making the announcement right then and there. The class would be free.

No business or tax ramifications.

He'd make copies of his service dog training certificate for everyone.

And… "Mr. Buzzing Bee?"

He heard the voice. It was close. Glancing down, he saw the pudgy-cheeked face looking up at him with a way too serious expression for a child that young.

He hadn't heard her approach. Glanced out over the crowd for Sage.

Or Scott.

First glance gave him nothing.

He had to glance down again. "Mr. Buzzing Bee? Who's that?" He sure as hell wasn't up on kid shows and their various characters. Past or present.

"Mommy says you're Mr. B, like the alphabet, but I like Mr. Buzzing Bee, that's who."

*Mr. Buzzing Bee.* His heart flipped. And then flopped.

Sage's daughter had given him her own name.

He looked for her mother. Didn't see her.

"Are you mad at me?"

Peering down into those big, soul-deep eyes, Gray dropped down to his haunches. "Oh no, never," he told her. Not because Sage had told him to be nice. Or because he feared her child would ruin their truce by saying he was mad at her.

But because...nothing else came to mind except making certain that he did not, in any way, have an adverse effect on the child.

"You know why I could never be mad at you?" he asked, sifting through a dozen reasons that popped immediately to mind, so he gave her the best one.

"Mmm-hmm." She nodded so big her chin touched her chest full of unicorns with every downward pass.

"You do?"

Her gaze at him was steadfast. "Yep."

"Why?"

"Because you're Uncle Scott's friend and Uncle Scott loves me." The little one's tone of voice sounded as though she was talking to a child who didn't understand. The answer was clearly obvious to her.

And not one of the twelve or so he'd come up with. A lot of them dealing with her mother. But Leigh's version was also true. And worked just fine.

As the little girl ran off, Scott took a long sip of beer. And digested the fact that Sage, and/or Scott, had chosen not to mention that Gray had also, once, a long time before, been friends with her mother, too.

# Chapter Twelve

Leigh ran up to Sage as she was coming back from gathering up dessert supplies and tools. "Mommy, Mommy... Mr..." The child stopped, saw the bag hanging over Sage's wrist and the tools in her hand. "It's s'mores time! Yay!" Leigh ran off—to tell any number of people that it was time for dessert, Sage was sure, when suddenly the child turned back around.

"Mr. Buzzing Bee isn't mad at me!" she announced gleefully and headed back to the crowd.

Not everyone wanted the toasty snack. On the contrary, most didn't. But people pitched in to help create Leigh's favorite treat, and Sage caught several smiles in Leigh's direction from the residents settling down to their lawn chairs, as conversations broke up to twos and threes, and quieted.

That was when Sage noticed Gray, sitting in the chair Scott had loaned him, a bit closer to the beach than anyone else. Sipping his beer.

Having clearly pulled his chair back after everyone else had settled.

Iris jumped up from the chair next to Scott's empty one. "I've got this," she said to Sage, nodding toward the marshmallow Scott was grilling, and Leigh, who, with chocolate on her face and sticky fingers, was waiting to carry a plate with the beloved treat to Dale, who'd asked for one.

The photographer nodded toward Gray and said, "Go."

She couldn't go.

Didn't want to go.

Iris nodded toward Leigh's empty chair. And back toward Gray. As if to say, scoot.

Leaving Sage the choice to make enough of a scene that someone, worst of all Leigh, would catch on that something was going on. And included in that choice, leading Iris to believe that Sage couldn't handle a few minutes alone with their new neighbor.

Or, pick up her chair and join Gray for a couple of minutes of casual beach chat.

With a mental promise to verbally decimate her twin for telling anyone about her past with Grayson Bartholomew, Sage picked up her chair.

Gray saw her coming. He could have prevented a quiet conversation in the dark, with nice people gathered in front of them, and the ocean flowing in steady, soft waves behind them.

But it was time to man up. To realize that the love he'd felt for Sage in the past had been the real thing. Ill-fated, yes. But not going to die.

He hadn't left her because he hadn't loved her. He'd left her because he couldn't be the man she'd needed.

And still couldn't.

It was time to come face-to-face with that fact. Put it right there between them—a solid, unbreakable wall.

She didn't ask if she could join him. Just unfolded her chair and set it next to his.

He took a sip of his beer. To appear nonchalant. And for liquid bravery. It was only his second. He'd never been all that big of a drinker.

"Where's your wine cooler?" he asked, building up to making the wall. Wine and wine coolers were all he'd ever known her to drink. And neither any more heavily than he'd ever imbibed.

"I left it in the house when I went for the s'mores," she told him. "I only ever have the one, and rarely finish that anymore. Being a parent...changes things."

Bingo. Bullet to the target.

Or, more accurately, plaster to the two-by-fours. Wall construction complete. And he hadn't had to lift a finger.

He took another sip of beer. Painting the wall, he told himself. He wasn't changed. Still had his two beers.

"She told me you weren't mad at her," Sage said from next to him, facing the same crowd he was. Probably seeing it all very differently. She was part of a family there on Ocean Breeze.

He was a stranger in a very nice land.

She'd said *she*. Not Leigh. As though they both knew that the existence of that child was proof that he'd made the right decision to walk out on their wedding.

"I'm Mr. Buzzing Bee," he offered, with a motion of his beer bottle in her direction. Like throwing up a hand.

Or...throwing in the towel. Topping the wall with it.

"I'm sorry about that..."

"No," he interrupted. "I don't mind. Seriously." The wall was high enough. "Truth be told, I kind of like it." He didn't grin, but in another world, he might have. "You've done a great job with her," he continued. "She's bright, and aware. Self-confident..."

He stopped himself before he went too far. Said too much.

Sage nodded. Didn't even look his way. But said, "It does my heart good to hear you say that. Thank you."

Her heart.

He couldn't go there.

Had somehow started to climb that wall between them. He needed to get himself back down to the ground. Lock himself in place there. Permanently.

Sage had an ex someplace. Or, at the very least a co-parent.

Perhaps even still in her life.

He hadn't been around enough to know if Leigh saw her father on a regular basis. Perhaps the man had had her for the night one night that week even. Or would get her for the entire next weekend. It wasn't like Scott would ever say so.

It wasn't any of Gray's business, of course. But that was the absolute best material for wall building.

"I have to ask…just because…it's like the old elephant in the room… Where's her father in all of this?"

He expected Sage to stiffen, at the very least, and maybe issue a very professional pronouncement that he was crossing the newly established line between them.

A line that seemed to keep moving, somehow.

Not because he wanted it to. And he was damned sure that she didn't.

"I have no idea." Her words were…shocking. Horrible.

His heart stopped as he considered that she'd been forced. By a stranger. "Wait…you weren't… Oh, my God…"

"I don't know because her birth mother didn't say…" Sage's words kept falling next to him. As hard as he was trying, he couldn't quite catch up with them.

Not quickly enough. He was too busy fighting off the need to go find and strangle any man who would have forced himself on Sage.

"She's adopted."

Adopted.

*Adopted.*

But…that couldn't be.

It could not be.

For an entirely different reason. Gray felt like a racquetball, bouncing around a small, enclosed room, hitting wall to ceiling, wall to wall, wall to floor…

When he'd freed Sage from himself, she hadn't gone out and found the man she'd needed? The one who would…

So yeah, he'd figured that there'd been a bump in that road…the woman was living alone, raising a child, but… marriages broke up for various reasons.

He glanced at her. Saw her following Leigh's antics playing with the collie, Angel. Smiling. The first true Madonna smile he'd ever seen in real life.

And when Sage started talking about the advent of her very special daughter into her life, Gray saw just how much having a family had meant to her.

Way more than he'd even realized.

More than he ever had, for sure.

"I'd been on an adoption list for a couple of years," Sage said, "and then one night I get a call. A woman had picked me just that afternoon. She'd gone into premature labor, had signed necessary papers and had died giving birth. A blood pressure thing. The baby was mine if I wanted her. There'd be some legalities, of course, but, if I was interested, they needed me to get to the hospital right away. Because…"

She stopped. Couldn't go on.

She'd thought telling Gray about Leigh would cement the closure. Sever whatever thing kept trying to bud up inside her.

But as it turned out…she couldn't let him see her that deeply. That clearly. Not anymore.

"Because why?"

The tone in his voice, the soft depth that had always

reached her…pulled her gaze away from her very safe and happy child, to peer into the eyes of the man who could have been her child's father.

"They didn't think she was going to make it. I…um… wasn't going to lose my place on the adoption list if I took her. They just wanted to let me know…because technically, and more, morally, I had the right to be with her…and they didn't want the baby to die alone if she didn't need to do so."

"You went." He didn't guess. Or ask. He told. They'd been apart for ten years, and she'd changed some, but the type of person she was…he knew that person almost as well as she knew herself.

She nodded. "Scott didn't think I should at first. It was the middle of the night, and my call woke him up. But when I told him that they expected the baby to live for a month or more, not just a day or two, he supported my decision to be there for her. And…there was a chance that she was going to make it to a more normal lifespan. What kind of mother would I be if I just presented myself for the sure thing? The celebration? Without being willing to be a part of the fight?"

She couldn't read Gray's glance. She saw no approval there. Or disapproval, either. No judgment. Not even a knowing, like he'd have expected her to make the choice she had. It was almost as though he was studying her. Which made no sense at all.

He'd started the conversation.

And she finished it. "I lived at the children's hospital for almost three months. Took a leave from my job. Touched her when I could. Learned how to change tubes, how to re-insert them, how to read monitors and finally, how to hold a baby hooked up to so many life-maintaining machines. I talked to her all day. Kissed her good-night every night, even when they could only be blown through glass. They'd said she'd probably have brain damage. Would be slow to develop. And for the first year, they were right. About the development part."

She could be done. The happy ending, Leigh, was yards away in front of them, looking as though she was trying to employ all her cuteness to coax one more treat out of her uncle. At the moment, Sage didn't care if Scott gave in or not. One more piece of sugar before bedtime wasn't going to hurt the little girl.

Leigh had fought so hard, been through so much…

"She had to have six surgeries that first year," she said softly. "But they didn't seem to faze her. Every time I'd smile at her, she'd smile back. And now, she doesn't even remember that year. She calls her scars her birthmarks…"

Sage didn't pay attention to the tears on her cheeks. Didn't care.

Until Gray reached over to softly wipe them away.

What in the hell was he doing? Walls were in place for reasons. You didn't reach through them.

In the dark, with friendly people right there, with Sage's daughter right there, he didn't feel the danger.

Rather, he saw a new beginning. A place where he and Sage Martin could be friends.

Because Leigh was the wall between anything else that could have tried to re-blossom between them.

And she was as much of a guaranteed constant as they'd ever get, right there in Sage's world day and night.

She'd glanced over when he touched her. Was still looking at him. And he couldn't look away from her, either. As though they were signing another document, seeing each other anew, in different capacities to each other than they'd been. "It was your gestation period." He told her what seemed obvious to him. "She wasn't inside you, but you were wrapped around her as she developed. Your voice was her everyday constant. Your love for her probably grew every day, as I imagine it does when a woman has a baby in her womb. By the sounds of things, you were focused on her, as a woman has to be when a baby has taken over her body, and she kind of changed all of your normal choices, too, since you were spending days sitting in a hospital for her, eating hospital food, changing your normal physical habits…"

Tears formed in Sage's eyes again, and Gray stopped talking. Figuring maybe more had changed about the two of them than he'd known. He didn't know her as well as he'd thought. Had lost his ability to read her.

Until she said, "Thank you, Gray. I think that's the most incredible thing anyone has ever said to me."

And he swelled up like a geeky high school kid who'd just been kissed by the head cheerleader.

# Chapter Thirteen

Sage dreamed about Gray that night. Not one solid story. Or dream. Instead, it was a night filled with various sides of him. Flashing vignettes. Like letting go had opened up a floodgate of memories she'd been refusing to acknowledge for the past ten years.

Closure, releasing, meant setting it all free.

Sunday was the day to get ready for the week and after watching kids' church online with Leigh, she took the little girl out to lunch and then shopping, ending up at the grocery store, before heading home to relax for a few hours.

As chatty as always, Leigh kept Sage's thoughts occupied, often jumping from one topic to the next, as she saw things or other thoughts occurred. Their conversations ranged from Uncle Scott not being lonely now that Mr. Buzzing Bee was there, to nose picking. With a whole lot of *whys*, *how comes*, *I wants* and *can I haves* thrown in. Sage figured there might come a day when she'd crave mental quiet time, hours to entertain thoughts of her own, as she'd read in a few of the online forums for young mothers, but she wasn't there yet.

Sunday afternoon was dog time on the beach, with owners home, not working and wanting to give their companions time to run and play freely. Folks mostly stayed on their own porches, or in front of their own properties, which made everyone out of hearing range, but the dogs pretty much ran freely. And came and went, with a huge celebration every time someone new arrived on the scene.

And then there was Leigh.

Who ran through the front door of the cottage to the back, as soon as they got home. Saw her uncle, and as Sage came in with bags of groceries, announced that she was going to play with Morgan.

Scott generally made his way down to spend time with his niece, most particularly on Sundays. The two of them having quality time together, as near daily as possible, was the whole reason Sage had moved to Ocean Breeze. So that Leigh would have a father figure in her life, teaching her things Sage didn't know or care much about. Growing up twins, going through school together, Sage and Scott had been close. And at the same time, she'd been all girl all the way. Loving the frills. And Scott had been all boy.

Generally speaking, when it came to the mechanics of things, Sage didn't care how it all worked. She was just glad it did. Scott could explain in real detail how a car started just because you pushed a button. She'd deferred that question to him just the week before.

Scott also challenged the little girl to try, when Sage would have issued more caution. Gave her different insights, different ways of approaching problems, different thinking skills.

Where Sage tended to react emotionally in certain situations, Scott was more practical. Like the time Leigh had fallen, running on the beach, had hit a lawn chair and needed stitches in her head. She'd been less than two. Sage had been fighting tears on the way to the hospital, hating that Leigh was having to go back, to suffer more, and Scott had spent the time making funny noises and singing silly songs as he drove.

When she'd asked him about it later, Scott had told her that he knew Leigh would be fine. Stitches were a part of growing up.

And he'd been right, of course.

Still, Sage had suffered every second of discomfort right along with her little girl. Wishing she could experience the pain in Leigh's stead. And Leigh had wanted only her mother with her, holding her hand when the doctor had been stitching up her head. Staring at Sage, the toddler had whimpered as the numbing spray was applied, but after that, she'd just lain still. Watching her mom.

Because of those months of *gestation* as Gray had called it the night before?

He'd put a lovely spin on what had seemed such a heartbreaking time.

And...she wasn't going to do more than acknowledge that she was happily adopting the new perspective, giving him credit, with gratitude for giving it to her, and moving on.

No glomming on the gift giver, she reminded herself as she put away all the household items she'd stocked up on that day.

Though, didn't closure open the door to a new possibility? That of the two of them as friends?

She didn't hate the idea.

She was still toying with it in her mind as she finished up and went outside to join her daughter and brother.

They were no longer alone. As often happened, Angel and Iris had joined them. The professional photographer lived in the cottage next to Sage, and the two women had been friends since the first day Sage had looked at her new home. There'd been several places to choose from, some already renovated, some that could be done to her liking. She'd ultimately chosen the one she did partially because of Iris Shiprock.

The woman had lit up when she'd seen eight-month-old Leigh—in spite of the two tubes still connected to the small-for-her-size baby. She'd gushed and engaged—and had shown real compassion, too, though not in front of the baby.

And...Iris had also been a twin. She'd lost her sister in a car accident, Iris being the only survivor, and had moved into the cottages when she'd been ready to start her new life.

Sage had always figured her and Scott's twin status had been why the three of them had bonded so quickly.

That afternoon, as soon as she saw the game of chase ball that Scott was instigating with his niece and both dogs, Sage took a seat in the sand right next to Iris.

She was on a mission to set her friend straight.

"I'm guessing, from the way you were pushing me on Gray last night, that you were thinking about our history."

With almost twenty-four hours to consider it, she didn't blame her brother for confiding in Iris—most particularly if he'd been concerned and had wanted perspective.

"Noooooo." Iris's eyes were alight as she pulled out the word with a sound of anticipation and interest. "You know him?" she asked, then answered with, "Well, obviously, I know you knew him since you and Scott said he'd known him since high school...but history? As in, you *know* him know him?"

Cringing inside, Sage gave herself demerits for overre-acting. And creating an issue for herself where there needn't have been one.

She should have trusted her brother to hold her privacy sacred. He always had.

"Come on, now, you've spilled the beans. Do tell!"

She didn't want to tell.

Not even Iris. Didn't want to talk about the past. She'd just gotten closure. Hadn't even had a full day to savor the freedom.

Hashing up the past so soon just seemed…dense. Ignorant. Like nothing good could come of it.

Which was why she'd intended to let Iris know that no matter what Scott had told her, there was absolutely nothing between her and Gray.

She'd needed the woman to let go, just as she had.

And to that end… "I just…the way you shoved me over there last night, visually at least…if you didn't…why did you do that?"

Iris hadn't known? And she'd still…

The *why* suddenly took precedence over what she'd sat down to do. Letting Iris know that there'd never be anything between her and Gray, other than a possible lighthearted, very casual friendship, and to stop pushing them together.

"Seriously, Sage…the vibes between you two? They were setting the beach on fire!"

"They were not." They couldn't possibly have been.

And… "You think everyone thinks that?" Horror rushed through her so strongly, she didn't even try to keep it out of her voice.

"I wouldn't say that," Iris allowed slowly, ostensibly watching the antics on the beach between dogs, man and child, but Sage saw the glances Iris was stealing…all aimed at her. "The rest of them don't know you like I do."

True. Iris knew all about Leigh, had sat with Sage late one night, asking questions, shortly after she'd moved in. Had wanted to see all the pictures. And was always up for watching Leigh if Sage had to work late.

The woman had done some pretty phenomenal photo sessions with the two of them, too. Both individually and together. Catching an essence Sage had never seen in herself.

But one that she'd been trying to get to know better ever since.

Partially appeased, Sage nodded. "Get it!" she called out to Leigh when the little girl was racing her uncle for the ball. And followed it with, "Good girl!" as Scott let the preschooler win.

"Back to Gray," Iris said, and it was like Sage could feel the other woman's insistence. Her need to know.

"There are no vibes between us." She had to get that straight, make it perfectly clear, right up front.

"You can say so," Iris told her. "But my eye doesn't lie, girl. I know what I see."

Right. Iris's photography was so good because of all the things the woman noticed that others didn't. Slammed by her own previous thoughts of just minutes before. Still… "No one's perfect, Iris. Even you have to get it wrong once in a while and this is that while."

Iris didn't even seem to consider the possibility. The strength with which she shook her head further abased any hint of her being wrong.

"You can deny it all you want. I know what I saw. And, I might add, not just on you."

Sage stared at the other woman. She thought Gray was lusting after her, too?

Now that was just ludicrously…not hitting her as negatively as it should have been.

Shaking her head, shooing away any chance that there could be a little bit of truth hiding in Iris's erroneous perspective, Sage asked, "You feel like leftovers for dinner? Scott and I both have fridges filled with salads. From potato to broccoli…"

Broccoli salad made by Gray. She'd made sure what wasn't eaten had made it back to Scott's refrigerator. Not her own.

"No way, Sage. You aren't dissing me on this one. Seriously. You and Gray have a past. You just admitted it by thinking Scott had told me about it."

Yeah. But that didn't mean she had to spill her guts if she chose not to. Even to her closest friend.

"It might help, having someone impartial to him who could have an eye out for you." Iris's words fell softly then, all teasing gone. "Obviously, it's something of a big deal to you or you wouldn't be avoiding talking about it."

Silently entertaining the thought that if Iris knew she was avoiding the topic, she'd be kindest just to leave it alone, Sage homed in on the rest. Someone having her back. Just in case.

Someone who could save her from herself if she slid back out of closure…

A woman who could talk womanly emotions with her. Things like, say, lust. A topic she and Scott had never and would never address.

And so, trying for as few words as possible, she told her friend, "We were engaged. Ten years ago. I wanted a family. He'd said a few times that he didn't get the whole family thing. That he was open to getting it, but wasn't sure he'd be a good father. Things like that. Never with any explanation, you know? Even when I asked why he'd say those things. He'd just shrug. And then two days before the wedding— a two-hundred-guest affair, which we'd been planning for almost a year—he tells me that he doesn't ever want to be a father, doesn't want a family and since he knew how important it was to me to be a mother, he thought it best if we called everything off."

There. She'd talked about it.

Saw the change come over Iris. Compassion and support, rather than teasing or egging her on toward a possible hookup.

And Sage finally had closure.

* * *

The next week passed in a flurry of business. Gray made the decision to start up a series of clinics, assuming he had enough vets willing to put their names on the dotted line, rather than just into conversation. He'd reached a goal and didn't want to be scared into sliding backward into one affordable clinic that offered basic care and surgeries at a cost lower- to middle-class families could afford.

And he was calling them Buzzing Bee Clinics. It was a great name for animal clinics. Made him smile. He'd texted the name to Sage, a bit apprehensive that she'd read too much into his adopting her daughter's name for him for his new start. He needn't have worried. She'd simply texted back a smiley face, and got to work on filing for the corporation. Drafting bylaws. An employee manual. Composing contracts for all veterinarians to sign, making them wholly responsible, separate and apart from Buzzing Bee Clinics, for their own choices and actions. They'd be contractors. Not employees. And could be terminated for not following contracted mandates.

Each separate clinic would have a manager, who was hired by Gray and reported directly to him.

The list of protections went on, and while Gray wasn't sure he'd ever find anyone who'd sign on with him under the proposed guidelines, at least not with his reputation currently in tatters, he'd been bolstered by the conversations he'd had the week before and had to try.

All because of Sage.

Before she'd called him to talk business, he'd been thinking in terms of applying to become a government employee paid to work at the shelters where he was currently volunteering. Abandoned animals didn't give a snoot about reputation. They just wanted to be helped and loved.

Both of which he knew he could accomplish.

Just until the courts were done with GB Animal Clinics and he could see what was left to start over. At which time he'd go back to working the shelters for free.

The house selling had bought him more time.

And Sage…

Heading up the elevator to her office to go over the final draft of the new corporation business portfolio on Thursday afternoon, Gray thought again of his conversation with Sage Saturday night on the beach. He didn't let himself dwell.

Much.

Hadn't been home to see her or her little miracle on Ocean Breeze since that night, but he did occasionally have to stop and readjust his thinking of her to a brand-new version.

A beautiful version.

But one that more clearly didn't fit as a partner in his life. Being a mother was Sage's life goal.

Being a wife had been a means to that end.

Her door was open and with a light knock, he headed in, closing the door behind him. Sage, on a call, waved at him, and he took his usual chair over in the conversation area of her office.

They'd established a routine. Knew each other's expectations.

It was nice.

In a black, slim-fitting, above-the-knee skirt, tight white tank and short black jacket, she came over to join him.

He didn't react.

A definite sign of successful wall building.

Of recovery.

Holding up the folder he'd carried in, the house sale papers she'd requested him to bring, he asked, "Which do you want to do first?"

She'd brought a pile of folders over with her.

"The house." She didn't even hesitate on that one. Held out a hand. Their fingers brushed as he passed it over. And... he didn't get hard.

She'd become only a friend. No more heightened senses around her. No more tension as he worked hard to be everything she needed. To get every bit of everything right.

And no more open door to sexual memories, either.

He watched her pore over the pages, was fond of the focused look on her face as she read every word of a very standard, very boring real estate contract. And then copies of title papers that he'd be signing as soon as he left her.

The tip of her tongue snuck out to lick her bottom lip. He noticed. Stared at it for the second it took him to realize he was doing it and stop.

And he didn't get hard.

She read the last page, nodded and said exactly what he'd expected her to say. "Everything looks good."

He nodded. Not surprised. But pleased to have her expert opinion just the same. He had hundreds of thousands of dollars on the line. Even after all his years of success, he didn't feel the wealth lightly.

Putting the pages back in the folder, Sage didn't hand it back to him as he'd expected. Half sitting forward to take it from her, he watched her put the folder on her lap, her hands clasped over it, and sat back.

Was something wrong? Making her hesitate? He didn't ask. If there was a problem, he didn't have to pull it forward. It would find him.

"Are you sure you want to do this, Gray?"

The compassion in her expression as she met his gaze hit him hard. He hadn't been expecting it. "You think it's a bad move?" He was pretty good with numbers…and getting more than market price on a cash deal.

"Not financially," she said. "Of course not. You come way out on top here. It's just that…" She glanced away, and then back. Taking him back.

To that damned surfboard.

Which couldn't be happening.

But he'd seen the look before. The time he'd told her he'd sold the board for the earrings. He hadn't thought about that transaction in a decade, and suddenly it was there twice in a week?

"This house…it's everything you always wanted, Gray. Your dream home. And it's not like they're a dime a dozen around here. Obviously. Based on what the new owners are willing to pay to get it. I just hate to see you give it up."

He opened his mouth to speak. Stopped the words that were about to come out because he'd be mirroring a scene from a lifetime on the other side of the wall.

"I'm pretty sure we're going to be able to get you that income fund, Gray. The deposits all line up exactly, as you'd said they would. We've already talked to the judge. A hearing is scheduled, which is part of what I have to talk to you about today." She nodded toward the much larger pile of file folders on the table in front of her. "You don't have to do this."

Maybe not in her world. In his…he didn't have his account back yet. His own fault for leaving the money in the corporation at all. And Gray didn't live on hopes and probablys. "If I renege on this offer, I might not get another one as sweet," he said. And then, feeling cornered, finished with the blast from the past. "I just don't have an attachment to things, Sage. If I need another house on a cliff over the ocean, I'll find it. And pay what I have to pay to get it."

He knew, even before he'd finished, that he should have kept his mouth shut.

The expression on her face...he'd seen it before, too. A mixture of sorrow and something more. Not horror. Nothing as acute as that. But a total lack of understanding, for sure. Like maybe she was looking at a creature from outer space.

Almost as though there was something wrong with him.

Only this time, he didn't feel threatened. He no longer needed her to see him in his best light. Didn't have to feel like he had to downplay the details of who he'd been, where he'd come from. He'd never lied to her, or Scott, about his youth. They knew the basics.

In that moment, with her looking at him as though there was no wall separating past from present, he said, "When I was growing up, everything in my home, every possession I had, had a price tag on it. Any given day, any given thing could disappear if money was needed for groceries or to keep the electric on." He wasn't looking for sympathy. He was about to be a very rich man again, whether she got him his income savings back or not. Some part of him just needed to clear up a mistake from the past.

Not for her.

But for himself. He was done selling his own truths short.

"Any time I quit playing with a toy for more than a couple of weeks, it was put up for sale. Either with a sign on it in the front yard, or through word of mouth."

Her mouth hung open, her eyes wide with the horror he'd escaped earlier. "I'm so sorry, Gray, I had no idea...you never said..."

He cut her off with a wave of the hand. "I'm fine with it, Sage. That's the point. I learned young that I'd have what I needed to survive, and the rest...the wants...they were dispensable. But I also learned that things could be replaced. Through my own hard work."

Speaking of things he wanted, he held out his hand, looking at the folder on her lap. With a quick glance down, she picked it up. Held it out toward him. But when he'd taken hold, would have pulled it away, she held on to her side. Placing her free hand over his.

"Your surfboard meant more to me than the earrings, Gray," she said softly, shocking his equilibrium straight to hell. She'd remembered.

He met her gaze. Couldn't look away.

"It meant more to me because you'd worked so hard to get it. You were so proud of it, used it all the time. It was more than a surfboard. It was a reward for your dedication and hard work and you deserved that joy."

Her words, her eyes, her touch… Gray was starting to flounder again.

As though she was reading his thoughts, she said, "I still have those earrings. I kept them because they're a symbol to me of hard work and dedication—and the joy to be gained from both."

As she finished, she squeezed his hand.

And Gray got hard.

# *Chapter Fourteen*

Using her newfound closure to get her through the meeting with Gray, Sage shut her office door behind him the second he exited. Sagged back against it.

*Why hadn't he told her?*

The question had been ripping at her heart for the past hour.

Even as her brain had focused on the business at hand.

Gray had spent his entire childhood having had his possessions sold out from beneath him—his toys even?

As shocking as that was, the fact that he hadn't shared the experience with her...

Sage made it back to the couch. Sat. Felt the start of tears and didn't stop them. Instead, she buried her face, holding her forehead with her fists, and rocked.

Trying to assimilate. To be then and now.

To understand. How could she have loved the man as completely, as wholeheartedly, as deeply, as she'd thought she had, and not *known*?

She'd asked about the surfboard. He'd shrugged her off. She'd let him.

Why had she let him?

Sitting up, she stared at his empty chair.

And remembered her conversation with Iris on the beach four days before.

*He'd said a few times that he didn't get the whole family thing. That he wasn't sure he'd be a good father. Things like that. Never with any explanation, you know? Even when I asked why he'd say those things. He'd just shrug.*

And she let him. She hadn't pushed.

Worse, she couldn't remember needing to know more.

She'd simply accepted that he was different from her and that that was okay. She hadn't judged. Or worried. Hadn't tried to make him more like her.

She'd accepted the man he was. Loved him for who he was.

There was no doubt in her mind about those things.

And yet…what he'd just told her…

It was like, in the space of five minutes, the man she'd known since she was eighteen was no more. He'd morphed into…more.

So much more.

Standing abruptly, filling with anger, she strode to the window. Was pretty sure she could pick out his SUV leaving the parking garage so far down below.

Didn't matter that there were hundreds of SUVs that looked identical to his on California roads.

How could he say he loved her and wanted to marry her, but hadn't even shared himself with her?

How humiliating to have blabbered every thought, every emotion, every want and fear all over him, only to find that he'd withheld even basic facts from her? And not just innocuous stuff, either. What he'd just told her…that was life-shaping information right there.

Why hadn't he told her, dammit?

Leaving the window, she went to her desk, reminding herself of the paying clients who were waiting to hear from her yet that day.

She had the work done. But the calls were equally important.

Communication was the key to trust.

And…he hadn't trusted her.

He hadn't trusted her?

Why hadn't he told her?

She could ask herself a thousand times and she wasn't going to get the answer. She didn't have it. Gray did.

So why hadn't she pushed? Tried harder?

Why had she let him just shrug her off?

Deflated, Sage flopped down into her chair. Slouched back, staring at…nothing.

She should have tried harder.

Like Iris had with her Sunday on the beach. People needed coaxing sometimes.

And sometimes they needed to know that the place was safe for revelations. Iris had made her feel safe. Letting Sage know that she saw her friend in need of support and was willing to offer only that.

Had she somehow failed to give Gray that same sense of support?

She sat up straight.

Did the fact that Gray had confided in her that day mean that he felt safe with her in the present, when he hadn't in the past? Was her offer to help him, her ability to come through on that offer, building a trust in him that hadn't been there in the past?

She hadn't meant to take his hand a bit ago. And definitely hadn't had any thought about squeezing it. She'd moved on reflex.

From an open heart brimming with more than ten-year-old love.

She'd seen his hard-on. The way he'd been sitting, legs

spread to lean forward…she'd glanced down, needing escape from the sudden depth of emotion flowing between them.

She'd seen.

Felt an instant, answering pool of warmth flooding her.

They'd both pulled back so quickly, she grabbing files, he covering his lap with his own, starting right in on business, that she'd almost convinced herself the seconds hadn't happened.

Certainly, they shouldn't have.

Nothing had changed between them in terms of hooking up. They weren't right for each other.

But if through closure, she could gain a very dear, beloved, very close friend…or even just be regular friends with Grayson Bartholomew again…

Sage reached for her cell. Hit the new, temporary speed dial she'd set up on her screen. Beneath Scott and Iris.

Listened to the ringing. Again and again.

Reminded herself he'd been going to the title company straight from her office.

Opened her text app instead. Needing to connect with him right then, right there, before she talked herself back from a moment she knew was too important to lose.

I should have known. I shouldn't have just accepted shrugs and non-answers. Please know that it wasn't a sign of not caring.

She wanted to tell him what had prompted a response that seemed a bit careless to her all those years later.

Couldn't explain, even to herself.

Hit Send.

Put her phone down. Reaching for her office phone to get

back to work and connect with one of her most important clients, while she waited to hear back from Gray.

He could be with the title people for a while.

Her phone beeped a new text before she'd started to dial.

Setting the receiver back in its cradle, heart thumping, she picked up her cell.

Don't, Sage. Don't look back. Don't start to wonder. Don't open that door. It won't end well.

She read the words once. Twice. Again.

Thought about pushing him, even while she knew that she'd lost that chance.

Knowing, too, that he was right, no matter what differences they resolved, or mistakes they tried to repair, in the end, nothing had changed.

And trying to prove otherwise wouldn't end well.

On Friday afternoon, late, Gray pulled his newly purchased handheld heavy-duty tape dispenser one more time. Sealing the last of the boxes of things that were being picked up and transported to the storage bin he'd rented.

He'd been working all week, in between business meetings— driving through camera flashes as he pulled onto the property.

He wasn't currently making headlines, but past experience told him that when the GB Animal Clinics case went to trial, any one of those photos could show up in major news sources, and on personal social media accounts, too.

*Boy from government housing made good, gone bad.* He'd read a couple of them when his clinics had first been shut down but had stopped almost immediately. They were energy sucks.

As was the house he'd once thought proof of him having

reached the pinnacle of his success. Thirty years old—at the time of purchase—and he was at the top.

Stacking the last of the boxes by the front door, he locked up for the last time, left the key for the Realtor—who was going to be at the house to meet the moving company the next day so Gray didn't have to deal with any possible paparazzi—got into his SUV and didn't look back.

An hour later, he was sipping a beer on Scott's back porch, inhaling long breaths of salty air. Relaxing for the first time all week.

"He's here! He's here!" The childish voice floated up to him before he noticed the bodies walking up the beach. Scott and Morgan had been gone when he'd arrived home—the prosecutor generally took the corgi for a jog on the two-mile-long beach after work. He'd figured them for visiting someplace, one direction or the other.

He didn't stand as Leigh, in leggings and a pink, short-sleeved ruffled smock, bounded toward the cottage. Her mother, also in leggings, with a loose-fitting white T-shirt and that long hair flowing in waves down her back and over her shoulders, didn't appear to be in nearly as much of a hurry.

Assuming they were looking for Scott, he was caught off guard when Leigh's voice, raised for her mother to hear, said, "Hurry, Mommy! We gotta hurry! Mr. Buzzing Bee's here!"

He stood then.

Sage was looking for him?

The woman had stopped a few yards from the porch. Leigh, however, was taking the steps—her hand on the rail helping to pull her up—one foot on each step.

"Like big people do!" she pronounced when she reached the top, her hair depicting a halo of golden ringlets in the setting sun. "Hi!" she said, stopping a couple of feet from Gray, looking up at him.

She wasn't smiling.

"Hi," he said back, glancing over the railing at Sage, still down on the beach. The woman shrugged.

Giving him no clue at all what was expected of him.

"Can I help you?"

"No. I did it all by myself," Leigh said, pointing toward the stairs. "I'm a big girl now."

"I can see that." Another glance toward Sage. Another shrug. "If you're looking for your uncle Scott and Morgan, they aren't here."

With one finger on her chin, Leigh appeared to be pondering that situation. "They're probly still exacizing," the little girl told him. "Morgan needs it."

Smiling, Gray stood there, feeling like a giant towering over the tiny human being, and said, "Why does she need it?" Just to hear the response.

"I dunno." Leigh squinted up at him. "But Mommy says you're a doctor for animals."

A third glance at Sage showed him a woman who was definitely keeping her distance. And an eye on her child, too. "That's right, I am."

Leigh's little fingers reached toward him and before he realized what was happening, she'd taken his hand. Gave it a good, four-year-old-size pull. "Good, then can you come pwease 'cause Baby is broked and Uncle Scott said he could fix her, but she's my best doggy and I fink she should have a real doctor."

Not sure what the child was talking about—Sage was one of the few Ocean Breeze owners who didn't have a dog—Gray filled with purpose.

There's no way he could, or would, refuse. That little brow, scrunched in the seriousness of the matter, had him leaving his beer behind without a thought as he allowed the youngster to lead him back down the steps to the beach.

In no universe would Sage have encouraged, or even suggested, that her daughter seek out Grayson Bartholomew. But neither did she attempt to dissuade the child from seeking the best care she thought she could get for her broken, battery-operated stuffed toy.

Staying on one side of Leigh as the little girl, with her hand still in Gray's, leading him with great purpose, told the man all about Baby. "She can bark and walk and wag her tail and do fwips," Leigh was saying with a sweet earnestness that brought tears to Sage's eyes. "'Cept now she can't and can you fix her?"

"I can sure try," Gray said, his head bent toward the child, his attention all on Leigh. He hadn't even glanced in Sage's direction as he'd come down the steps.

Hadn't given her the chance to mouth the *I'm sorry* she'd had ready for him.

Nor did he follow Leigh into their home when they reached Sage's place. "I'll wait right here on the steps," he told Leigh, sitting down after she'd climbed up. "Bring Baby out here. Maybe it would be good for her to get some fresh air."

More like he needed it, Sage guessed. And stood out in the sand, in front of him. "I'm sorry," she told him. "I could have dissuaded her, but she was so adamant. And also, just FYI, she thinks you're lonely down there all by yourself. I've tried to tell her you're not home much because you're so busy helping dogs be healthy." She was jabbering again. A pre-closure thing. Just… "I just don't want you to think I'm pushing her on you, or encouraging this behavior."

Gray looked up at her. "The thought never entered my mind."

Nor, apparently, did the fact that he was blocking her entrance to her porch.

"You're welcome to come in," she said from further outside her home than he was.

"I'm fine here." The refusal should in no way have hurt her feelings. And yet, it did.

"At least come up on the porch. I've got two chairs." He'd been sitting on Scott's porch. It was a thing he chose to do. If he refused...

Whether Gray was following her train of thought or not, didn't want to give her the impression that he had a problem being there with her or not, she couldn't tell. But felt better, anyway, when he stood and availed himself of one of the two chairs.

The one she always used.

But freeing up the steps so she had access to her home.

She just wished there was a way he could free up the space he'd captured in her heart.

# *Chapter Fifteen*

He fixed the toy. The wiring attaching the battery compartment to the parts that needed energy had frayed and come loose. A tiny cut with his teeth, to remove some colored coating, a few twists, and Baby was once again barking and flipping and wagging her tail.

"Yay!" Grabbing up the dog off the porch floor, Leigh hugged it. "I knew you could do it!" With the dog under her arm, she grabbed hold of the porch rail, as if to head down the steps.

"Hold it!" Sage's voice stopped all movement.

With one glance at her mother, Leigh said, "Oh yeah. Thank you, Mr. Buzzing Bee."

He grinned. "You're welcome," he said, figuring he should have been more solemn. Manners were a serious business.

He should be getting down those steps, too. Heading back the way he'd come. To the place he'd been invited to stay.

"I guess it's pretty obvious that my earlier stipulations… regarding our…interactions…aren't realistic." Sage's tone of voice came easy. Her words hit him hard.

He started to stand. "It's okay," he told her, figuring she was, in her way, apologizing again. Was getting kind of pissed that she thought she had to do so. For whatever reason.

"You want a wine cooler?" she asked before he'd fully left his chair. Throwing him for another loop.

Dropping his butt back in place, he figured it would be churlish, bad neighborly get-along vibes to refuse, and accepted the offer.

With a silent caveat that if she started in on him as her text the day before had implied, wanting to rehash the past, he'd leave the wine cooler, and her porch, behind.

She wasn't the only one, it turned out, who needed stipulations.

To move the conversation in a direction he figured she'd willingly follow—and keep her away from the areas he'd decided he would not go—he asked more about Leigh as soon as she handed him the bottle of lime-flavored beverage.

And as Leigh played in the sand with her newly fixed toy, chattering some scenario she'd concocted, Gray heard about the little girl's day care, in the building where Leigh worked. About the girl's penchant for correcting others when she thought they were wrong. Her cheerfulness. Her stubbornness. Her sweetness. Each characteristic coming out through stories Sage told.

And through questions he asked. Half an hour passed like minutes, and he began to wonder what she'd put in his drink, he was so relaxed.

Knowing full well that Sage Martin wouldn't spike a drink for any purpose. Except maybe, if a gun were put to the head of someone she loved.

She'd loved him once.

Silence had fallen between them. He figured he should go. Wasn't getting up yet. Still had a quarter of a bottle of wine cooler sitting with him.

"You think it's possible for us, me and you, to grow into something new?" Sage's words were like a slash in the early-evening glow. Back to the day before. He never should have given her that snippet of his childhood. Not when he hadn't done so when he'd been engaged to marry her. She'd picked up on the discrepancy. Wanted things he didn't choose to give...

He looked at her daughter yards away, playing happily in the sand. Leigh could jump up and join them at any time.

Sage wasn't pushing. Her question hung there, but she wasn't forcing anything.

Nor would she get into it with him or start something that could potentially blow up on them with the child right there.

As his mind worked its way back to reality, he entertained her question again.

*You think it's possible for us, me and you, to grow into something new?*

"I think the way life works, it's impossible not to grow into something new. Things happen. We experience them. They change us. Every single day," he told her.

"Yeah, but I mean us, Gray. I'm finding that, as we've let go of the past and put it behind us, I'd like to not miss you as I have over the years. These past two weeks have been nice."

All senses on alert, Gray warned himself about allowing wants to create a no-win situation. And felt Sage calling out to him in a way he wasn't sure he could deny.

They couldn't be a couple. They both knew that.

"What are you envisioning?" he asked. Their past, the way he'd walked away, the way he'd missed her, the things he still felt, forced the question.

"Friends." She gave the answer with no hesitation at all. Leading him to figure that while he was still grappling with her conversation, she'd already been through it in her head. Knowing Sage, probably multiple times.

He waited for her to continue. To give him what she'd come up with. While he tried to stay afloat. He'd had no such preparation time.

But being honest with himself, had to admit that he'd given Sage in his life again way more thought than he should have done.

She was there.

And she mattered.

Two facts he couldn't deny.

He glanced over to see her watching Leigh. Not him. And turned his visual attention outward once again as well.

"Like Iris and Scott." Her words came with confidence. "My brother and Iris and I have been friends since I moved in here," she continued. "You know Scott…after his disastrous marriage…"

"For which he takes the appropriate amount of blame," Gray interceded. When it came to her brother, he was a whole lot more in the know.

"I know. And you obviously know that since then his relationships with women are all casual. He's married to his career and wants it that way."

"I do know that, yes." He was way more curious to see where she was going with the conversation than he was to be discussing his friend at that moment.

"But with Iris…he's just like he is with you. Or more accurately probably, with me. They're close friends. Period."

Without sex. Gray heard the unwritten small print implied in her words.

She set her bottle down and touched Gray's arm. Drawing his gaze to hers before he thought better of it. "Because they both know that any more than that would come between them and they don't want to lose each other," she said, as though issuing a final, rehearsed line.

But one that rang with a strong core of truth.

Except for one thing.

That touch on his arm. Her fingers holding any part of him. And Gray wanted more than *just friends*.

Gray's eyes, holding steady on hers, felt like coming home. Feeling like she was treading water without a life vest, could be saved or sink at any moment, Sage didn't look away.

With one part of her, she heard her daughter's voice, still in storytelling mode, talking to Baby as Leigh dug in the sand. Building some imaginary world. She knew Leigh was close and safe.

And the other part, or another part…something inside her that had once been so strong…couldn't tear her gaze from the eyes boring into hers.

"I'm not going to lie to you." His voice, his words, started out so ominous, she sucked in her bottom lip. But stayed on board. She had to hear him.

Not just listen, but hear what he didn't say. Something she'd thought she'd done so well in the past, but clearly had not.

"I don't want to lose contact with you a second time…"

Thank God. She had to blink to keep from tearing up.

"But…"

No! Sage's brain went blank for a second. Not wanting the *but*. In the next second, she realized that the *but* was exactly what she needed if there was going to be any world for her and Gray after closure, and she prompted, "But?"

"If you keep touching me, I can't promise to be like a brother to you…"

Oh.

Well, then.

There was that.

"Then I won't touch you." Sage said the words with complete conviction. And was certain she saw a cloud of disappointment pass over Gray's expression.

Unless…she'd just imagined it because she'd wanted it to be there.

Scott had a date Sunday night. A woman he'd been seeing casually, on and off, for over a year. An FBI agent he'd met on a case who was part of a team that traveled all over the country. She was a little older than him. Widowed. With no interest in anything but companionship with occasional benefits.

The woman fit Scott to a T, Gray had told his friend the first time he'd heard about the agent. Gray had been a little jealous, had asked if Sheila had any friends, but had only been querying in jest. He preferred to find his own dates.

Had been thinking about doing so as he walked the beach at ten o'clock that night. Scott was staying at Sheila's, and Morgan needed her nightly "go" time. While Scott generally let the dog out the back door, and Morgan was trained to make and get right back inside, Gray had opted to go for some fresh air. To commune with the ocean. The air. The waves.

With the moon bright enough to show him the way— and any harm that could potentially come to Morgan—he'd walked from Scott's away from Sage's place to the end of the beach. On the return trip, still thinking about dates and such, he'd passed Scott's and continued the other way, passing Sage's and Iris's without pause, and made it clear to the other end of the two-mile-long stretch.

Thinking about Iris and Scott. The way they were able to make friendship work. Now that he'd met the woman, he didn't get it at all. Iris was gorgeous. A little tall for Gray, but perfect for Scott. And yet, seeing them together...it was obvious they were just friends.

The corgi never faltered in her trot beside him. Asked no questions. Or passed any judgment, either. She was just there. Keeping him company.

Her companionship was nice. As was the quiet solitude of the beach. Right there. For him to enjoy at a moment's notice.

And he got to thinking. Then to looking.

The cottage at the far end of the beach, several past Sage's and Iris's, stood dark. Dilapidated. What had once been luxurious, admired, sought after, revered, was standing alone in the dark. Deserted.

Much like Gray. Like his business. His life.

The cottage, along with several others, was available. For a price. And subject to the owner being willing to abide by a pretty stiff set of covenants, conditions and restrictions that bound the entire Ocean Breeze neighborhood.

He could renovate the thing himself. Hiring contractors where necessary, but he knew how to do a lot of the work. Had put himself through college by working construction. Him and the cottage—lives renovating together.

With his house sold, and if Sage really was able to free up his income account, he'd be able to afford the cottage. Didn't give a whit about needing to follow restrictions. Would welcome the protection and privacy they provided, actually, as he told Morgan aloud.

The dog, standing next to him, circled around, staring up at him.

As though looking for answers.

Most likely to "Can we go home?" Followed by "I want a treat."

But it could also be, "What are we doing next?" Followed by, "This is fun."

That was the thing with dogs and cats. While they relied on humans to make sure they had food and water, they could be left alone for hours and be fine to fend for themselves.

On average, dogs slept eighteen hours a day, so really, not much responsibility in caring for one.

So why didn't he have one of his own?

He'd always told himself it was because he worked so many hours in a day. But Scott did, too. Of course, Scott lived in a unique mecca where others were there to walk or feed the dog, others whom the dog knew and loved, in his absence.

In his semi secluded showplace on the cliff...not so much.

If he bought the cottage, though...

A huge *if.*

First and foremost, even before financial considerations, he'd have to run the idea by Sage. No way would he even consider the idea if it in any way made her uncomfortable. Ocean Breeze was her home. Her happiness.

He'd snatched the life she'd planned from her once.

He would die before doing so again.

And yet...she was the one who'd brought up the idea of a new friendship between the two of them. Like Scott and Iris. She'd specifically pointed to them as an example.

And they both lived on Ocean Breeze.

Maybe that was the trick. Living in the same neighborhood. Seeing each other every day. Having ready access when and if both parties desired, but with no pressure, expectation or obligation.

No strings. Just neighbors sharing a beach.

And no mystery, either. It was all right there. Taken for granted. Plebeian.

Morgan circled his legs. Letting him know she was ready to quit standing around doing nothing. And Gray returned to real life. Pulling himself back half a dozen notches.

Living on Ocean Breeze? Renovating the cottage himself? He was getting way ahead of himself.

Maybe he should just concentrate on putting out feelers among the neighbors for a service dog water rescue program before he started moving in on them.

And give Sage time to adjust to his return to her life before jumping into any idea of a long-term friendship between the two of them.

Any idea of permanently sharing her beach would just have to wait.

# Chapter Sixteen

The next week flew by. Sage was busier than usual at the firm, juggling the depth of detail in Gray's pro-bono project with her usual workload. And Leigh's preschool was gearing up for a Halloween party that required parent volunteers. Of course, she was one of the first to sign up. Being a parent *anything* gave her as much of a glow four years into her life with Leigh as it had the first day she'd been told she'd passed all regulations and was on the list to get a baby.

There were glitches that week as well as joy. Most definitely. A time or two when she'd instinctively reached out to Gray, only to snatch her hand back.

In an obvious fashion that appeared to have the same effect on him as a touch would have done. Or rather, had had a similar response to his effect on her. Flooding with desire wasn't something she went around and did on a regular basis anymore.

And the one time she hadn't pulled back in time...they'd both recoiled as though singed. And that instant was better left to burn to ash and drift away. Out of their memories.

Then there was her new Buzzing Bee Clinics brainstorm. A project she'd already researched. Two events. One for investors. And the other, a smaller affair, for potential contractor veterinarians. She'd just heard back from her public relations expert. Sage would handle all the legalities, of course, and was ready to present the ideas to her pro-bono client.

On Friday of that next week, she texted Gray to call her when he got a chance, and smiled when her phone rang within seconds—with his ID popping up on the screen. They'd seen each other a few times that week. A couple of waves, followed by brief small talk—mostly chatter by Leigh—on the beach. And once, in her office.

"I have a friend who's in the PR business, Marissa. She excels at putting on events, publicizing them and getting attendees for her various clients."

"She's a party planner."

"Actually, no, she owns her own PR firm. She hires out the actual planning of the party part."

"Go on."

"I was thinking that…if you're interested…" She drew out that last word…worried suddenly that, with all the negative publicity, she was going at proposal delivery all wrong. Talking to him more like a friend than a client.

"You can stop right there, Sage. I'm not interested. I don't care if she's the Princess of the Moon, is the most beautiful woman in the world and owns every bank known to man… I don't need you setting me up."

Standing there with her mouth hanging open, Sage fell back to her chair. Setting him…what?

"Frankly, it just feels…kind of creepy. Wrong. You, selling me on another woman. Selling her on me…"

She almost burst out laughing. Except that there was nothing funny going on.

"Um, Gray? Never ever, even for one second, in any universe, have I ever even thought about hooking you up with another woman."

Another woman. Oh, God. There couldn't be another unless there was one. Her. And she wasn't, currently. She just… had been.

And it hit her, sitting there, with her hands sweating, that she still thought of herself as Gray's woman. In past tense. Yes. Of course.

But still his.

For part of her life, she had been.

What did closure have to say about that?

He wasn't talking. Neither was she. Pulling back her cell, she checked to see that the call was still connected. Flooded with relief to see that he hadn't hung up.

And took action. "I spoke to Marissa about Buzzing Bee Clinics." Her daughter's creation—that name. Leigh.

Closure settled over her. Suffocating desperation. And she continued with a professionalism she was trying very hard to connect to. "She mentioned doing two events…" Sage figured she talked for two minutes. Didn't even remember coming up for air. Discussing details of a project he hadn't even spoken to yet. Because she didn't pause long enough to give him time.

Until she'd run out of words. And finished with, "What do you think?"

She held tightly to her phone. Hoping they hadn't just ruined things between them.

Gray's voice sounded loud, coming from the silence that had been hanging so long on his end. "Whatever it costs, I'm in."

And Sage let out the breath she'd been holding.

He needed a date. A woman who entertained him. Who enjoyed being with him. Who wasn't looking for a future that included family. Gray couldn't think of any other way to get Sage out of his system long enough for their friendship to take root.

But couldn't think of any woman he wanted to ask out. Partially because he on a date meant that he exposed whoever was with him to the possibility of cameras flashing at any given moment. With any narrative attached. True or completely fabricated.

He could get creative. Rent a day cruiser, drive south to pick it up and pull into a private marina someplace to collect his date. It could be all hush-hush and romantic.

The idea raised nothing but dread in him. All aspects of it. From the effort to finding the woman.

A guy with his life crashed around him, with the debris still being picked through...he just didn't feel like exposing that to anyone he knew. Or someone he didn't know, but could meet. If he kept himself open to doing so.

The women he dated generally came with a good dose of compassion. And that led to expressing their understanding and sorrow, or offering to help, or, worst of all, questions. He just wasn't into it.

So why in the hell had he given Sage the impression that he thought she'd think he was good dating material?

With a package that she'd praise to a friend?

Unable to rest easy with the huge gaffe he'd made that afternoon, Gray changed into shorts and a polo shirt after work and, sliding into flip-flops, headed down the beach. Scott was out with Morgan. He may run into his friend or not. They'd actually talked about sharing a meal that night, since they hadn't done so since Gray had moved in. After his conversation with Sage that afternoon, Gray had been thinking about making an excuse to avoid the sit-down with her brother.

Instead, he was heading down to fix the situation. With rain from the past couple of days having slowed beach activity, and gray skies still overhead, Gray was surprised to see how many people were out and about.

Until he considered the fact that dogs had to go, rain or shine. And dog owners had a tendency to congregate as their canine companions looked for just the right spots.

Leigh wasn't out, anywhere he could see, but Sage was. Sitting on her porch with a glass of what looked like tea.

She waved. Instead of waving back, he veered straight toward her cottage. "You got any more of that?" he asked, climbing the steps without waiting for an invitation.

She stood. Heading toward the door, from which some child's song was playing, being sung by what could only be cartoon characters. "Sure," Sage said, adding, "It's sweetened."

Telling. Not asking if that was okay.

Because she knew that he was a sucker for sweet tea. Though…he'd never told her why. All part of the putting his best foot forward with her.

She thought she knew him so well…down to his addiction to a particular kind of tea.

The past kept creeping in on them. Wrapping them in some kind of personal and very cozy blanket.

And so, as soon as they were both seated again, sipping tea, he told her something she didn't know. Throwing off the blanket—in his mind at least. "My grandmother always had sweet tea in the house. No matter how bad things got, how bad a fight she and my mom might have had, or how much pain she was in, she always went for the tea. It was like the panacea for anything bad. Icing on the cake we didn't have. She'd said it was because it was so cheap. Tea bags, a gallon jug, sugar and water. When the sun was shining bright, she'd always make extra, to account for rainy days…"

"I saw a jug brewing out on Scott's porch earlier in the

week," Sage said softly. In a tone he knew. Had used to think it was just for him. He didn't look at her.

Couldn't chance that she'd be looking back.

Nor risk a conversation that veered toward her wanting to know why he'd never mentioned the tea thing to her before.

A consequence he'd failed to consider before he'd started his soliloquy.

"He drank most of it," Gray said, with an eye roll. And then started right in with his reason for being there. "I was thinking about starting a class here on the beach, residents only, to teach water rescue to any of the dogs who might be candidates to learn. And whose owners would like to join in."

First steps toward a possible, more permanent, place for him on Ocean Breeze. Baby steps.

His grandmother used to say that baby steps still completed the journey. She'd been a very wise woman. Something he'd been too young and unaware to appreciate at the time.

"I didn't realize you knew how to train service dogs." A benefit he hadn't foreseen. Space between them. Built by the more than ten years they'd spent apart.

And…interest, rather than any negative reaction to him establishing himself, in any way, on her beach.

Encouraged by how easy his chat with Sage was going, Gray told her about his work with service dogs over the years, starting with having had one as a patient shortly after he'd opened his first clinic. And outlining some of the things he'd done since. Making certain to list his credentials in there, his service training certification, so that she'd know that he was legitimate.

Just as he'd do with any residents who chose to enroll in his free class, if he were to actually offer it. Which was how he ended his long-winded explanation.

By stating the free to Ocean Breeze residents part.

"I'm talking about water rescue dogs, here, not water search dogs," he clarified as it finally dawned on him that Sage seemed genuinely interested in what he had to offer. "Water search dogs are trained to smell human remains. That's not this. Water rescue dogs learn to swim out to a human in distress and by various means, get that person back to their handler, whether the handler is on shore or in a boat."

"Like if Leigh got washed in by a wave..."

He nodded. Didn't share that he'd had the thought several times since his scare with Morgan. Watching the little girl on the beach. But he did say, "Or adult residents who might get a cramp or hit by a surfboard," and then added, "It will also help if any of the Ocean Breeze dog brigade get swept away. The dog will instinctively know to get to its handler. And other dogs could help. Assuming we train them to go after each other."

"When do you propose starting?"

He glanced at her, saw the genuine interest in her gaze, saw a friend, and spent the next half hour working out details with her. She'd present the idea to all her neighbors personally. Would be in charge of paperwork and signing off on liabilities. The class would be held on Saturday mornings. And would run for as long as there was interest.

Neither of them mentioned that Gray's time on the beach was limited.

Nor did he introduce the idea of him sticking around. Buying a place.

Assuming at least one resident was interested, there was going to be a class.

He and Sage were heading it up as friends.

They were taking a baby step.

He left her porch with his stomach full of tea, a smile on his face and only a little bit turned on.

# Chapter Seventeen

The meeting with veterinarians interested in contracting with Buzzing Bee Clinics turned into a lovely lunch, Friday afternoon of the next week, hosted by a local country club. Tables were set in a private room in front of a glass wall overlooking the golf course, and beyond that, over a cliff, the ocean.

Fixtures were gold, silver felt real and napkins were linen.

Sage arrived just after everyone had finished eating, for the business portion of the gathering. She spent a couple of minutes with Gray, to go over their program details, and then stepped back as the man—looking way too gorgeous in his dress pants and lab coat, with his longish dark hair framing his face—was called over to a table by a woman Sage recognized as one of his former veterinarians.

She didn't watch their exchange. Didn't want to know how he interacted with beautiful professionals in his field. Straightening the short jacket over her slim-fitting navy pants, she helped herself to a glass of water instead.

Gray spoke first to the sixty-two veterinarians who'd attended. Marissa had put word out beyond the local area, and outside Rockcliff and San Diego, people didn't care as much about the local scandal. They did seem to care about affordable pet health care for middle-class families.

Sage knew that Gray could sell his concept. And as he

spread his passion around the room, she couldn't help but gravitate to him. Unfortunately for her, it wasn't the veterinary aspect of him that she absorbed. The man had always been able to touch parts of her no one else ever had. Even in the decade they'd been apart. She'd dated plenty. Most particularly before she'd decided to go the adoption route. On the lookout for a father for her family, she'd tried again and again to find a man who raised even half the ardor in her that Gray had. Or a hint of the physical ecstasy he'd brought her.

Just listening to him talk—even about science and medical practices—instilled a warmth in her that she couldn't ignore.

But she could focus on other things.

And she did, following him up with the less passionate part of the meeting—the contractual legalities involved in being a part of Buzzing Bee Clinics. The practical aspects that would be required for next steps. Finishing with a potential income report recommending that each applicant have it vetted by individual financial advisers.

She gave all attendees her contact information, not Gray's.

Then she left to go back to work, hearing later that they'd garnered forty-five applications for the eighteen positions Gray was currently offering. Three veterinarians a piece at a total of six clinics. He'd be a floater. Choosing to work at all six locations. He'd said he wanted to be inside, part of the workings of each one. At least to start.

While Friday afternoon's event was a win, Gray needed the black-tie fundraising event scheduled to take place the following night to be an equal success if he was going to get six clinics up and running at the same time. He'd found potential sites to rent in four strip malls, and two other free-standing buildings.

But with investors, the brunt of the sell landed on Sage. With the day's win, she was experiencing a decidedly uncomfortable bit of tension as she considered the following evening.

She'd already been a bit jittery at the thought of attending the dinner/entertainment event with Gray. The two of them, decked out. Maybe having a cocktail. At a venue they'd been to multiple times as guests of her father back in the day.

Adding in the new pressure of Gray's leap into his new life resting completely on the money they might raise, and she wanted to grab up Leigh and run to Disneyland for the weekend.

Sort of. As wonderful as fantasy time with her little girl sounded, most particularly considering how much Leigh loved the resort, a part of Sage needed to be right where she was. Helping Gray.

Logically, she couldn't explain the internal pressure to herself. She owed Grayson Bartholomew nothing. But logic and heart didn't always coexist in complete harmony. Sometimes one had to rule the other long enough for the lagging member to catch up.

Trouble was, she didn't know which part of her was behind. Her heart or her head. And couldn't seem to get either to pony up.

Sitting on her porch Friday afternoon, she had a legal pad on her lap, a glass of tea on the little table beside her and a bit of a headache.

An impromptu volleyball game was taking place on the beach, with the four players in sweatpants and T-shirts in the cooling late October air. Neither Scott nor Iris were there, but Harper was. And Morgan—the only dog—with Gray. Leigh was the runner after the ball when anyone missed.

Which was why she'd been watching the game, paying no attention whatsoever to the work she'd brought home to do. Harper had called Leigh over to *help* with the game. But

Gray had been the one to look toward Sage's porch for a nod of permission. And then he met the little girl in the sand and walked her down to the game.

Such a small thing.

No different than taking a young patient to a room to greet a pet that had had its teeth cleaned. She couldn't let the sight of Gray with her daughter touch her heart.

"Hey!"

Sage jumped, turned her head as the sound reached her from the beach to the left of her. "Iris!" And Angel. As soon as Morgan or Leigh saw the visitor who'd just arrived, they'd both be barreling their way over.

It was a testament to Sage's upset state of mind that she hadn't even been aware of the photographer's approach. Something that Sage noted with serious exclamation points. She had a child to consider.

Could not sink into an emotional quagmire.

Mostly, she was glad to know that Leigh would be heading back her way momentarily.

Right until she remembered that Morgan was with Gray, not Scott. Which meant that he'd be the one to collect the dog.

And she'd be fine. They'd seen each other several times on various porches and the beach since they'd decided to hold water rescue classes. The first one was due to start the following week.

"Really quick, while Leigh's occupied," Iris said, glancing down the right side of the beach as she took the empty chair beside Sage. "You have that fancy thing tomorrow night, right?"

"With investors, yes," she replied, highlighting, for herself as well as Iris, that while the decor and trappings, the entertainment Marissa had arranged, were fancy, Sage's part in the event was strictly business.

"Adults only."

"Right. I've got Harper staying with Leigh." And hadn't told Gray. His first night on the beach, the sight of him and Harper on Scott's porch had stung. Still did.

It shouldn't. She was super fond of Harper. And wouldn't accept Gray as more than a friend even if he asked, which he would not. Still…

"So, I've got this thing…" Glancing over toward the game and back again, Iris met Sage's gaze. "I was going to ask you, but since you were busy, I asked Scott, since we'll need a second chaperone for part of the time, but I really want to bring Leigh. I'm photographing behind the scenes at the San Diego Zoo. She'll be able to be right close with dolphins, even pet them if she wants to, with a trainer right there, of course. And Scott. He said he'd ask you, but I need to know that you're really okay with it…"

Leigh was addicted to dolphins the way a lot of little girls adored unicorns.

"I'm doing all the aquatics and monkeys tomorrow afternoon, and evening. And then some of the larger animals early Sunday morning before the zoo opens, so I've got a suite down by the beach. It would mean her spending the night. The suite has two rooms, of course, both with two queens, so Leigh could stay with me or Scott…"

Iris adored Leigh. Had had the little girl over to spend the night a couple of other times Sage had to be out late.

And once when she'd been on a date.

But, as uncomfortable as she was about Gray's event, the thought of coming home afterward to a house without Leigh didn't sit well.

What in the hell was she thinking? "Of course she can go," she said, with force.

The day she started putting her own needs above her daughter's opportunities was not going to arrive. Ever.

Scott was just getting home from work when Gray returned with Morgan to the cottage. The two men had managed to coexist, with their separate bathrooms, without running into each other all that much. A lot of the ease came from Scott's schedule being pretty much set in stone, and Gray's largely being fluid. He worked around the man who'd taken pity on him.

"Harper says to tell you hi," he said, coming in to see Scott grabbing a beer out of the refrigerator. Sage's brother handed one to Gray as well, without asking, as Scott passed Gray on his way into his room to change.

Scott had assumed correctly. Gray wanted the beer. Uncapping it as Scott's door closed behind the prosecutor, Gray leaned against the kitchen counter and took a long sip.

Leigh had told him, when he'd walked her back up the beach, that Mommy had told her not to bother Mr. Buzzing Bee, but she didn't think she was. "Am I?" the little girl had asked.

He'd quickly assured her that she was doing nothing of the sort. And went on to tell her that she could never be a bother to him, but he wasn't sure she fully grasped what any of it had meant.

He'd grasped it, though. With a pin in his heart.

He didn't want to be that guy...the one mothers thought didn't like kids...or that kids *bothered* him.

Yet, what could he expect? It was the message he'd inadvertently sent Sage. With what he'd said. And what he'd left unsaid, too.

He thought about changing out of his sweats. Sniffed his underarm.

It didn't stink.

And sauntered out to the porch. Harper would be taking Aggie out. She might stop by. Giving Scott and the woman a chance to chat. He had a feeling the woman might be interested in the owner of the cottage.

It might be amusing to watch the interchange.

Lord knew he could use the distraction.

Scott, dressed in cotton pants, a short-sleeved pullover and flip-flops, made it out to the porch before Harper was out walking Aggie. Gray had heard his friend calling Morgan and knew that as soon as he left the porch, he'd be heading down Sage's way.

Because he always did. Pretty much every night. The man took his uncle duties as seriously as anyone Gray had ever seen. A quality he admired immensely.

"So tomorrow's the big night," Scott said, leaning on the porch rail by the stairs.

Gray shrugged, tapped his beer bottle on his sweatpants. "Could be."

"With Sage and Marissa putting on the show, you can pretty much count on it," Scott chuckled. Gray would have liked to feel even half as confident.

The way his life was skyrocketing, so much potentially great stuff in such little time, had him a bit uneasy.

He'd learned the hard way that what went up, could come back down again.

And investors? That was a whole new thing to him.

"You driving, or is Sage?" Scott asked, one thigh up on the porch rail at that point. Looking as though he'd be content to hang out and dissect Gray's life for some time, while Morgan sat contentedly waiting to go for another walk. The longer one she'd get with Scott.

"I'd figured us both for driving," Gray told him. It wasn't like they were attending together.

"Why waste the gas?"

By Gray's calculations, they could probably both afford the gas. He knew he could, and Sage was in a better position than he was at the moment.

Besides, unless things had changed, Sage drove like the road law patrol. One mile under the speed limit so she didn't risk going above, and always turning exactly when GPS told her to—even back when that help had been a device plugged into the cigarette lighter and attached to the dash. Brows risen, he glanced up at his friend. "What's going on?"

Scott shrugged. Had the grace to look away, and then, bringing his gaze back to Gray said, "I worry about her, being out late without anyone with her, driving in the city alone on a Saturday night..."

Gray nodded. Should have had the thought himself. "I'll drive," he said with a grin. "No way I'm riding with your sister."

"I got you there, bud." Scott's parting chuckle could still be heard as he walked with Morgan down the sand.

# *Chapter Eighteen*

There was no way Sage would have agreed to ride with Gray to the function on Saturday night if Scott hadn't been the one to tell her that Gray had said something about driving her. Her brother had been vague, but when Gray's text had come in, with Scott right there, she'd look churlish, or worse, cause more of an issue than she wanted to deal with, if she refused.

They'd been alone together plenty of times in the weeks Gray had been back in her life. Mostly in her office with its soundproofed walls and the door closed. Just the two of them in a car, with Gray having to focus on his driving, could hardly pose a threat.

Even to a libido out of equilibrium.

Still, as she put on the sleek, slim-fitting long black sheath, leaving her hair wavy and long around shoulders covered only by spaghetti straps, and stepped into three-inch glitzy black heels, she was aware that Gray would be the first one to see her that night. And took a second long glance in the mirror, turning to get side and back views as well. Assessing her sexiness.

And then, not.

Maybe it was natural to want Gray to eat his heart out. To see what he could have had, even ten years later, if he'd been…

What?

Someone he wasn't?

How fair was that?

And more to the point, how could she possibly say she'd loved the man if her love had only been good for as long as he'd been what she needed him to be, not who he was?

And she had loved him.

More than a decade later, she still had no doubt on that one. Head and heart in complete agreement.

Leigh had left earlier in the day, and Sage had been quite pleased with all she'd been able to accomplish with the unusual freedom. From housecleaning to casework, she'd managed to complete more tasks on her list in half a day than she normally got done in an entire weekend.

Including be ready a good ten minutes early, with nothing to do but pace. And think about the last time Gray had come to the door to pick her up for anything.

That night just forty-eight hours before the big day she'd spent an entire year anticipating. Or a whole life, if she considered her girlish and teenaged dreams of her wedding day.

He'd rung the bell of her apartment, and when she'd pulled it open his back had been turned to her. She should have known then.

No. Rehashing stopped with closure. That was part of the deal.

With nine minutes more to wait, she heard her text sound, and grabbed her phone out of her clutch as though it was an oxygen mask to a suffocating person.

As tight and tense as her chest was feeling, she was finding it kind of hard to draw an easy breath.

I'm heading down now. Meet you outside.

He wasn't coming to the door to get her.

Like any other rideshare, he was merely going to wait out front.

Drawing strength from the reminder, Sage slid the long, thin strap attached to her clutch over her shoulder and locked up.

The night was going to be fine.

She just needed to relax.

Gray was sure that Sage's looks had stunned him in the past. He had no specific memory of the sight of her literally taking away his breath.

But as he watched her move around the carpeted floor, from table to table of black-coated men and gorgeously adorned women after her speech, answering questions, smiling, generally passing out confidence and security, instilling trust, he had a moment where he could hardly draw in air.

He'd always found her beautiful. And way too sexy for his own good. Her petiteness perfect for his own shorter stature. Letting him stand a good manly eight or nine inches taller than her.

His penis, as usual, had spent the night growing taller by her, too. By her. Across the room from her. Watching her sincerity reach the audience of seasoned investors...

And that smile, with lipstick under bright lights making it harder to ignore—he'd lost count of the times he'd been thankful for his buttoned suit coat.

Not that he didn't have himself under control. He wasn't walking around like some kind of letch. But the sudden infusions that quickly dissipated would have been a bit awkward if anyone else knew about them.

A guy couldn't help what he couldn't help.

While the night had been designed so that there would be no business transactions taking place at the event, with a designated web address printed on business cards and passed out to every attendee to express interest, Gray had several people come up to him at various points, wanting to meet him and shake his hand.

To tell him that they were interested in his concept and in doing business with him.

Sage's firm was setting up a specific investment program, as opposed to selling stocks, that would pay initial investors back with percentages of profit sharing in addition to interest.

Gray lost track of how many hands he shook. His face started to get stiff from smiling. But he didn't tire, for one second, of Sage's continuous conversation, rehashing different aspects of the night, all the way home.

She spoke of unusually high percentages of attendees who expressed interest, about next steps, mentioned that the comedian Marissa had hired had done a great job pulling in the audience with investment jokes.

Purely professional, and still, in the glow from the streetlights under which he drove, she glowed. Even in the dark, her eyes seemed to sparkle.

So much so that he wanted to ask her if she'd like to stop at the place up on the hill, just above Ocean Breeze, for a nightcap. But didn't want even a hint of impropriety. Of him taking advantage of the moment or putting her on the spot.

He didn't want to ruin what was easily one of the best nights he'd had since he'd left her world all those years before.

"You want to stop for a drink?" Sage asked as he pulled onto the road that would take them down the cliff, past the elegant Rockcliff Restaurant and Bar, to Ocean Breeze.

With the invitation coming right on the heels of his own thought, he didn't give any consideration at all to refusing. "Sure," he told her, made the turn, parked and walked around to open her door for her. As he'd done countless times in the past.

She'd already let herself out.

Taking the reminder in stride, he walked beside her, not close enough to touch, and didn't have to worry about getting the next door for her as there was a uniformed employee trusted with that task.

The bar, a quietly lit place with light walls and upholstered booths, with a few matching table and chair sets scattered about, was surprisingly busy. Making it easier to slide into a booth across from Sage and relax. She ordered a glass of wine—not her usual spritzer—and he asked for a scotch. What the hell, they were celebrating.

Even if the evening ultimately produced no money, they'd thrown one hell of a party, attracting the attention of respected people, without any snoops getting wind of it. Might be just for the one event, but he felt as though he was alive again. In the world he'd spent so many years building.

He'd gotten some of his confidence back.

And he had her to thank for that.

The wine calmed some of the adrenaline coursing through Sage after the great evening. It relaxed a bit of the excitement generated from signs of early success based on attendee comments and reactions, and Sage hadn't felt so personally successful in a long while.

Surprised by that, she took the second while Gray was in the restroom to check herself on the thought. Ran through a mental checklist of professional landmarks, happy clients, awards...but couldn't find a single standout. Nothing that made her feel even half as alive as that night had done.

No, it was thoughts of Leigh that did that. The little girl's happiness, her development. The odds they'd helped her beat together. Those were her highs.

But...she was more than a mother. Leigh was growing up fast already. Asserting her independence in all kinds of ways.

And if Sage's whole world was just her child, it wouldn't be good for Leigh. Would it?

Shaking her head as she saw Gray coming back toward her, Sage determined not to ruin the night with her usual ruminations. There'd be time later, when she was herself and not coming off a high with a glass of wine added in, to assess her future success as a mother. And a person.

"You looked like you were having deep thoughts," he said as he slid back in across from her. His gaze held hers, filled with interest. And…warmth.

She shook her head. Nodded when the waiter passed by and asked if she'd like another glass of wine. She had the whole night to herself. Didn't need to worry about being responsible for anyone else. And looked back to see Gray still watching her.

Like maybe he was seeing her for the first time. And she wondered, if they'd met in their current lives, if things would have been any different for them.

And had a flash of the story he'd recently told her about growing up. His lack of attachment to things. Wondering what else he might not have shared.

Thinking of her strong desire to be a mother—the elephant that was always in the room between them—a desire partially born from her closeness to her own female parent, she asked, "Did you ever know your father?"

Even as the words slipped out, she braced for his pullback. The way he had of straightening his shoulders, his head rigidly held on top of them…and hadn't realized until that second that that had been his tell.

And the thing that had stopped her from ever pressing for more. He'd stiffen, pull back and…

But he wasn't stiffening. "I never even knew for sure who he was," he told her, slowly moving his stir stick around the full glass of scotch that had just been delivered. "My mother was in high school when she got pregnant with me. All I ever knew was that no one but Grandma stood by her. Mom had a hard time with it all. Working at the restaurant. Raising me. By the time I was old enough to demand answers about my father, she was gone, and Grandma swore she didn't know." While Sage's heart broke, digesting things she'd never guessed, Gray paused, and then said, "I sometimes thought it was a blessing when my mother was killed in the car accident when I was ten. She always seemed so tired…"

Holding back tears, Sage stayed front and center with Gray. Right there, in that moment, she knew real closure. And a strange kind of opening, too.

Not only had he never known his father, he'd also watched others suffer for his father having deserted them. Maybe not the reason Gray didn't want to be a father. But the fact that he'd never witnessed, firsthand, what being a father was all about—good or bad—brought clarity to something she'd never been able to understand.

Gray's leaving her—hadn't been about her.

He'd said that, of course, but everyone usually did in a breakup situation. Or at least did commonly enough that it was understood that it didn't mean anything.

In his case…maybe it had.

And while it didn't change their past, or their future, didn't change the people they were—a man and a woman with very different needs—knowing still made a difference.

Sage's eyes brimmed with warmth, but no pity, as Gray finished talking. Normalizing what could have quickly turned into a derailing of all they'd been working to build.

"I was super close to my mom," she told him. "She was lovely, and kind. Always busy doing something for someone.

And involving me in it somehow. Teaching me how to live a good, happy, giving life without my even knowing it was happening." Her gaze took on a faraway look, leaving Gray more alone than he'd been, and wishing he could travel to that place. That he'd known her mother.

And then she was back. Looking him straight in the eye, as though calling him to attention. She'd had his attention from the moment she'd stepped back into his life again.

"I was just starting puberty when she died..." Her voice trailed off. Before he could find any kind of right words, she started up again. "Dad expected me to pick up the reins, and I could. I knew what to do, in some of her volunteer work, and, of course, at home. It's like I became my own mother. And there was comfort in that..."

The parental relationship she was describing, the mothering...he knew exactly what she was talking about. Recognized it. From her dealings with Leigh. And he settled inside.

Leaning a bit forward, she continued, "It's like I was keeping the best part of my life, Mom's warmth, her love, alive, right there, every day..."

Sage blinked. Gave her head a brief shake.

And then with a frown said, "What am I doing? I'm so sorry, Gray. I didn't mean..."

Frowning right back, Gray leaned forward, too. "What? Didn't mean what?" He'd barely started in on his second drink, but felt like he'd passed out or something. Regaining consciousness having missed something huge. Except that he'd been sitting right there. Still sober enough to drive.

"You..." She shook her head. "You tell me how hard it was at home. Your mother...always tired. And I jump in with the perfect mom story. Oh, my God." Her eyes widened, looking aghast. "Is that what I did to you in the past?

Was I this callous to you? Shoving this great upbringing, this privilege, at you?"

"No." He said the word with force. It needed to be there. And took her hand across the table, looking her straight in the eye. No blinking. Head-on. "You were, are, one of the most sensitive, strong, caring women I've ever known. You didn't shove, Sage, you shared. Any privilege you might have had, knowingly or not, was as much mine as yours when we were together."

Moisture filled her eyes. She blinked. Nodded. But her chin had that telltale tremble.

"It's not your fault, Sage," he told her then. Words coming forth out of his need to own up. Man up. "You were right a little while back, when you realized that I'd withheld…certain aspects…of things. You seemed to think it was because of something you did or didn't do, but it was not. I very carefully, very consciously, showed you the me I wanted you to know. I didn't ever lie to you. I gave who I was when I knew you. But I chose to shed a lot of things. And since I'd shed them, I didn't share them."

Great job. Couch it all, still. Couching the couching. Manning right up.

"It wouldn't have mattered how much you nagged me. I wasn't going to give you any more. Because in my mind, I'd left the past behind. The last thing I was going to do was dredge it back up again." Feeling the warmth of her soft fingers in his, he let go.

Sat back and said, "But I see now why being a mother is such a huge part of you." And saw, too, that some things were never going to change.

# *Chapter Nineteen*

They left before either of them had made it through half of their second drink. Sage knew he was right to call it a night. And was still sad to see the evening coming to an end.

A completely adult night.

She had so few of them.

"You feel like a walk on the beach?" Gray asked as he turned onto Ocean Breeze. Almost as though he was reading her mind.

She wasn't dressed for beach walking, but then neither was he. "I do." She said the words, smiling, and then almost immediately stiffened.

The words she'd been rehearsing, dreaming about saying to him, and then had been robbed of the chance.

But they fit. And she'd had closure on the past.

He pulled into Scott's place. "This tux is on loan," he said to her. "If you don't mind, I'll just run in really quick and get out of it."

"As long as you don't mind me overdressed." She grinned. "At least until we make it down to my place."

The look in his eye as he turned to her sent an instant flood down to pertinent parts. He'd opened his mouth, as if to say something, but it just hung there for a second, before closing abruptly.

"I've got no complaints," he said, his back to her as he let himself out of the car. She got out, too. Could put Morgan out as he changed. And bring the dog back in. Adults only wasn't the life she wanted for herself. At all. Fully clear on that one.

But sometimes…

Morgan completed her business and ran right back up the porch steps just as Gray came to the doorway, in swim trunks and a T-shirt.

*Seriously?*

After letting the corgi back in, he secured the door behind him and joined Sage on the beach. With her heels hanging from the fingers of one hand, she squished her toes in the sand, feeling the coolness of the last Saturday night in October there, too.

And shivered.

"You are not going swimming this late at night, alone, in the ocean."

With a grin in her direction, he said, "You could always watch out for me."

"I mean it, Gray." She had no smiles at the moment. "You know as well as I do, with the tide, an undertow, or…who knows what in the water, hunting for food…"

"How about let's take that walk and think about it," he offered, heading off slowly in the direction of her house. With his hands in the pockets of his trunks he said, "I've actually swum regularly, at night, since I've been here. Not for long, just a dip in before bed. And I don't go out far. I respect the ocean as much as anyone. It just…makes me feel good."

His words appeased her somewhat. Enough that she relaxed again. She didn't want anything to ruin the night.

And most certainly didn't want it to end badly.

So she walked, uncaring that the sand was sticking to the bottom of her dress, or, for that matter, that she could only take smallish steps. She felt beautiful. Womanly. And a tad wild, too, out on the beach all dressed up.

Like some kind of worldly woman who had it all.

When they reached her cottage and Gray made no move to head up to it, her sensation of freedom escalated. Because it was momentary, not purporting any kind of change that she didn't want, she kept walking, too.

Responsibility was important. Necessary. She'd be lost without it.

And a few minutes of time out of time, of vacation from real life, was necessary, too, she was finding.

She couldn't drive if she didn't refuel her tank.

Something her mother had once said to her father. Telling him he'd needed to relax a little bit. She couldn't remember her father's response, but also didn't recall any time that he'd followed any advice but his own.

Or had taken a vacation.

And…oh, God…had her years with only him as a parent rubbed off on her more than she knew? Had she become him?

"Do you think I'm too much like my father?" The question burst out of her.

"No." Gray's answer was swift. And certain-sounding. Comfortable. "You're nothing like him."

"I'm responsible. All the time. I work and I come home and lots of nights, after Leigh's in bed, I work more." Fear engulfed her for a second.

Until Gray took her hand, pulling her to a stop. Faced her to the ocean and pointed. Then turned her around to gesture to her cottage in the distance. "Can you see your father living here?"

"Hell, no." He'd wanted the view, but… "He hated the sand."

"What did he enjoy?"

Standing there with him, staring at the ocean, she had to

think a minute. "I'm not sure." She couldn't remember her father ever just hanging out and relaxing or bursting out with uncontrollable laughter. "Work, I guess. And being a father."

He'd taken pride in his kids. Spent a lot of time with them.

And her words… She swung toward Gray, horrified at herself again. "That was in no way directed at, or intending to be, a dig at you…"

He lifted a finger, touched it to her lips. "I know."

She heard his voice, but all she was aware of was the warmth of his touch on her lips in the Southern California chilly night air. And bare shoulders that were no longer as cold as they'd been starting out.

She burned.

And when his face came closer, haloed by moonlight, she watched. Her mind blank.

Her body filled with want.

The touch of his lips shocked her system. Like water when she was dehydrated. She recognized the sustenance, felt the desperate need, but had been without for too long.

More docile than normal, she stood there, letting him kiss her. Drinking from the sensations flowing through her, and nothing more.

He pulled back. "Sage… I… I apologize. I'm sorry." He turned away, and she came to life.

"Don't, Gray," she said, not recognizing her own voice. Not sure what she was expecting from him. Or herself. "Don't walk away from me."

She grabbed his arm.

And held on.


*Don't walk away from me.*

It was the second time in recent weeks that he'd heard the words.

Turning around, a shadow in the dark, on the long-deserted beach, Gray looked for something within himself to grasp hold of. To steer him.

Still in front of her near-acre of property, he stared at her. "I won't," he heard himself say. Yearning to be heard. And reeling from the possible lie he was telling. Moving in closer to her, he cupped her face with both hands. "I promise, Sage. I won't ever walk away from you again."

She might leave. They might both turn their backs on the friendship they were trying to build. But that promise, come hell or worse than hell, he would keep it.

Only just beginning to understand the damage he'd done to her by walking out two days before their wedding...

He'd been saving them both from love turning to hate. From disappointment. Arguments. Resentments. Walls. Inevitable divorce.

His course had been so clear to him.

And nothing was clear anymore.

"I'm sorry," he whispered, holding her face, but not moving in for more. "I'm so sorry."

"For what?"

He wasn't sure. All of it. "For not being what you need," he said. "For not figuring it all out sooner."

"Gray..." Her whisper floated away on the wind before he could hear intention in the tone.

"I'm sorry for loving you so selfishly, and for accepting your love, for letting you love me..." Maybe the stiff scotch had loosened his tongue. It hadn't rattled his brain.

The words had been there a long time.

Needing to be said.

Sage's hands flew up to Gray's as he started to let go of her. She held his hands against her, staring up at him. "You didn't let me love you, Gray. You had absolutely no say in that matter. The choice was mine." Her words came with all the strength she had in her.

"You don't get to take that away from me," she said more softly, as he stared down at her.

Standing there, so close, with the rest of their bodies not touching, those seconds were everything. And not enough.

"Loving you then…helped grow me into the woman I am now." She was staring at his lips. Didn't want to look away.

Gray wasn't moving. He just stood there, staring at her, his expression still holding pain. A lot of it. And she leaned forward. Doing what a woman did.

She put her lips to his, to kiss the pain away.

After that…everything was a blur. Her hands dropped Gray's to slide around his neck. To hold him close while their lips said other things that had to be said.

And did so in ways they both seemed to need. And to understand.

Her mouth opened first. Or his did. Didn't matter. They both had tongues reaching for each other, and when they met again, she felt Gray's tension ease into something much more welcome.

More pleasurable.

In that kiss they bridged the pain with which they'd left each other, back into the joy they'd once found in each other, and Sage hadn't found enough of it yet.

They fell to their knees together. And down to their sides, lips still touching. Even as top lips parted enough to gasp for air, bottom lips still touching.

Tongues continuing the conversation.

Her breasts strained for his touch, hurting to the point that she took his hand and placed it over her nipple, showing him her need. He knew exactly what to do. She'd shown him years before.

She nearly wept when she felt his touch, on first one breast then the other. Even through her dress, he made it happen. He hadn't forgotten.

Just as she knew what his straining pelvis against her thigh meant. He was ready to explode.

Aching as much as she was, needing his touch so desperately, and finding the bliss again in his touch as he gave it to her, she couldn't deny him the same...recognition.

The same glory.

Lifting her body enough to get her dress up, she watched him breathing hard as she yanked at her panties, and then, pulling the elastic band of his trunks, she lowered them enough to release his penis and straddled it.

He thrust as she lowered, a dance they'd perfected many years before.

One that lasted only seconds, before they were convulsing around and within the other. The final stanza, the last step.

Before reality returned.

# *Chapter Twenty*

It took about ten seconds for Gray to recover enough to know that he'd made a colossal mistake.

Sage was already off from him, rapidly yanking her dress down to her ankles. A sure sign, if he'd needed one, that the world had just turned blacker than the night.

He'd had sex without a condom. Something he hadn't done since…Sage.

And he'd had sex with Sage.

Who, thankfully, had been a stickler for remaining on birth control. Due to her cycle, not her sex life.

Which did nothing to protect against the splintering of a very fragile, incredibly important, newly forming platonic friendship.

Nope, he'd just blown that straight to hell.

No matter who'd climbed on top of whom. He'd had a chance to say no.

As thoughts splayed across his mind, Gray lay on his back in the sand, tempted to just bury himself right then and there, but when he figured that would be akin to walking away from her again—something he'd promised never to do—he righted his trunks and sat up.

He wasn't going to tower over her.

The next call was all hers.

"Okay, well, I guess that was bound to happen. Got it

right out of the way, there, didn't we?" Sage blurted, walking a small circle around herself, as though looking for something. Her shoes were already hooked around her fingers. The clutch she'd been wearing all night hadn't come off during their romp.

But then the whole thing had taken less than a minute.

Definitely his worst sexual moment of all time, in terms of respect, consideration, caring, relationship.

And one of the most powerful, incredible minutes he'd ever experienced.

Sage came to a standstill over him. Just stood there. Looking down.

He'd never felt lower in his life.

"Are you waiting for me to apologize?" Her words started out strong. Segued to something akin to petulance by sentence end.

He glanced up at her. "What for? We're two adults. Clearly consensual." So why did he feel like he was the one who owed a million apologies?

"I came on pretty strongly," she said, when he wished she would just let things go and…sit down beside him for a minute or two.

Let his body…and his mind…regroup.

Glancing up again he said, "Yeah, well, my pheromones have been invisibly bombarding you since the first day in your office," he told her. Knowing why the fault was his. "I've been turned on pretty much since that first second by the elevator and shooting out the silent chemicals ever since. Mind you, they were firing without my blessing, but…" His neck was hurting, staring up at her. "You mind sitting down?" he asked. And then added, "It's not like we're in danger of crossing any lines here…"

Nope, that damage had already been done.

But the consequences seemed a tad less fatal when she lowered herself beside him. Not close enough to touch. But not piranha distance, either.

"So that was kind of random, huh?" she asked, knees drawn up with her dress pulled down over them to her ankles. With the dress's slim line, not an easy feat.

That together with the fact that she was hugging those knees with both arms wrapped around them told him enough. She'd closed herself off to him.

There was relief in that.

And a certain amount of disgust for the relief.

"As you inferred, it was probably inevitable." With no good way out. How did you proceed with a friends-only plan when you'd failed to keep to protocol at the first viable opportunity not to do so?

"It doesn't change anything," she said then. "Not going forward."

The words lightened his load a ton. Until he glanced over at her and got turned on all over again. She was Sage. The one woman who did it for him above all others, apparently.

And a woman who needed far different things than he was equipped to provide. He got cold sweats even thinking about being the family man that would complete her picture.

"You think it's possible...to go forward as planned?" he asked her. Realism was the one thing he could trust.

And they could most count on.

"Because I can't guarantee that if we have a repeat somewhere down the road, of a night like tonight, it won't happen again."

If she could be the guarantee then, fine.

He was watching her, but she didn't look back. "I don't see how we have any other choice."

Weak. A lawyerism—avoiding a fact due to having no

good answer but refusing to commit to that information. She used to tease her brother about using them.

"So we just let the emptied pot fill up again, and cook, until it reaches boiling point and then see what happens?" The pot calling the kettle black. And they were the pot. Right there. Them together.

Sage finally turned to look at him, and while he couldn't see the expression in her eyes due to the night's shadows, he definitely recognized the firm set of her chin. "We're too far in to disappear from each other's lives." She pointed out another truism. "And I'm not sure I have the strength to try, in any case."

*Whoosh.* The chills that passed through him were decidedly the pleasant kind.

"So the only solution is to be on guard and make certain that we don't ever let ourselves end up in the position we were in tonight. I'd planned to drive myself and I should have done."

And he had some good news there. "I planned to drive separately as well," he told her. "Scott was the one who asked..." He stopped, realizing he was hanging his friend out to dry. And finished with, "He was worried because he was going to be gone, and we'd be coming home late..." Hoping he was digging the twin out at least a little bit.

Sage's facial muscles moved some. And while the night kept most of her expression from him, he had no trouble picturing her rolling her eyes.

"From now on, we know our parameters," she said.

He wanted to grin. To take a swim. Or just run circles on the beach. "Agreed," he said. Putting his whole system into the one word.

She'd found their way out of the muck.

Thank God.

* * *

As soon as they'd agreed upon a new plan to manage their gaffe, Sage jumped up, excused herself and left Gray sitting on the beach.

He'd offered to walk her up.

Her *no* had been a bit harsh, but understandable, given the situation. They'd settled instead for her flashing her kitchen light—which could be seen from the beach—twice when she was inside and locked up safe.

She got there and done with impressive speed. And into her room to change just as quickly. As though they were burning her, she stripped off the dress, the noticeably wet underwear, and throwing the gown in the dirty clothes, put the panties in the trash. Practically jumping into sweats and a T-shirt, she walked through the dark front rooms to the kitchen, peering out to see that Gray had left her portion of the beach.

And then, opening a wine cooler, slid outside to sit on her porch. She needed the fresh air, the sound of the ocean. The sense of freedom. Hoping to hell, together with the wine, she'd find a way out of the panic coursing ruthlessly inside her.

What had she done?

They hadn't used birth control.

And if she...

He'd think she'd jumped him on purpose.

A part of him would have to always believe that she'd tried to trap him.

Oh, God, there was no proof otherwise.

Every bit of the evidence pointed to her guilt.

*Had* she done it on purpose?

Absolutely not. Unequivocally. Her instant panic, the

second she'd realized what she'd done, was testimony to that fact.

Somehow—while flooding with fear-instilled desperation—she'd managed to hold it together and get away in a calm, rational manner.

But...

Oh, God. Oh, God. Oh, God.

The only consolation was that he'd think she was on birth control. She'd once forgotten her pills when they'd been on a weekend getaway on a chartered boat, and she'd insisted on nixing the plans to go back for them. Her cycle used to be so painful, and profuse.

Something that had waned over the years. And her doctor, for her own health, had suggested, since she wasn't sexually active enough to need them, that she go off them. He'd advised that a condom would work just fine.

If one used one.

Oh, God.

The morning-after pill. She had to get it somehow. Call someone. Find a free clinic. Or a woman's health office. Call a friend...

She'd brought her phone out with her, but it wasn't the late-night hour that stopped her from searching the internet or dialing potential sources.

It was the idea itself. She had friends who'd used the morning-after pill. Supported their choices wholeheartedly.

Would use it herself in a heartbeat if she'd been forced, or...

If it wasn't Gray she'd just had sex with.

Because she loved him. And wiping out the possibility of life for a child conceived in love?

Most particularly when she considered how strenuously Leigh had fought for her life? And then pictured the result of that fight. A child she was raising up to be a loving, fun, aware, contributing member of society.

She was mother incarnate. Her own mother incarnate. It was just who she was.

Truth was, even if she hadn't been in love…if she ended up pregnant, she'd probably have to have the child. It was just who she was.

But she absolutely did not want to be. Not with Gray.

For his sake. The idea would strangle him.

But for her own as well. She didn't want to grow a baby, bear a baby and raise a baby whose father didn't want him or her.

*Him or her.*

The image brought to mind a slightly larger version of Leigh the first time she'd laid eyes on her daughter. A picture minus the tubes and tapes. Maybe a boy. Or another little girl.

And she sat with it.

Tears dripping down her cheeks.

As she tipped her bottle and swallowed.

Gray wanted to have sex with Sage again.

And again and again and again.

He'd once wanted to surf across the ocean, too.

And he'd wanted his mother to meet a man she loved, who loved her, and get married.

He'd wanted his grandmother to be well enough for him to be able to leave her to go to his junior prom. He'd already asked the girl, and she'd said yes.

He knew how to live with unresolved desire. How to move forward, past it. To focus on things he wanted that were within his ability to achieve. To stay there until the sting of disappointment dissipated. At least for most of his conscious hours. Until pushing aside the need became habit.

He was very proficient at the habit-forming part of it all.

He focused every ounce of his energy in other, more positive endeavors. Like vetting all the applications that poured in formally after the luncheon.

And watching the dollar amounts rise in the investor accounts, too.

He surfed. A lot.

Stayed off the beach, otherwise.

And when all else failed—as it did a week after their night on the beach—he scrounged for immediate diversion. He'd arrived at Sage's office right on time that next Friday afternoon, completed his business with her—trussed up in one of his most conservative suits and fully knotted tie—and was sitting in the chair with her desk between them. He was mentally preparing himself for the next session that was to include one of her partners, when her phone rang. Said partner had unfortunately been forced to take an emergency call, thought he'd just be a few minutes and asked if they'd wait for him.

It was the first time they'd been alone, with no business to conduct, since the unmentionable occurrence on the beach. The other couple of times he'd seen her that week, he'd left as soon as they were through with whatever had called him up to see her.

He watched her on the phone with her peer, frowning as the conversation progressed. When she'd hung up and dialed a receptionist to let her know about the partner needing not to be disturbed—he couldn't help but wonder if she seemed a bit edgier than usual. Even more so than she'd been the first day he'd been there in her office.

Or was he just imagining things?

To ask would ensure that she was edgy.

They weren't bringing up that night. At least not until

some of the burrs had been worn down enough for them to do so with a shrug or a chuckle at their immature behavior.

Feeling the tension growing in him, he went over his final eighteen veterinarian applicant choices one last time. Sage would be contacting them all by email to start the paperwork process as soon as her meetings with him were through for the day.

He knew to redirect unproductive thoughts with issues of importance to him. Most particularly with emotional attachment—like him getting his life back a hell of a lot sooner than he'd ever even hoped could be possible.

Life back meant finding a new home.

Which brought him back to the beach. And the possibility of buying the still-dilapidated cabin at the end of the road.

He spiraled down from there. Found himself staring into space—gaze pointed directly at Sage—a fact he noticed only when she said, "Is something wrong?"

Unhinging, he dug deep and blurted, "I couldn't go to my junior prom."

*Flipping wonderful.* Way to save the day.

Sage's frown was full-blown and filled with confusion. "What?" He wanted to smooth the lines from her forehead. And kiss those lips again. For a long time. As he had the other night.

He quickly jumped to the most recent thoughts that would counteract the inappropriate desire surging through him. "I was just thinking about my prom," he said then, instilling as much casualness into the words as he could muster. Hoping it was enough. "I was lost in space, and you asked what was wrong," he continued, as though they were discussing bubble gum machines.

Nodding, Sage's expression cleared, wiping away those

lines he'd seen himself soothing. "So, why couldn't you go to your junior prom?"

"My grandmother wasn't well. She had a lot of things wrong, some things that flared up unexpectedly. A neighbor, who'd been a good friend of hers for years, would come over during the school day, if there were issues, but she worked nights, caring for an older woman in her home, and there was no one else but me."

He heard how ridiculous he sounded. A grown man, spilling his guts like a teenager, but the feelings he was invoking inside himself were doing the trick. A bit of humiliation was well worth that.

"So…you thought you were going, but she had a flare-up?" Sage's expression had taken on her lawyer-at-work look. Interested. Concerned.

But professional.

He welcomed it. Felt success in his grasp.

"Yeah," he said. "There was this girl in my English class…"

"Trina? The one who turned out to be suspicious and possessive and started showing up at your locker at school, and at your house and calling you to see if you were home when you said you would be?"

He'd forgotten he'd told her that part. It had been early in their relationship, when they'd talked about dates they'd had that had gone wrong. About things they didn't want in a relationship.

He hadn't mentioned his abhorrence at the idea of having kids. Hadn't mentioned children at all. No, he'd talked about not wanting to feel like he was being stalked.

He gave his standard nod. "Yep, that's the one." And because he couldn't afford not to, he continued. "I asked her to prom, she accepted. It would have been our first date. But I couldn't go."

If he had, maybe he'd have found out sooner how desperately possessive the young woman had been. At a dance, with all the other classmates there, dressed to the nines... he'd have wanted to hang out with them. Trina had been big on it always just being the two of them.

Which mattered not at all. He was digging deep for emotional triggers that would keep him away from thoughts of reacquainting himself with Sage Martin's body.

The woman was frowning again. Shook her head. "And you were lost in thought about this now?"

One more nod.

"Why?"

Well, now, that part wasn't for the sharing.

He glanced over at her, still standing behind her desk from where she'd risen to reach the applicants folder. Standing above him.

Much like she'd stood above him in the sand...

And it hit him. Bringing up the prom...he was more on task than he'd realized. Was just taking some time to get up to speed with himself. It was the exact topic they needed.

Him coming clean. Out loud. To the one person who most needed—most deserved—the rotten part of his truth.

## *Chapter Twenty-One*

Was Gray about to tell her that he'd met up with Trina again after all these years? That the woman might be showing up with him at the beach?

The idea was ludicrous. But she couldn't get it to blink away. The thought of him bringing any other woman to Ocean Breeze was…just…wrong.

Chest tight, she watched him, and knew the second he'd made a decision. Was shaking inside by the time he started to speak.

"My grandmother had multiple sclerosis, among several other things. I knew from the time my mother died that my grandmother wasn't expected to live a normal lifespan. She'd wanted me to know, to be prepared. To be ready…"

Sage fell back to her chair. Staring at him.

"And by ready, I mean she instilled in me a need to make my own way, to strive and achieve and not settle. To make more of my mother's having lived by succeeding and making a difference in the world."

He stopped talking, took a couple of quick swipes at his chin, and Sage swallowed back tears. Gray would neither want nor understand them. He'd see pity. Where she felt…love.

She hurt inside for his having hurt.

Growing up with that helplessness…with a loving guardian who taught him to be capable, but not being able to fore-see, to prevent, her death.

"Every good ounce in me is due to her," he said then, meeting her gaze head-on.

It was a tragic tale, and a beautiful story, too. "I'm guess-ing she's looking down on you. And is so proud of you, Gray."

The shake of his head, his unrelenting gaze, stopped her words.

"After a while, living like that, with no real sense of con-trol over my future, or even daily activities...I resented it sometimes."

"Of course you did. Who wouldn't?"

"She knew. In that last year, every time I had to stay home, she'd apologize to me. There she was, having given the last years of her life wholly to me, losing her daughter because of me...in pain...still getting up, cooking and cleaning, any-time she could. She gave me her last breath...apologizing be-cause I couldn't go to the damned prom? Because she *knew* I resented her for that."

Sage quieted inside. An almost deathly quiet.

More was on the way. She could feel it emanating from him.

"I'm great at the small stuff, Sage. The momentary things. I can care about all my patients and relate to their young human companions. Because it's only for the moment. Or the hour..."

She could see the train about to wreck. "That's not true," she butted in. Trying desperately to stop the oncoming crash. "You do it all day, every day. It's your life, Gray." She waved to the top of her desk. "As embodied by all of the energy going into getting it back for you."

He wasn't listening. His shaking head told her so. But she just kept talking. "Not just from me, and others who knew you, but, because of what you'd already built, you're getting new energy from total strangers, too."

"The job is my responsibility," he told her. "Not the individual. I can always call off for a day, have another veterinarian fill in for me."

"Have you ever done that?"

"I'm also off every evening, weekends, anytime I take vacations…"

She had a flash to her sense of freedom the other night. How much she'd missed a little time for herself. "Everyone needs time off, Gray. Even I…"

He stood, cutting off her words. "No, Sage. Hear me. I can't bear the thought of being responsible, full-time, for another life. It makes me feel like I'm suffocating inside. The idea of living my life waiting for the resentment to hit…it's like someone who's terminal, waiting for death."

As his grandmother had been. As he'd watched her be. Sage saw him standing there and didn't recognize him for a second. He was Gray. And was changing right before her eyes.

"That's why you broke our engagement…" She wanted to stand, too. But didn't trust her legs to hold her. "You were resenting me."

"No!" His obvious frustration had her attention. And sent relief shooting through her, even while she remained on full emotional alert. "Children are wholly dependent. Vulnerable. Unable to take a different path than the one you put them on until they're grown."

He stopped, ran a hand through the always messy, thick strands of hair that she'd once envisioned being free to touch for the rest of her life.

And then continued, "You're missing my point, Sage. When you're an adult, you're responsible for yourself. But children…you have them, and then the things that happen to you that are out of your control, it'll affect them adversely, shape the entire rest of their lives, and you won't be able to do anything about it. I just…"

Dropping his hand to the top of her desk, he just quit talking. Standing there. As though giving up.

Reminding her of something he'd said about his mother. About her death being a blessing because she'd always been so tired.

"Wait a minute. Are you talking about your mother resenting you? Or you resenting having to care for your grandmother?"

The look he gave her was odd. Something new. As though he didn't understand her. Didn't know her well enough to figure her out. He sank back down to his chair, continuing to watch her.

As though, if he looked long enough, the answers would suddenly appear, written across her forehead? Or she'd speak them.

She waited. Couldn't let him off the hook.

"The thought of being like my mother, responsible for shaping a young life, knowing that if I screw up I screw the kid up forever, I just can't see that. Even if I only make his future more difficult, or don't have the capacity to love him enough, it's not fair to that little one who had no choice in the matter." He shook his head. "And after caring for my grandmother—knowing that I have the propensity to resent someone I love—I can't allow myself to create a life." Another head shake.

And then he looked her right in the eye, chin up. "I guess the answer to your question is…both. I won't risk children's lives on a chance that I'll ever feel about caring for them as I felt about caring for the old woman who'd been the only good in my life. I won't know, until someone is fully dependent on me. And I can't take the chance that it would happen again. Nor can I risk not knowing if I'm capable of loving a child enough. My father didn't care enough to stick around. Or at least check for consequences for what he'd done with my mother. And she clearly didn't seem to find having me worth the sacrifice…"

Sage stilled. Too full of conflicting emotions raging through her to do anything but feel them all.

After all those years…she finally understood.

Was seeing him differently.

And it didn't help.

Didn't make anything better. At all.

She'd thought they'd been so close that, other than their familial needs, they'd been open and honest with each other. That she'd known him better than she'd known anyone. Even her twin brother.

She'd given him all of herself.

While he'd been hiding himself from her all along. If he'd only let her in. Talked to her, at least. Let her love the whole younger man while he grew into the successful man he'd become. Maybe he'd have seen life differently, through the eyes of faithful, every-day love. Maybe not. But at least, if he'd have given her a chance, given her the truth and let her make her own choice…

"I'm sorry." She heard sorrow in his tone. Didn't meet his gaze. Whether he'd followed her thoughts, or was just sending out a general politeness, Sage couldn't even try to tune in to find out.

"I'm sorry, too," she told him. Needing the conversation to end.

In her current, somewhat broken and shocked state, all she knew was that her life with Gray, any kind of future relationship they might have, had just changed forever.

Most particularly in light of a possible consequence from their few seconds of stolen pleasure on the beach.

Gray went straight back to Ocean Breeze that night. No more stopping for a long dinner and a beer, or a sports bar, watching a game he didn't care about, and having a beer. No more looking at homes he didn't want, or sitting with the architect to draw up plans for renovating the interiors of the various Buzzing Bee Clinics locations he was in the process of leasing and buying. He'd managed to eat up Sunday through Thursday nights, to avoid any chance of time with Sage on the beach, but Friday night, he just didn't have it in him to run anymore.

He'd been at it since he was old enough to know that his life wasn't like his friends' lives. He'd very likely lost Sage's respect because of it.

So he was running to avoid becoming what he was. A product of a nontraditional, sad and painful, but still loving home. There'd been enough to eat. He'd always been warm and fed. Clean. And treated with kindness.

He'd never had a hand lifted to him.

Or, as far as he could remember, a harsh word spoken to him inside the walls of his home, either.

Opening up to Sage…had opened up his past to himself. Allowing him to see alternate views of his reality. The woman had always had a way of making him feel…all the things he'd never felt at home. Safe. In a nonphysical sense.

But in the space of one sentence, that had changed.

Nothing Sage had said. It had been his own words.

And between the capital letter at the beginning, and the period at the end, he'd finalized his own life sentence.

*My father didn't care enough to stick around. Or at least check for consequences for what he'd done with my mother.*

Six days before, he'd had unprotected sex. A first for him. A major, unforgivable first. He was assuming Sage was on birth control. But he hadn't asked. Had been too busy running from what they'd done, trying to avoid the consequence he felt he may have created. He did not want to lose their friendship over a glorious minute in the sand.

He'd felt a change come over her that afternoon. Felt her withdrawing from him.

And knew he had to ask about the birth control.

He would not be his father. Period.

He'd suffocate, have his lungs blown out, go on oxygen twenty-four seven, chain himself to within a few miles of the kid at all times, if that was what it took to assure himself he'd stick around. He'd never have a child of his growing up without a father. Wondering where he was.

He'd never abandon a woman pregnant with his child.

Most particularly not Sage Martin.

He'd promised her he'd never walk away again.

Scott's car was in his spot as Gray pulled in the empty space next to it. The cottage was empty. Friday, early court day. Scott was already out on the beach bringing in November with Morgan's long walk. Or, he'd finished it and was hanging out four houses down, nursing a beer and enjoying the company.

A private, low-key gathering of friends any night of the week. All dog lovers, too.

Ocean Breeze was most definitely a one-of-a-kind neighborhood.

He couldn't find anywhere else to live that even came close to it. And hadn't mentioned buying the cottage at the end of the road, either. Not even to Scott.

He'd inquired about it, though. Knew it was still available. At a way higher price than the building was worth, in its current state. But he'd pay twice as much to be able to come home to it every night.

Gray changed out of his suit and into casual, dark cotton pants and a short-sleeved lighter pullover. He was just reaching for a beer when he heard a knock on the door.

His stomach sank a notch. Harper.

He liked the woman. But he didn't need adult female companionship at the moment. Even just the friendly version.

He went to the door, though. Doing so was just who he was. You didn't turn your back on...

It wasn't Harper looking at him through the glass. Gray had to look a lot lower down to meet the wide-open and very serious and determined big, blue-eyed gaze of his visitor.

Figuring Scott for being within hearing distance, maybe watching Morgan on the side of the cottage, he slid open the door.

"Can I come in?" the child asked.

Sage would not have put her daughter up to the visit.

Would she? She'd clearly been set to show him a thing or two about life, just before her colleague had interrupted them that afternoon.

At least that had been his take on her expression. Her firm stance.

Didn't matter one way or the other. No way he'd reject a four-year-old.

"Of course," he said, standing back. Glancing out again to see who was out there listening in. Who'd be coming around the corner to the porch steps any second.

Leigh, in leggings, a long-sleeved purple T-shirt to match and tennis shoes, took one step inside. Peered up at him and asked, "Mr. Buzzing Bee, are you mad at me?" And before Gray could do more than kneel down to her level, she continued. "Sarah got mad at me at school today and she stayed on the other side of the room and wouldn't come over and play with me and you don't come play anymore, neither. And I thinked about it on the way home 'cause Mommy was busy in her head."

"Busy in her head?" He tended to the least minefield-feeling part first.

"Yeah." The child nodded, looking a little less severely focused. "When she's got work in there and doesn't always hear me and I have to say it over and over."

Gray managed to choke back the chuckle that burst up through him. But couldn't prevent the smile that split his lips, and he said, "No, Miss-Leigh-who-pays-attention-to-everything. I am not mad at you. And don't think I ever could be." He told her something that just seemed clear in that moment. "You are kind, and caring, and you're very good with dogs," he told her, words coming up out of him.

"Then why didn't you come out to play all these days? I saw dolphins and petted a monkey and met a elephant doctor and been waiting to tell you 'bout that last part."

She'd met an elephant doctor…

"Leigh!"

"Leigh?"

"Leigh!"

Screams, at least two female and a male, all hit him at once, from farther up the beach. Instilling instant remorse. Scott wasn't around the corner. Sage hadn't put her up to…

He should have checked.

"Uh-oh." The little girl's voice hit him hard, too.

"Don't worry," he told her, picking the child up, settling her on his hip as he'd seen Sage do. "We're both in trouble on this one, and we'll take our punishment together, okay?"

Those blue eyes, so close to his own now, implored him. "Do I gotta?"

"Yes. Without any argument. You disobeyed your rules."
He was already out on the porch. "Deal?"

"Okay…"

He heard the grumble in her voice.

Might have smiled at it if he hadn't already been shouting
out, "She's here! She's here!" at the top of his lungs.

As he galloped down the beach with Sage's child in his
arms.

# *Chapter Twenty-Two*

Sage's heart went from pure, undiluted panic to relief so quickly she stumbled as she raced toward the man heading for them.

That it was Gray holding her rescued daughter gave her a further measure of warmth. With wide eyes she reached the two before Scott and Iris, but just barely.

Sand flew as she stopped abruptly, reaching for her daughter. "Are you okay?" she asked the little girl, checking every inch of her for stains, signs of blood, bruising, distress. And then, looking up at Gray, "Where did you find her?"

Then back at Leigh, hugging the little girl tight. "Thank God," she said, and burst into tears.

"Where'd you find her?" Scott's voice spoke just beyond Sage.

"Is she okay?" Iris asked right after. As Morgan and Angel circled around them barking.

Sage hung on. Squeezing her eyes shut to stem the flow of emotion welling over. She didn't want to scare Leigh.

The thought materialized, just as she heard Gray say, "I didn't find her. She knocked on the door."

The dogs had quieted.

"Mommy, you're hurting me!" Leigh's voice, strong and a bit irritated, accompanied the little girl's proclamation as she pushed against Sage.

"I'm sorry, sweetie," she quickly responded, putting the child down and looking her over again head to foot as both dogs came forward and did the same. Morgan licked Leigh's fingers. "You're sure you're okay?"

Because if she was...then what...

"I breaked the rules and Mr. Buzzing Bee said I have to take my punishment and him, too, together. I don't know why him. It's my rules." At that, the little girl turned to look at Gray, who'd been talking softly with Iris and Scott, while standing right there, within touching distance of Sage.

"How come you get in trouble? It's in my rules?" she asked, frowning.

"Because I'm a grown-up and I know your rules, and I didn't check to make sure you were following them, which makes me in trouble, too."

As Sage slowly got up to speed, her mind spun in all new directions. Which built different tensions. With a hand on her daughter's shoulder, she stood and faced Gray. "She broke her rules to visit you?"

Why that was in any way his problem, she had no idea.

"Am I punished now?" Leigh asked, looking up at the two of them.

Scott, who'd stopped talking with Iris and was watching the interchange, stepped forward, looking at Sage, and then Gray, before taking Leigh's hand. "I think Mommy needs some time to figure that out," he told the little girl. "Why don't you come with me and Miss Iris back to your house and wait for her?"

He glanced at Sage at that last bit. She nodded. Fighting through the residual effects of the original trauma, to try to figure out what was going on.

She'd been standing right there, with Leigh playing catch with the dogs, talking to Scott and Iris about an apparent potential buyer for the cottage at the end of the road, and next thing she knew, Leigh was gone.

"Our first water rescue class is tomorrow," she said, inanely. But not. "They can't come soon enough as far as I'm concerned. I thought..."

Didn't matter what she'd thought. She'd failed to watch her child.

"She said she snuck away on purpose," Gray told her. "She thought I was mad at her because I wasn't on the beach anymore. Apparently, one of her little friends at school got mad at her today and stayed on the other side of the room and wouldn't play with her."

"Sarah, right. I heard about that."

"She told you?"

"No, her teacher did. Sarah apparently told Leigh that since she only has a mommy she comes from a broken home. Leigh was adamant that her house wasn't broken and stomped her foot, insisting that Sarah take it back. Sarah didn't. And Leigh told her she didn't like her anymore. From what I heard, Leigh later apologized, but Sarah didn't respond and wouldn't talk to her."

Basic kid stuff. All except for the broken home part.

"I once had a kid tell me that the police were going to come and take me away," Gray told her. "We were about Leigh's age. He'd heard his mother call Child Services on my behalf. Kids repeat what they hear." He shrugged, meeting her gaze as he dropped yet another bombshell glimpse into the young life that had shaped the man he'd become. "I heard my grandmother give that woman some words that I've never forgotten," he added with a grin. "Right after Child Services had done their thing and cleared my home and upbringing as clean and loving."

Watching him, Sage asked softly, "What did she say?"

So not the most important topic at hand. But he'd said he'd never forgotten.

"Love matters," he said back, holding her gaze. And then with one of his nods, grinned again. "Right after she told her that it might behoove her to mind her own business a little more and ours a little less. Her son had just been caught stealing grapes off what he thought was a neighbor's fenced-in vine. Turned out the neighbor caught him and stopped him from eating them as they were common moonseed, not grapes, and poisonous."

Love did matter. And sometimes you loved someone enough to know that you weren't good for them. You took responsibility and walked away.

Sage got his message loud and clear.

Gray's instincts were pinching him uncomfortably, strongly urging him to retreat back to Scott's cottage and nurse his beer.

The man his grandmother had raised stood on the beach with a question hanging there, waiting to be asked.

Was she still on birth control?

"I'm sorry Leigh bothered you," Sage offered before he could force the words past the constrictions in his chest and throat. "As you've probably noticed, she pretty much has the run of the beach down here, in terms of neighbors. She thinks everyone is family and therefore fair game. I'll be giving her a lesson on that one as soon as I get home."

Gray's spine straightened. "You don't trust me with her?"

Maybe he couldn't blame her, considering his resistance to having a family, but he'd made it quite clear that he was good with kids. Enjoyed them. Just… "Because I didn't think to make sure someone knew she was with me," he finished before she had a chance to respond.

"No!" Her response, the irritated drawing together of her brows, spoke more strongly than the one word. "In the first place, I think I just overheard you telling Scott that you thought he or I were just outside..."

He had. And nodded.

"And in the second, my God, Gray! You're a renowned veterinarian. So much so that even when social media is trying to cancel you, you've got investors lining up to support your new start. You can't be that good with animals and not be good with kids. Beyond that, Leigh likes you, and she might be only four, but she's a pretty good judge of character."

He looked at her then. Waited.

"And my brother and I are good judges of character, too," she added, somewhat sheepishly, while Gray's mood took an upward soar.

"Then, please, let Leigh know that she is welcome to visit me anytime, with your knowledge and permission, of course, and I will be delighted to be counted as one of her friends."

A friend. Not a parent.

*That* he could handle.

With honest anticipation. Sage's little girl was a hoot. "She's a captivating conversationalist," he said, because thinking of Leigh's way of looking at the world made him smile.

And he needed all the smiles he could get.

Sage nodded, thanked him profusely for keeping Leigh safe and turned, as though to go. Gray called her back. "Hey, hold on a sec."

Turning, she raised her brow, but wasn't going anywhere.

"I just want to make sure we're ready for the morning," he told her. "You've got all the paperwork ready?" The excuse was cheap. See-through. The group was meeting at her back porch, where they'd sign necessary forms, and then the rest of the morning was all on him. Sage wouldn't even be there.

She didn't have a dog.

"Yes, everything is filled out. Just awaiting signatures."

He knew that. She'd mentioned the fact that afternoon.

She turned to go again.

"Don't be too hard on her," he blurted next. "I really should have checked that someone knew she was there."

"Did you really tell her that you'd take your punishments together?"

"I did. When I told her that she had to own up to her mistake and serve her time without argument."

Sage's face softened, and she smiled. "I'm probably going to let her go with a stern warning on this one," she said. "So here's yours. If ever there comes a time when she's too much for you, or pestering you, I want your word that you'll let me know."

"That sounds more like a question than a warning."

"I mean it, Gray."

He got the warning loud and clear that time. In look and tone.

"It's not going to happen. But if it ever did, I would absolutely let you know."

She nodded. Watched him a second longer and turned to head back up the beach.

"Are you on birth control?" The question shot out. Hit her in the back.

Shoving his hands into his pockets, finding it hard to breathe, Gray waited.

Sage froze.

Was tempted to just start walking again. Go home. Pretend she hadn't heard Gray's parting blast.

Something in his tone played back to her. A kind of emotional desperation. Reminding her of their conversation in her office that afternoon.

Wasn't such a shock. She'd been replaying it in her mind, over and over, ever since. Figured that damned conversation was why she hadn't noticed Leigh missing until the little girl had had time to get to Scott's, knock on the door and have a conversation with Gray...

That afternoon...he'd mentioned having a father who didn't care enough to see if there'd been consequences for his actions.

Gray wouldn't be that guy. But if she chose to keep something from him...

That would be on her, and he'd be free...

Sometimes loving meant being responsible enough to know that you weren't good for someone and walking away. Her inability to take the morning-after pill...that wasn't on him. She'd made the choice.

She'd have to cut all ties with Gray. At least for a while.

She had no right to make another person's choices for them. Period. Just as he hadn't when he'd chosen to walk away rather than be honest with her about his aversion to being a father. The causes. The reasoning. The conditioning that had built inside him over a period of years.

And maybe a whole lot of misplaced guilt, too. Feeling resentful sometimes, even as an adult, was normal. And for a teenager, all alone caring for an incapacitated grandmother...tenfold.

Thoughts flew as she stood there, looking at sand, seeing nothing. Maybe, if she didn't move, he'd just slip away, and they could pretend his question had never happened.

Sage slowly turned. Looked at him.

And knew he already had his answer.

Her initial response…her hesitation…was enough information.

"Are you…"

What, pregnant? She held his gaze. Felt a need to defend herself. With no opposition coming at her.

"It's too soon to tell."

He nodded. That series of short bobs that covered up so much. And continued to hold her gaze. As though they could somehow both disappear from the situation. Or it would disappear. All of it. The past.

Those seconds on the beach.

The huge question hanging there without an available response.

"But you could be."

She nodded.

"How likely?" She used to be super irregular. He'd known that once. Had been attentive to certain plans, and wonderfully kind and attentive when she had bad cramps.

The memories washed over her.

And the truth came out. "I've regulated over the years as I aged. Like clockwork."

"And?"

"Timing is right for me to have been ovulating." There. He could blast her all to hell. Accuse her of trapping him.

She'd clearly been the aggressor. She couldn't blame him for being suspicious of her motives. What a hell of a get back, right? He breaks your heart, ruins your life plan, humiliates you with a cancellation two days before the wedding—and ten years later you trap him by forcing him to be a part of the reason he'd walked away.

Sage hugged her arms. But didn't turn away again. She was a lawyer. She had his argument already worked out for him. Would take it with her head held high.

Tell him she hadn't planned a second of it. Would never have trapped him. And leave him to believe what he might.

Better that he think her duplicitous and walk away than that he stick around and feel trapped.

Gray's lips pursed. He'd been standing there nodding, his gaze blank. Eventually, those piercing brown eyes seemed to focus on her again.

"When are you due?"

That was it? He was going to take it on the chin, like he had everything else in his life? Keep it inside, and then, when he got to the point of suffocating, take off again?

"Next week." He'd probably already figured that. A woman's cycle wasn't all that much of a mystery.

"Okay, well, keep me posted."

Hands still in his pockets, Gray turned and headed slowly back down the beach.

Sage watched him. Tears in her eyes.

Wanting to call him back.

But didn't.

There was nothing she could say to make things better.

# *Chapter Twenty-Three*

Gray didn't sleep. He tossed and turned. Dozed and woke up with a start, heart pounding. Several times. At three, he got up, slipped into sweats and a long-sleeved shirt, grabbed his flip-flops, and tiptoed to the back door.

Making it outside without alerting Morgan.

And then he walked. Up the beach, back down again. Once. Twice.

Scenarios chasing themselves through his mind, bumping into and toppling over each other. Melding. Segueing. Interrupting.

He couldn't land.

He could be a father already. Done deal. No choice.

Sage's baby.

Knocking on his door and asking Mr. Dad if he was mad.

Sage telling the child not to bother him.

That wouldn't affect the kid at all. Being told not to knock on Dad's door.

Or, more likely, Father. It took more than biology to make a dad.

Semantics. Who the hell cared what he'd be called?

If there was a baby. There might not be. The possibility was valid. Some women tried for years, having sex based on ovulation tests even, and still didn't get pregnant. An old sit-com favorite came to mind on that one.

The couple had eventually chosen to adopt.

Just as Sage had done.

Sage.

She had to be…what?

Getting what she's always wanted? To have a child of her own. Conceived with a man she loved?

Had loved?

Did she still love him?

Did he love her?

No point going there. The questions were moot.

He'd reached the far end of Ocean Breeze. Where the road and beach met sharp, rocky cliff. And where, in between the two, sat the dilapidated cottage that he'd inquired about purchasing.

He hadn't made an offer. The neighbors would all be told at that point. They couldn't affect the outcome. Just…according to neighborhood bylaws, a notice of pending sale would go out.

As he stood there in the dark, hearing the ocean roaring behind him, his toes rubbing grainy sand against the leather of his flip-flops, he decided.

He was going to make the offer.

He'd talk to Sage first, let her know. And if she grew distressed? Begged him not to buy?

He'd cross that bridge when he came to it. If he did.

The cottage spoke to him in a way no other building ever had. It was like the broken-down thing was calling him home.

And if Sage was pregnant…if he was going to be a father…he had to be close.

To the child.

And to the sea.

He'd get a dog right away. Had to have it trained before the child visited. And, hope to God, the canine would train him, too, in how to be responsible every single day, without growing too resentful when the dog's needs overrode his own desires or plans.

Of course, there were a lot of wonderful places he could board a canine companion when he had to get away.

Not so with humans.

Walking up to the cottage, he made his first in-person, up close inspection. Stood in the cracked and broken parking spaces. Touched the knob on the front door. Noticed shingles missing from the roof. Saw some rotting wood on one side.

And eventually ended up sitting in the sand, leaning up against what had used to be a sliding glass door, an entry-way that had been boarded up.

He'd have to dig out to have a porch.

He wanted a porch.

The place was small. Much smaller than Sage's or Scott's cottages. That was partially why it hadn't sold, the Realtor had told him. The woman had also shared that all cottages had right-of-way for additions. Sitting on almost an acre apiece, there was certainly room for the structure to grow.

He had to tell Sage he planned to make an offer. As soon as possible. He didn't want to lose the place.

Sage.

Possibly pregnant Sage.

He'd had some hours to come to grips with the idea. She'd had almost a week. Had obviously known, the second she'd climbed off him—or shortly thereafter—that there'd been completely unprotected sex.

And she hadn't said a word. Protecting him?

Or afraid to tell him?

Sage, afraid? Not when it came to telling someone the truth. Easy or hard, the woman was a rock when it came to delivering provable fact.

Even to a man who'd left her at the altar because he'd been so resistant to impregnating her he'd had to break her heart. And his.

But she'd wait until she knew.

And she'd spend every minute between the possibility and the knowing…distraught.

There were some things a guy's gut just knew when it came to the woman who'd once been his soulmate.

He'd never actually said the word. She had. But that truth had resonated so deeply within him he'd accepted that it was so.

Sage would rather die than trap him. And because of a few brainless seconds in the sand…she could be forced to do just that.

Ten years after they'd both suffered so much to prevent the imprisonment from ever happening.

Irony at its worst?

Fate's worst joke on him ever?

An early Thanksgiving nightmare?

Or just something that had happened because he and Sage had made a choice without considering the consequences?

Gray leaned his head back against the house, closing his eyes so he could concentrate more fully on the sound of the waves as he let the questions roll over him.

Figuring he'd have his answers, at least the pertinent ones, soon enough.

The first water rescue class took off to a hearty round of applause at its conclusion. Using Morgan as his demonstrator, Gray had started with giving dogs treats for quickly entering the water at a splash. From there, Sage got a little lost, but noticed that all six residents enrolled in the class were attentive. And participating.

Sitting up on her porch, she made certain that while Leigh watched from the sand, she didn't approach or interrupt the class.

Gray had said he needed to speak with Sage when class was over. With lead in her stomach, she waited, preparing for the worst.

Knowing that she'd handle it, whatever it was. She'd lost Gray once and survived. Had thrived.

If he planned to sue her for trapping him into an insurmountable situation, she'd offer to settle out of court.

And if she was pregnant...

The thought scared her to death. A single mom of one, that she could do. But two? Tending to Leigh and a newborn? Up all night? Working all day?

Scott would help where he could. And Iris. And Harper and others, too.

She'd be fine...but...would she always be doing it alone? Going to bed alone? Waking alone? Raising children alone? And later, after they were grown, living alone?

Was that the penance she paid for falling in love with the wrong man?

And if she wasn't pregnant?

She wouldn't be growing a child inside her, giving birth or tending to a second newborn. Life would continue just as it had done before Gray's advent on the scene. She'd been happy. The happiest she could ever imagine being.

Before she'd fallen in love with the man all over again.

Sitting up straight, Sage stared only at Leigh. Refusing to allow her gaze to stray, for even a second, to the far too handsome vet on his haunches, spreading his gentleness all over as he taught lifesaving measures.

She had not fallen in love with Gray all over again.

She wouldn't be that brainless. Wouldn't make such a self-destructive choice.

Hell, she'd just really met the man the day before. When he'd shown his true self to her.

And…had fallen in love with him more deeply. More intensely, for understanding the man more deeply.

She couldn't do it. Couldn't trap him in a situation that would ruin his life. He'd fought too hard to get out of circumstances that had controlled him.

Scott approached the group five minutes before the class was due to end. Or rather, approached Leigh, took her hand and led her down closer to the group. Let her play with the dogs as they came up off the wet sand—a place she was forbidden to go unless one of her adults was holding her hand— and then, as the small crowd dissipated, he took Leigh's hand again, as Leigh's head turned up toward his.

Sage saw her daughter nod. Saw her brother look up her way and wave.

Leaving her only non-churlish option to wave back. Which she did.

She stood up, seeing the man she'd purposely been not looking at heading her way.

She'd expected to have Leigh close by, inside watching the movie she already had cued up and ready, while she and Gray had a glass of sweet tea on the porch.

He'd say what he had to say.

He'd leave.

And she and Leigh would head into town for some shopping.

She'd had it all planned. Was off her mark, even thinking about being alone at her house with Grayson Bartholomew.

The possible father of her possible child?

When he hadn't known, she'd been able to keep herself contained. But with someone else clued in…

How could something that wasn't even real yet, might never be real, suddenly seem more real?

She was standing in the sand, as though guarding the entrance to her porch, when he approached. "You arranged to have Scott take Leigh?" she asked.

"I did." He didn't even attempt to prevaricate a little bit. Which tightened the knot in her stomach. The man meant business.

In a manner that had to be out of earshot of children.

"Did you ever have a dog growing up?" she blurted out. Hating that she kept losing her tongue around him like some frilly thing that didn't know better. Leigh wore frills. Sage hadn't since her mother died.

She was avoiding the coming confrontation. He'd know it. How humiliating.

"No."

"Did you want one?" Leigh wanted one. But seemed happy to settle for having nearly a dozen of them wandering in and out of her days.

"Yes. And before you ask, we couldn't afford it." His words were somewhat short, but not with a mean bend. More like impatient to move on to his meeting agenda.

She didn't invite him to the porch. Or offer the tea she'd been prepared to serve.

"I won't keep you," he said, and she nodded, grateful that it would be quick. The beheading of whatever dreams she might have been secretly harboring.

"I wanted you to be the first to know I've found a place. I intend to make an offer later today."

What? Sage's mouth dropped open. That was it? He'd been looking at homes since before his had closed. Had planned to purchase, and then move after the GB Animal Clinics case went to court…

"Um, good!" she said, catching up to him. "Great! Where is it?"

Please, God, overlooking the ocean. Gray's one stipulation, whenever they'd talked about where they might live, had been that he have an ocean view.

"It's right here, Sage. On Ocean Breeze."

Right there?

He thought he was going to move in with her?

Had he lost his mind?

She wasn't saying no. Or even trying to shake her head. Mouth hanging open again, she just stared at him.

Then, closing it, studied him. And eventually asked, "You're serious?"

He nodded. That short series of bobs. Looking her right in the eye. As though he could climb inside her and make certain she understood him.

But…he couldn't just move in with her. They weren't together.

She didn't even know yet…

And something else hit her. Iris telling her and Scott that she'd heard that someone had expressed interest in the dilapidated place at the end of the road. No formal offer had been made, but she knew.

"It's you," she said aloud, wide-eyed.

"It's been me since I walked up. You just figuring that out?"

"No, it's you who expressed interest in the cottage at the end of the road. You're going to buy it?" She couldn't keep the excitement out of her voice. Couldn't stop happiness from flowing through and out of her.

His grin came slowly. "I take it you don't have a problem with it, then? With us being permanent neighbors?"

Permanent neighbors. Not lovers.

Or parents.

Neighbors.

Something else struck then. She'd heard about interest in the cottage *before* she'd told Gray that she could be pregnant.

And had heard that the potential buyer had inquired about the place several days before.

Their sex on the beach, her possible pregnancy, hadn't changed anything as far as his wanting to live close was concerned.

At least not yet. He might change his mind, run for a cliff house someplace, if she found out she was pregnant.

And he might not. Maybe, living down the road, without full responsibility, or the ability to affect the life inside a home, would be enough to keep him around.

Her smile was a bit tremulous, but she got it out there. "No, of course not," she said, both hands clasped at her lips. "I have no problem with us being permanent neighbors."

No problem that she'd put on him, at any rate.

She was in love with the man. Possibly carrying his child.

Felt a little like she'd just been given a little Thanksgiving miracle. Something extra to be thankful for that year.

She might be a fool to want him around, even just as a neighbor, but the truth was, if that was where he wanted to be, she wanted him there.

Neither of them mentioned the very real danger inherent in having Gray living so close permanently. That at some point, they could find themselves in a situation similar to the previous Saturday night.

They both knew it was there, though.

And that afternoon, when she went shopping, she slid a new item into her cart.

A box of condoms.

Just in case she wasn't pregnant.

# *Chapter Twenty-Four*

$W$as she or wasn't she? Gray woke every morning of that next week with the question in mind. Sage could start her period any minute of any day.

Then he'd get up, focus on the day's tasks and refocus every time his mind strayed. It was an exhausting process, but it worked.

And though he was incredibly busy, he made a point to be on the beach three of the five evenings. He may have been a little tense around Sage, needing answers, feeling as though his entire future was in the balance. But there was no way he was going to have little Leigh think that he was mad at her, or didn't like her.

Why his opinion seemed to matter to her, he had no idea, but knowing that his absence had affected her negatively, he made certain not to be absent.

His plan had only been loosely formed. It wasn't like he was thinking he'd head down to Sage's and hang out with them. On the contrary.

He was trying not to think about the woman he'd been carelessly ecstatic with on the beach.

As it turned out, the four-year-old took care of the situation for him. As soon as she'd see him, she'd run up, give his legs a hug and run off. Or call out to him asking him to "Watch this!" He'd been treated to everything from somersaults to throwing sand as high in the air as she could. She showed him she could skip. And at one point, had crooked her finger at him, instructing him to bend down, and had whispered that Mommy had forgotten to punish her for running down to see him and so could they please keep it a secret so neither of them had to take a time-out.

He'd agreed immediately. With the caveat that she'd never run off again, and he would always tell if he knew she was breaking a rule. To which she'd solemnly agreed.

He saw Sage, too, but only in a group on the beach. Never alone. He caught her eye a time or two, but one or the other of them would look away.

They talked on the phone several times, pertaining to business. They'd been granted a hearing with the judge assigned to the GB Animal Clinics case the next week, and would know, possibly even that day, if he'd be affluent again. She'd received twenty-two signed commitments from investors; money was rolling into the Buzzing Bee Clinics account, enough to allow him to sign leases on three of the four properties and make offers to purchase the other two.

Two of his eighteen veterinarian contractors had changed their minds about joining him, but two others had immediately accepted the spots, and Sage had appointments to finish up paperwork with all of them that next week as well.

Each time he'd seen her on the beach, met her gaze, he'd looked for some kind of nod, letting him know she'd started her period. Each time he'd answered her call, his first thought was to hear her say she was calling to let him know she wasn't pregnant.

The week passed, and she made no mention of their secret situation. None.

Leaving him to ruminate on things in a way he never had before. Was she scared? She'd be happy if she was, right?

Having a baby was the one thing she'd always wanted most. Two would be twice the happiness, right?

And twice the work.

Was she praying she wasn't? Was that why she didn't talk about it? She was in denial. Telling herself not to worry. Unless she found out otherwise, there was no pregnancy.

If she'd just said something, anything, to clue him in to her state of mind, maybe he wouldn't have spent so much time on the topic. He'd never been good with the not knowing. Get all the facts. Weigh them. Make the decision.

He'd learned practicality in the cradle. For necessities, you found a way to provide. And you moved on from the wants you didn't need.

Pay the bills you had to pay, eat whatever you could afford after that. Even if it was oatmeal three meals in a row because all it took was oats and water.

Find out if you got the woman you'd once loved to distraction pregnant, and if you had, then figure out how you were going to live with yourself for the rest of your life.

As the week passed, he was slowly starting to see a picture gelling on that one. He'd be living down the road. Not in the house.

No way he'd be the main source of example, or the one a child looked to for early-development security. Although, he knew a lot about not having that. Knew what the child would need. Might not be a bad thing to be close, just to help Sage in case something came up in that area.

Give his advice. His point of view.

Still, living down the street…he'd have a step back. A step out. Precluding the need to worry about forming resentments that others could sense.

Like little Leigh. He'd rather die than have her ever think he resented a second of her sweet spirit filling the air around him.

His problem in the past, with his mother and grandmother, had been that he had no way out. Though, thinking back, he was sure, even if he had, he wouldn't have taken it. He'd been where he belonged.

And the cottage at the end of the road...that night he'd found out that Sage hadn't been on birth control, when his life had been careening out of control, he'd been unable to sleep, had walked down the beach to the cottage, slid to the ground, leaned against the broken-down building...he'd found home. A sense of peace he wasn't sure he'd ever had.

In the midst of the worst storm in his adult life.

Facing his worst nightmare. Possibly being a father.

He'd put his head back, listened to the waves and had actually fallen asleep. Waking hours later as dawn was breaking.

He'd made the offer on the place as soon as he'd had Sage's blessing.

All the Ocean Breeze residents had been notified and all seemed genuinely glad to have him join them. He'd received an official invitation to the Thanksgiving gathering on the beach. And a flyer telling him about the holiday lights that went up right afterward. Apparently, Ocean Breeze was known throughout Southern California for the beach light display that could only be seen by those living in the private neighborhood, or by boat. The sheet warned of the hundreds of boats that would be appearing in their waters, outside their reef, every weekend during the holiday season.

He'd never done holiday lights in his life.

Was on the end of the beach where it wouldn't matter much if he didn't shine as bright.

He'd figure something out.

Most of his time on the beach that week had been spent being joined by different clusters of neighbors, welcoming him to the neighborhood.

Wanting to join his water rescue class.

Asking him when he was getting a dog.

His usual answer, that he had an entire practice filled with dogs who needed him, worked long hours and lived alone, had sounded a bit weak to the Ocean Breeze residents. At least in his own ears.

All the Ocean Breeze residents were single professionals. The majority had dogs. But not Sage.

She had the only child on Ocean Breeze.

Class on Saturday morning had two new students, and several of the dogs were already running into the water on command to get a treat. He'd had it easy for the beginning steps. All of the dogs on Ocean Breeze were already used to the water and were comfortable in it. And all the ones in the class already responded immediately to basic commands. That had been a prerequisite for joining the class.

Standing in the wet sand after the session, talking to his students' owners, Gray laid out a brief overview of their goals. Next step would be to play games with the dogs while in the water, building up to retrieving a toy for a treat. And later, retrieving it off a boat. Progressing from there to bigger object retrievals, and then a person floundering in the water. Owners would have to work with dogs one-on-one. And Gray would have private sessions with all the dogs who showed proficiency for actual rescue operations when they got to the more advanced stages of training. The dogs would be expected to work with distractions going on, to learn to ignore the distractions.

And, of course, only the stronger and bigger dogs would be capable of adult rescue. But the smaller ones could still alert to a potentially life-threatening situation...

Morgan ran from his side, and he turned to see that Sage

had joined them. Her presence jarred him, stole his train of thought. Sage…she didn't attend the actual class.

She had news.

Because he'd interrupted himself to stare at her, everyone else was watching her, too.

It wasn't their news.

"I just wanted to let you all know that I put together a package of toys and other objects you can use for your individual work with your dogs. I found everything on sale and got bulk rate on shipping. Anyone who's interested, let me know…"

It *was* their news. She'd even talked to him about it that morning, just before class. When he'd asked where Leigh was.

She'd been in the house getting ready because Uncle Scott was taking her to the park to play.

Gray had seen Scott just before he'd come out to the beach. They'd stood in the kitchen, sipping coffee. Talking guy banalities. Scott hadn't said anything about taking his niece out for the morning.

And Gray had zero business feeling left out due to the fact that he hadn't. He had no business being *in*.

He hadn't been himself since he'd woken up that morning. Other than class time, when he was in his zone, doing what he loved, he hadn't been focused at all.

Mostly, he'd been trying not to focus on the one thing consuming his mind.

Sage's bodily functions.

Was she pregnant?

They'd reached the two-week mark. If she hadn't started yet, they could do an early test. He'd looked it up. Ten days after conception, home tests could often detect positive results.

And he had a right to know.

\* \* \*

She could have texted him. She knew Gray had to be living on the edge of cold blades, waiting to find out if his worst nightmare was coming true.

At the same time, she needed to take care of her. She had a little girl wholly dependent upon her and had to keep herself above water.

So she'd taken the night. And then had asked Scott to watch Leigh so she could have time alone with Gray—not that her brother had any idea about that.

Which had been part of the plan.

She didn't want Scott to know—and couldn't guarantee that, on a Saturday morning, her twin wouldn't wander in on a tense conversation and get suspicious.

"You got a minute to walk up to my place with me?" she asked, as the final laggers in Gray's class dissipated with their dogs. She held up the folder of class paperwork, some of which she'd just had signed.

"Just let me get changed," he said, barely looking at her, as he took a couple of steps backward while he spoke, heading toward Scott's place. "Tea on the porch in five minutes?" he asked, and barely waited for her nod before he turned and jogged up the beach.

Leaving her with more minutes of anxiety to get through. And…on the porch…

Not at all how she'd planned.

And she'd planned it all so carefully.

The segue in with class paperwork. Talking about how it was going. Keeping it calm. Casual.

Because she needed it that way.

And the privacy? That was all for her, too.

The last time things had ended between her and Gray, while starting out with a private moment between them, had precipitated the canceled wedding, the canceled life, and had been the most humiliating experience of her life.

While she'd been trying to hold together pieces of her heart and fighting anxiety as she'd tried to figure out, overnight, what her life was going to look like.

As she remembered back, the sympathetic looks and comments she'd received, even months later, had been unbearable. People had meant well, but their pity…had weakened her. Set her back notches in her growth.

It had held her in a place she hadn't wanted to be.

So…no chance for sympathy on the current time around. Most particularly not with Gray moving onto Ocean Breeze.

And with Leigh in the picture.

She loved them both so much. And if having Leigh in her home, raising her alone, with Gray on the outskirts of their family life, was what the future held—she was good with that.

Genuinely and sincerely.

As badly as she needed Leigh happy, she needed Gray happy, too. She loved him. The man he was, not the man he'd seemed to think he had to be for her.

Something that had been true back then, but that maybe ten years of maturity, and actually being a mother rather than dreaming about it, had shown her more clearly.

If Gray had been able to be completely open with her in the past, things might have been different. At the very least, any breakup would have been a mutual thing.

None of which mattered, she reminded herself—firmly—as she poured glasses of iced sweet tea and set them on coasters on side tables in the living room. Next to two chairs that faced the couch.

Getting through the next minutes with Gray believing she was just fine…that was the goal. No pity. The goal.

Being able to build a healthy life on the beach with Gray joining their close-knit group—that mattered.

As did having him in her life.

Truth be told, that mattered most.

She was watching for his approach. Stood inside, sliding open the glass door as he stepped up onto the porch. Inviting him in.

Leaving him little option was more like it.

And led him straight to the chairs in the living room. No couch. No even getting close to the hallway where her bedroom could be found.

No attraction. No tears.

Absolutely no regrets for what could have been.

Just friends.

In another pair of the cotton pants he seemed to prefer, with a light-colored, long-sleeved button-down shirt hanging loosely over them, Gray didn't touch his tea. Or sit.

He stood over her and said, "You know."

Sitting there with her tea glass held between her hands on her lap, the sweat getting her jeans a little damp, she forced herself to hold his gaze, and nod. Then smile. "I'm not."

She braced for the relief, the overjoyed light to shine from his eyes. Focused on keeping the smile pasted on her lips.

It was for the best. She knew that. Had been praying that she wasn't.

Just her heart…it had been sabotaging her all week. Hoping…

Figuring that it would all work out. Her with two children, giving birth to Gray's child as she'd always dreamed of doing, with Scott as the father figure, and Gray a close friend right down the street.

Unconventional, sure, but so what? If it worked for them

and the children grew up safe and secure, loved and happy and healthy...

Her spray of thoughts halted as she realized Gray wasn't shining joy all over her.

He'd dropped to the seat she'd left open for him, knees apart, elbows propped, his hands clasped and hanging in the air between them.

His sideways glance...didn't show her anything she'd expected. Or really even understood. "Gray?"

Had he decided not to go through with the sale on the cottage? Or be her friend? The scare had been too much for him? Chances of another one too much of a threat looming over him with them living on the same mile-long stretch of beach?

"I'm sorry, Sage," he started, and her heart dropped further. "I just... I know that a part of you...it's what you've always wanted, more than anything else, being pregnant."

No! She would not be pitied. Most particularly not by him.

"I knew I was meant to be a mother, Gray," she said softly, feeling the conviction of her words with all her heart. "And I am one. The possibility of a baby..." She stopped, glanced at him. And made a choice. "Yeah, I was disappointed, on one level. Gutted, actually. But on another...just as much relieved. I knew what it would do to you, Gray, and honestly, it wouldn't have been worth it."

The truth slid out—both from some hidden source inside her and into the room. Simultaneously.

Having a family had been vitally important to her.

But so had he been.

And while she'd never once considered giving up motherhood.

She hadn't fought for him.

Or for them.

# Chapter Twenty-Five

She wasn't.

Gray walked slowly back to Scott's place, thinking about sand in his flip-flops. How warm the San Diego sun felt even in November.

She wasn't.

An early Thanksgiving blessing. A whole two weeks before the holiday.

He hadn't stayed long. One long glance between the two of them, and Gray had downed his tea in one long drink. Set the glass down and hadn't been surprised when she'd rushed right with him, though good steps behind him, to the door.

They'd broken a cardinal rule there for a second.

Being alone in either of their homes.

He figured, over time, the attraction between them would fade. Or become so commonplace that they lived with it just like their enjoyment of alcohol. It was there, but you didn't partake of it in excess.

In their case—with the passion—any at all was excess.

She wasn't.

They'd escaped disaster.

So why wasn't he flying? Light as a feather?

He'd most definitely spent the week praying for the outcome she'd just delivered.

Even as he'd tried to prepare himself for a different answer. Tried to envision how he'd handle that other outcome.
Just so he'd be prepared in the event that she'd said she was.

He'd worked himself up to believing that it could work.
If it had to.

She wasn't.

And…hadn't seemed all that broken up by the fact. Shock-
ingly unbroken, actually. He knew her well enough to know
she'd been hiding from him.

And rightfully so.

She had to be somewhat disappointed.

Hell, even he was feeling a form of letdown after the past
week of anxiety.

Sad, that they'd watered their relationship down to the
point of not being able to be real with each other. To offer
comfort where it was most needed.

Only the two of them knew what they'd possibly had.
Only the two of them were feeling the effects of finding out
there'd been nothing there.

Yet, they weren't talking about it between the two of them.

The future was wide-open again.

She wasn't carrying his child.

Gray tried the reality on for the rest of that day, as he
drove from appointment to appointment, trying to be everything everyone needed from him as he and eighteen other
professionals started new chapters of their lives together.

With him at the helm.

Holding eighteen careers in his hands.

The thought took root. His chest got tighter. So much so
that he pulled off the road from one of the new clinic sites to
the next. His next on-site contractor appointment wasn't for
another hour. He'd been planning to get there early.

And instead, he sat in his SUV, staring at the ocean.

Why hadn't he seen it before?

All the vets who'd lost their jobs because of his one mis-hire at GB Animal Clinics. He'd seen a friend where a criminal existed. And he was just going to go and ask eighteen vets to sign on with him again?

And they were doing so? Some of them who'd already been burned by him once?

He grabbed his phone, intending to call Sage, and stopped. Calmed.

Sage. The seemingly endless bylaws and conditions and employee handbooks…she'd not only been protecting Gray from a second career disaster, she'd also been protecting everyone who worked for him.

He pushed her speed dial.

What kind of friends were they if they couldn't talk?

She didn't answer. Probably busy with Leigh.

He called another couple of times that afternoon. And a third as he headed home.

Sage didn't pick up.

And she didn't call him back.

Which pretty much told him what kind of friends they'd become.

Largely, because of him.

Sage took Leigh on a playdate on Saturday with another little friend from school, Jeremiah, and his mother, Maya, who was also single and a nurse practitioner in a medical office in their building.

Jeremiah wanted to go to the San Diego Zoo because Leigh had been talking about her day there with her uncle Scott and Miss Iris, and she spent the day telling her young friend all the inside scoops—in four-year-old terms—every time they stopped at a new enclosure. She named all the dolphins in the show, too. Telling Jeremiah how to tell them apart, and when one of the trainers recognized her, she invited both kids down after the show to let Jeremiah pet the dolphin in the private pool.

She'd had her phone off during the shows but had seen that Gray had called. He'd been meeting with contractors all day and would have things to discuss with her.

And while, in light of her newfound revelation—the fact that in the past she hadn't considered her role as a partner and wife nearly as much as she'd focused on becoming a mother—she might need to speak with him, that piece of news wasn't relevant when it came to work.

It was a bombshell she needed to work through before it became anything.

If it ever became anything.

With her time with Scott at the park that morning, and then the zoo during the afternoon and evening, Leigh practically slept through her bath, and was out before Sage had a chance to grab a book and sit down to read a good-night story. As Leigh called them.

Sage's heart filled to the brim, spilling over into a few tears, as she leaned down, kissed the little girl's cheek and pulled her covers up to her chin.

After turning on the baby monitor, and the night-light, she closed the door behind her.

Got herself a wine cooler from the top shelf of the refrigerator—the one Leigh couldn't reach—and thought about pulling the phone out of the pocket of her jeans.

She made a trip to the bathroom instead.

The bleeding that had purported the end to any pregnancy possibilities hadn't gone past the light flow that signified the beginning of her cycle. By the time Scott had brought Leigh home, it had stopped completely.

She'd left the office to buy the test earlier in the week. Had hidden it at the top of the linen closet in the bathroom.

And as she sat and watched lines on a piece of disposable paraphernalia, her life spun on a dime once again.

She sat there...stunned. Heart pounding.

Phone firmly in her pocket. Never coming out again.

And heard a knock on her sliding glass door.

*Scott.* She hadn't called to let him know she was back.

Didn't dawn on her until she was already in the kitchen, staring at the visitor on the other side of the door, that her brother would have just called her. If he hadn't seen her car in her spot, or lights on in her cottage...

Her heart rate, already accelerated, went into high speed, and she trembled as she pulled open the door.

Funny how fate had brought the man there right as her weaker self had been hoping to never see him again.

She slid open the door. Thinking she had to tell him what she'd just done. Overridden with anxiety as she contemplated the task.

His "Don't you ever answer your phone anymore?" gave her a shove back into reality. "Or return calls?"

Gray...at her door? He never...

"What's wrong?" she asked, feeling ashen, weak as she stared. "Is it Scott?"

He shook his head. Stood on the porch, leaning on the hand he had shoved up against the outside of her cottage. "Nothing's wrong," he said, more quietly. "I apologize for the drama."

That was new. Gray with drama. She'd thought he was there with urgent news.

And if he wasn't...

She needed to sit down. Went for the wine cooler she'd left on the kitchen counter. And turned before she got there.

For a few reasons. Most prominent, in that moment, was

the no drinking with Gray rule she'd given herself after the disaster her libating had caused two weeks before.

Grabbing the baby monitor off the counter instead, she headed back to the door, and motioning Gray to back up, stepped outside with him.

Sat in her chair, pulling her feet up to her butt, as though she hadn't a care in the world.

He'd come with a purpose.

Something must have gone very wrong at one of the sites. Which explained his current upset.

She had time to calm down while she heard him out. Dealt with whatever it was. But she started with, "I'm sorry about the calls. I was at the zoo with Leigh and Jeremiah, and his mother, Maya, and had my phone off." Babbling again. At the zoo with Leigh would have sufficed.

She'd have called him back a bit ago…if she hadn't had that life-altering detail to take care of…

Managed to cut herself off before that slipped out.

Sitting down next to her, leaning forward, as he had that morning, his elbows on his knees, Gray nodded. Looked over at her.

And then away.

His expression, even in the dark, had her heart pumping overtime again. She'd only ever seen him look that serious, in that deep, emotional way, once before.

The night he'd broken off their engagement.

"I've never been good at talking about my feelings, Sage," he said, and she froze. Ready to take what was coming.

Because she had no other choice. It was coming.

"And I realized this afternoon, I've also never allowed myself to admit that I need someone…"

Her sharp intake of breath brought his gaze to hers, and

he held up his hand, as though forestalling whatever she'd been about to say.

Which had been nothing. She was barely holding on to her thoughts in those seconds.

"So here I am, telling you, I realize that I need you in my life. I can't explain it. I'm sure some woo-woo theory would work, but I'm not all that up on that kind of thing. What I know is that where I fail, you succeed, and I think, in some way, I contribute equally to your life as well. Or did. And, I hope, can again. This…attraction between us… I don't know for sure how we handle it. My baser self would like for us to find a way to be occasional lovers, as needed, while living our separate lives in two separate homes. Preferably exclusive. At least on my part it will be. But if that's too much, if you need to be strictly friends, no touching, I'll find a way. I swear to God I will. I just can't lose you a second time."

The words seemed to tumble out of him, on top of each other, some louder than others, some barely discernible, in no way sounding like the Gray she knew.

Her eyes filled with tears. Her lips trembled.

"Please tell me you want us, too," he said, meeting her gaze then. "Tell me I'm not wrong in feeling like that's what you want."

He wasn't wrong.

But that wasn't what she had to tell him.

"I'm pregnant, Gray."

*I'm pregnant, Gray.* He couldn't have heard what he'd just thought. Was hallucinating back to the seemingly millions of times he'd heard her voice in his mind that week, saying those words to him. Rehearsing how he'd respond.

He'd never gotten that far—coming up with his own reaction.

And, as of that morning, hadn't had to.

She wouldn't have lied to him about that. He knew that as well as he knew his own name.

Which might be one of the few things he felt he knew for certain about himself at the moment. That and the fact that he shouldn't have had that third beer.

Granted, three wasn't anywhere near his limit. But was three more than he should have had before attempting his current conversation with Sage.

It had taken the third one to get off his ass and down the beach to actually follow through on the idea. He'd spent the second going over reasons for her unreturned calls.

"Did you hear me?"

Blinking, Gray glanced over at her. "Did you say something?"

She had. He knew she had. Just wasn't yet able to process the actual content.

"I said I'm pregnant."

Right. That. Except... He shook his head. "You aren't," he reminded softly. "Remember, this morning..."

It wasn't that he thought she was confused. It was that he was. He got that. Just couldn't find... He shook his head...

"I had some...bleeding...it stopped. This morning, actually. Before I even talked to you. I just didn't know it. All day, it hasn't started again. So I took a test."

She took a test.

*Oh!*

Oh, God. She took a test.

"You're pregnant." He stood, as though he could intimidate the words away. They were a threat to everything he'd come there to say. To do. To accomplish.

"It looks that way, yes," she said. "Both lines turned very solidly pink."

Pink. Both of them.

He hadn't known there were two lines.

"You're pregnant."

Sage stood, too, reaching out a hand toward him, but let it drop. "I know it's a shock."

"No! No, it's fine," he said, knowing that it wasn't fine at all. Knowing that she knew that, too.

"You're pregnant," he said one more time. Just couldn't seem to wrap his three-beer-addled mind around the implications behind the sentence.

"Yeah," she said then, wrapping her arms around herself.

Holding her child. Not reaching out to him.

"Okay, well, good deal," he said. Then turned, trotted down her steps and strode off up the beach. As quickly as his flip-flops in the sand would take him.

## Chapter Twenty-Six

Sage cried some Saturday night. More than she'd cried in years. For herself, a little. For Gray, and for the child who maybe wouldn't see the great man their father was, a whole lot more.

With tears trickling slowly, steadily down her face, she stayed out on the porch, waiting for him to come back. He'd walked the opposite direction of Scott's house when he'd taken his leave. Knew he'd have to pass by again to go home to bed.

She wouldn't let herself make judgments or worry about the mammoth changes coming in her own home life. She just sat with her newfound knowledge.

And waited.

Sometime after midnight, when she'd cried all the tears she had and still hadn't seen Gray head back down the beach, she'd figured out that he'd taken the road home.

He hadn't been able to see her.

She got that, too.

He'd been right when he'd said that he wasn't great at expressing himself when it came to emotional issues. But she was beginning to read between his lines a little better than she had in the past.

With the help of a little maturity, and a lot more insight where he was concerned.

The man had spent his entire life solving not only his own problems, but those of his caregivers as well, largely by himself. He'd taken on the burden fully alone.

Made most if not all his important choices on his own.

She couldn't expect him to suddenly change, just because he'd fallen in love with her.

He hadn't said so—that he loved her still. But she knew him well enough to understand that he'd never have come to her porch that night if he wasn't in love with her.

That move, more than any other, ever, spoke to her heart.

And it was that thought that she took to bed with her.

And fell asleep on.

Waking to find Leigh, in her so-sweet pink unicorn pajamas, crawling into bed with her the next morning. "I waked up before you," the little girl pronounced as she pushed herself under the covers and snuggled up, with her head on Sage's chest.

Filling her up in a way Gray had never known.

The thought of him, waking alone, broke her heart as she said, "Yes, and you did the right thing, coming in to get me." And gave her daughter a grateful hug, kissing the top of Leigh's head.

Just as her mother had kissed hers. Countless mornings.

She'd spent her childhood with love all around her, holding her up. Not just her mother, but with a twin. She hadn't even been alone in the womb.

Gray...he'd been loved, but alone...forever.

"What do you want for breakfast?" she asked Leigh, knowing that her day had to go on. Because life did.

That was how it worked.

And when Leigh sat up, scrunching up her forehead, her finger on her chin, she smiled, a real smile, and waited for the answer.

"Pancakes, I think, and then, maybe, chocolate."

"Uh?" Sage sat up. "Do we have chocolate for breakfast?"

"No, but we don't ever sleep in our clothes, either, and you're wearing your yesterday's shirt!"

Sage couldn't help the chuckle that bubbled out of her. "Got me," she said. "But we still aren't having chocolate for breakfast."

Just as she wasn't going to let her own heartbreak shower down on the precious little girl she'd been blessed with.

Or the little one inside her.

She'd made choices, commitments, and had others relying on her—for the rest of her life.

Gray had made no such commitments. And even if he could somehow find a way to be okay as a part-time dad to his own child, he'd need to be that for two, which was asking the impossible of him. Yet, no way would either of them allow Leigh to feel that she wasn't as important to Mr. Buzzing Bee as her little brother or sister would be. Gray would walk away long before he'd do that to her.

He'd already walked away.

She knew. Understood.

But she also knew, as she took Leigh through their morning routine, that she wasn't going to be free from the aches, the longing, the needs, the tears. Probably ever.

She'd provide a happy home for her children. Would undoubtedly know many happy times and even some perfect moments.

But she wasn't going to do what she'd done in the past— she wouldn't cut Gray out of her heart's awareness and reinvent herself. Focusing only on herself and the life she wanted. She would carry him with her. Stay present in her longing for him. Be willing to hurt. To be able to welcome him into their lives in whatever capacity he could be there. Even if that meant a Christmas card every ten years.

Because she loved him that deeply.

And because he deserved to be so loved.

The problem with cotton was that it wrinkled. Gray had the inane thought as he traipsed from his almost new home down closer to the water early Sunday morning. He'd awoken, sometime during the night, and had found himself sitting propped up against the house again.

Remembered the beer he'd consumed too quickly. Purposely allowed grogginess to remain as a buffer between him and his brain, had lain down proper in the sand, uncaring that even in his long-sleeved shirt, it was cold, and went back to sleep. He'd needed unconsciousness, rest, more than comfort.

But he'd awoken just after sunrise, fully conscious. Wholly aware.

And with solid purpose.

Waiting long enough for people to start to rise, one person in particular, he checked his email.

Clicked on the one from his Realtor. It had an attachment.

His accepted offer. The cottage was his.

And the timing was absolutely no mistake.

He felt no joy.

But satisfaction brewed a little deeper inside him.

One step in the plan done.

The plan—it was nothing he'd drawn up that morning. Or researched. He'd awoken with it fully formed.

Hands in his pockets, he made it to Sage's door with his flip-flops filled with sand, and resolution in his soul. Uncaring that his hair had spent the night splayed on the beach. He hadn't shaved or brushed his teeth.

He wasn't there for kissing. Or courting.

Lifting his hand to knock, he stopped when he saw Sage step to the door, staring at him, her hand on the latch.

Calling something to someone behind her, he couldn't make out what, she slid open the door, stepped outside and slid the glass closed.

"What are you doing here?" Her gaze swept him from head to toe. "Are you okay?"

He had no answer for the second question, but the first one fit his purpose just fine. He stared her straight in the eye. "I left here last night because I'd had a few beers and was in no state to discuss…the topic of discussion. I am present at the moment because I have now slept, am fully sober and expect it to be fully understood that I am not walking away from you. I made a promise not to do that again and I will keep that promise."

Probably not the best syntax. Or delivery. He'd gotten it out there. The rest would have to do.

Eyes wide, Sage didn't just stare at him. She studied him. He could see her pupils moving, taking in his face, down to his chest, and back up again. "Where did you sleep?"

"On the beach. At the cottage at the end of the road." His cottage. "I got an email. My offer was accepted."

She didn't burst into smiles. Or show any pleasure at the revelation. She was frowning. Shaking her head. "You don't have to do this, Gray. Seriously. I won't think you're walking away because I know that I have a special place in your heart, and you can't leave that behind. You be you, and I'll be me, and we'll always be us."

Yes. That. Exactly. He liked it. "You're better at the words," he acknowledged with a nod.

"I'll be fine here," she continued. "I have Scott, and Ocean Breeze, a great job and…exactly what I asked for—children to raise."

Her chin trembled, giving her away. She had it all. Every bit of it. Except, *we'll always be us*.

Trouble was, the two intelligent, professionally successful people they were, who'd created the lives they'd always wanted, had no idea how to be an *us*.

He knew one thing, though. "I'm going through with the sale. I want the cottage. I made a cash offer. It's a lot, but not compared to what I made on the sale of my house." She was privy to his current finances down to the dime.

Her frown was back. "Don't do it for me."

"I'm doing it for me," he told her. Solid on that one. "And for us."

She was pregnant.

He wasn't yet allowing his mind to wander in that direction. Had been jumping away from it every time it hit. But he was aware.

Sage was pregnant and the child was his.

"We need to talk," he said. As though they'd been communicating in some other fashion for the past few minutes.

She nodded. "Not with Leigh…" She broke off. "As soon as her show is over, she'll be out here…"

Right. Made sense. Leigh.

A big sister.

The *whoosh* that hit him left him a bit lightheaded for a second.

Siblings.

Shoving the thought away, he was hit with another. "Have you told anyone else?"

"Of course not."

"Can you hold off, with Scott in particular, until we have a chance to talk?"

"We, as in you and Scott talk? Or you and me talk?"

He looked at her. "Really?"

With a nod, and a hint of an eye roll, she said, "Yes, I'll hold off. I was planning to shop today. Usually take Leigh with me, but with as busy a day as she had yesterday, I could ask Scott or Iris to watch her. We could meet somewhere…"

The where…had to be someplace unromantic. With reminders all around of their changed status. No longer lovers. Or friends. But parents.

He shook his head. Couldn't grasp it. Wondered at a fate that would push them into such a situation. Even as he knew that he and Sage had made a choice a couple of weeks ago, a split-second decision to act rather than think…

"Let's meet at my cottage," he told her. "Text me with a time. I'll get showered and contact the Realtor for a key. You can give me pointers on renovation ideas. Tell your brother whatever you like," he added and turned to head down the steps.

He'd had no business asking for her silence. She might need Scott's shoulder to lean on as she and Gray traversed turbulent, murky waters.

Both feet on the sand, he stopped, turned slowly back. Sage stood there, watching him, and he couldn't figure out her expression at all.

She wasn't mad. Or crying. She was…there. With him.

"I'm not walking away, Sage." It was the only guarantee he could give her.

Her smile was odd, too. Trembly. But it was there.

With a nod, he strode up the beach.

He had a purpose.

# *Chapter Twenty-Seven*

Sage knew her twin was onto her the second she asked him to keep Leigh for her Sunday morning. She didn't say why. He didn't ask. The pause on the line was enough.

Also odd was when he asked where she needed him and when. As though only her schedule mattered. Accommodating her alone, not the both of them as was their way.

Something generally done only in emergencies.

And still, she didn't say where she was going, or why.

Which would be more of a "tell" to him.

She was pregnant. Was going to be a mother for a second time. And was going to be growing the child, inside her. Would feel her baby move there. Would breastfeed.

Sprinkles of delight burst through her.

And life quickly bottled them.

The oddest part, concerning her brother, was that he didn't ask if she was okay.

That one she didn't get.

But didn't push, either.

She didn't have an answer to give if he'd asked. She had no idea how she was. Except a mass of emotional confusion. A living, walking dichotomy.

There was so much to do. Thanksgiving on the beach was an easy thing, but Christmas! The lights. Shopping. Gray's cottage down the road.

Gray's *we need to talk* rang in her ears with every step she took. The phrase generally didn't bode well in relationship-world. But he was right. They did need to have a serious discussion as soon as possible.

She had Leigh to consider. What to tell the little girl. When to tell her.

After she'd been to the doctor, for sure. Had a blood test that would definitively tell her that she was carrying Gray's child...

Which, with the timing of everything, would happen mid-December. Before Christmas. A family holiday.

As the thought struck, she texted Gray with the time to meet.

An hour after she dropped Leigh off at Scott's.

No point in putting either of them through what was inevitably going to be a difficult conversation until she knew conclusively that there was a topic for the talk.

Dressed in black jeggings, a white button-down, form-fitting shirt and tennis shoes, Sage went to a twenty-four-hour clinic, got pricked, waited on the results and parked her car behind her own cottage. From there she walked the road to Gray's new cottage.

Just the thought, Gray's home...a small thrill went through her as she looked at the old place. She'd seen it a hundred times or more. It had just been dilapidated and sorry-looking.

That Sunday morning, it seemed to glow with possibility.

No matter what the outcome of the upcoming communication, Gray had found something powerful enough on Ocean Breeze to want to settle there.

Even before she'd dropped her bombshell.

He was waiting for her inside. Opened the door to her knock dressed in another pair of his cotton pants—dark ones, with a dark striped shirt with the tails hanging out. He still

hadn't shaved. His hair was mussed and kind of frizzy on
the ends like it got right after he dried it.

None of which mattered.

"I just came from the clinic," she said, as though he'd know
which one. The one didn't matter. She handed him the results.

"You are."

"Yes."

That signature nod of his...felt good. In its normalness.
Lord knew absolutely nothing else about the moment had a
hint of ordinary to it.

Years before, she used to dream about the moment when
she'd tell Gray she was expecting their first child.

Never, in any scenario, had she been having her second
child at the time. Or not been married to him.

Part of her swelled with excitement as reality set in. But
a smaller part. More, she was ravaged for him. And anx-
ious about her own future, too. She'd be fine. She knew that.
Just...getting from her current moment to the fine part. There
was so much to get through.

Telling her brother. Leigh. Carrying a baby. Keeping it
healthy. Having one.

But toughest of all was right there in front of her. Ready
to start.

She saw Gray's look of determination as she stepped into
the dusty and otherwise clean front room. Noticed the drywall peeling off walls. A hole in the ceiling with an exposed
beam.

Saw him standing there, in his new, falling-down home,
walked up to him, threw her arms around his neck and held
on.

A hug was the last thing Gray had expected. The tight
clutching, as Sage held their bodies together, was more than

he was prepared to overcome. Wrapping his arms around her, he held her with as much force. As though, through the strength of their arms, they could suffocate all the inconsistencies between them, kill all of the problems and just be together again.

As they'd been when they were younger. He started to get hard.

Until he became aware of her stomach pressing against his and pulled slowly, reluctantly, away.

She started to chatter then. Walking around his place, noting obviously needed repairs. Making suggestions. As though she thought he'd meant that they really would talk about revisions to his place when he'd suggested they talk about renovation ideas.

While Gray wanted to hear everything she had to offer on the matter, his mind was not at all focused on the work he had ahead of him. That he could handle just fine.

And sleep like a baby at night.

Baby.

That was the stumbling block.

Or dark, unending pit, from which he'd never escape.

The thought struck. And he gave it a mental eye roll. Maybe ten years ago, it had felt that way. Thank God he'd grown up some since then.

Funny, though, in a non-humorous way, how thoughts from the past, both good and bad, kept tripping him up.

Forcing him to sort through them.

Separate the true from the not so much.

And on to what was...

Sage was turning a circle in the living space, stopping in front of a half wall opening up to another large area off the kitchen. An eating nook, the Realtor had said.

"You could open up this wall—take it out—and have this be an e-shaped great room..."

"I intend to be in the baby's life, Sage." He couldn't prevaricate any longer. The truth was building up inside him, needing escape.

To be dealt with. Accepted.

"I can't promise that I'll want to do everything that's required of me, when it's required, but I *can* guarantee that I will do so. I will be where I need to be, when I need to be." He always had been. Another long-ago truth. The resentment had been a part of him, but so had the faithfulness. He'd never turned his back on his mother or grandmother. Never, ever seriously considered doing so.

He'd actually strongly resisted Child Services' attempts to give him, in their words, a better home.

"For better or worse, this kid has me for a father. We can't change that." Words he'd been rehearsing all morning. And on a roll, he continued. "What we can do is minimize the damage."

He was pretty sure Sage was blinking tears from her eyes as she turned to face him. He didn't let his gaze linger long enough to verify. "How do we do that?" Her question sounded like Sage. Calm, capable. Willing.

Right at the part where he faltered. "That's the part I don't know yet," he told her. "I'm going to be close...we know that. It's a given. Done deal."

"You still have time to back out."

"Would you quit saying that?" The sternness in his tone came as a surprise to him. But was legitimate. "I want this place. The first night I wandered down here...it was the first time in my entire life I felt like a place was home..."

He glanced over at her. Saw her mouth drop open.

Shrugged off his passion for a broken-down building, and

said, "We have real things to work out." So many of them, he couldn't seem to corral them. They just kept jumbling around in his head. Like kids jumping on a trampoline.

"Leigh should have a trampoline," he said then. Finding something that felt sure. "She loves to tumble, and the sand's not the safest place for that. They have them now with sides that go up so little kids don't bounce off them. I saw one at one of the places I looked at…"

He stopped. Stared at her staring at him. "Sorry. I'm new at this. And not even slightly good at it, apparently."

"No!" Sage gave him that trembly smile again. He started to wonder if it was a good thing. "No, you're doing fine," she said, nodding.

"I'm avoiding," he told her.

"I know."

He shrugged. She nodded again. Then took a sudden step forward, as though attached to some apparatus springing her into action. "But that's okay, Gray. I'm the one person everyone would have tagged for being over the moon with this news, and I'm struggling to wrap my mind around it all. The implications…what it will mean…everything that's going to change…it's overwhelming. Can I ask you to do one thing, for right now?"

He nodded. It wasn't like he had any choice. There were hundreds to do. "Can you please just let us take a few days to process? If something occurs to you, you text me. If something comes up for me, I text you. Maybe that's how we start to work through it all."

He liked that. A lot. A step back. Managing the fallout.

"That would be…yes, I can do that," he said. Then met her gaze. "Thank you."

She smiled.

And he said, "Now I have one thing to ask of you." One thing that was bothering the hell out of him.

"Sure, what?"

"Don't ever give me an out on my responsibility again. Not ever. I'm not that guy, Sage. I would have thought you, of all people, would know that. It was my somewhat twisted attempt to *be* responsible that led me to call off our wedding ten years ago. I'm not irresponsible. I just know squat about raising kids. I foam at the mouth, so to speak, at the thought of being responsible for one, because of that lack. And I tend to resent those I'm responsible for, on occasion."

"Did you ever think that maybe you resented your grand-mother's illness? Not her?"

The words stopped him cold. Semantics. And yet...

Something to think about. Sometime. Right then, "Okay, here's my first text. I'm in. Financially is a given. But I'm in for all of it. I need to know what's going on. Need to be privy to every choice, even if I don't have a say in it. And I need to know that if I say something stupid, or that won't work, you do what you do. Don't hold back."

Her eyes seemed to have gained a sparkle. "What do I do?"

"Be you. Kindly, calmly point out where I'm mistaken."

"And my first text back is, sounds good."

She smiled. He smiled.

And Gray looked around his new home. Figuring it for a very good choice.

Sage wouldn't let happiness bloom. Was afraid she'd lose sight of Gray's less overt expression of his needs. But damn, life suddenly felt...better.

With a world of possibilities looming that she'd given up on.

Their lives wouldn't be traditional. She wasn't getting married or raising a family with her husband.

But Gray was back. He was there to stay. He loved her—though he hadn't actually come out and said so in so many words—and he knew he loved her. He also knew she loved him. Looking at him, that was a given. And they were going to parent their child together. There were shadow sides, too. Like having to ruin a perfect moment with reality.

"Text number two," she said softly, as Gray stood there, looking around his space as though ready to start in on the renovations part of the meeting. "Leigh."

His eyebrows rose and his gaze settled on her intently. "Something's wrong with her?"

"No. She's four, Gray. And sensitive. We need to be careful, as we take on this baby somewhat together, that she doesn't feel…left out."

His head reared back as his eyes opened wide. "You mean me, right?"

She nodded.

"You're mother to both, I'm father to one. Do for the one but not for…" He was frowning. Shook his head. And as her heart was sinking, knowing that he was overwhelmed with being a father at all, he added, "See, this is what I mean. Things I don't know to think about. But I'd like to think that I'd have just gotten this one right without needing to talk about it. I'm already there for her. Right? We already established that one. So…" He glanced at her, looking as though an idea had just hit. "Do we tell her together? Let her know that I'm going to be in her life now, too?"

She hadn't gotten that far. Felt her heart flood with warmth. "I think she'd like that. And it would maybe make finding out that she is going to be sharing me with another baby a little easier to take. Knowing she gets you in the bargain."

"We could bring her down here. Tell her I bought the place, and tell her about the baby here, too. You know, outside the space that just belonged to the two of you. Let her be a part of things. I'm assuming…" His eyes lightened as his gave her a sheepish grin. "Who am I kidding, I'm only just now coming up with this, but I'll need to have kid things here, too, right? So that means her things as well as the baby's. For when you're working late and I'm on duty. That kind of thing."

He stopped talking. Seemed a bit like he was lost. But he wasn't overtly sweating. Or pacing. Or suggesting the meeting was over. He stood there. Nodding that nod of his.

"I think that's important, yes," she said, as her mind opened up wider. They were going to make it work. This new, more mature Gray, and the less selfish, more aware, more mature her.

"And maybe the new child can call me Mr. Buzzing Bee," he continued. "I really like that name. In case you couldn't tell."

Because he'd named his new clinics after it.

And there was her reminder. It was all working out. Just not as she used to dream she'd be raising a family. He wasn't ready to be Daddy yet. Might not ever be ready.

But if Mr. Buzzing Bee was who he needed to be, that was exactly who Sage would welcome into their family.

And be forever thankful that he was there.

# *Chapter Twenty-Eight*

As Gray had locked up his new cottage and walked back down the beach with Sage—keeping a body's worth of distance between them—Sage gave Gray another reprieve. She'd figured they should wait to tell anyone, including her twin, about the baby for another couple of weeks, at least. After Thanksgiving.

She was only a couple of weeks along. Anything could happen. She hadn't even seen her doctor yet. And they'd wait even longer before telling Leigh. At least until the baby started to show. Nine months would be far too long for a four-year-old to be patient. And…the first trimester was most at risk for miscarriage.

*Miscarriage.* The word offered the possibility of not having to be a father.

And didn't seem like a win to Gray.

Because he knew what it would do to Sage?

He wanted to think so. But as Sunday rolled into Monday and then further into the following week, as he and Sage texted random thoughts and questions to each other, Gray was finding himself—not suffocating.

Of course, he was spending a good bit of his time with contractors, and an architect, working on buildouts for his clinics, and for the cottage as well. He wanted everything in place for work on his new home to begin as soon as the sale went through title, which could be by the end of the week.

Some of the texts pertained to cottage questions. Where Sage had three good-size bedrooms, he only had two. She'd have hers, and a room for each of the kids—though she'd be giving up her home office. She also had a large, windowed alcove off the kitchen, outside the laundry room, that would work just fine for her desk and files. She'd put in a pocket door, for privacy.

But him, with only two rooms...he decided to have another added, and two closets put in. One for each child's things for those random occasions they had to spend the night. And there'd be beds, for when they had to take naps.

But not a crib. Sage had assured him that the baby could sleep in something called a Pack 'n Play at Gray's house.

And they'd texted about Christmas lights for the beach. The decorations would be going up before they shared their news with everyone. She'd offered to help him pick out what he needed. Had sent him a list from an online store. He'd clicked and purchased all of it.

She'd scheduled her first doctor's appointment. He'd be attending, though not in the room for the initial examination. His choice. She'd seemed relieved with it.

He'd be there for the birth, though.

One night his text had asked if she was scared. She was a little. So many unknowns. So much could go wrong.

He'd told her not to borrow trouble. Something his grandmother used to say to him.

He'd found that he handled the situation much better if he just thought in terms of Sage. She was pregnant. She'd be going through a lot of changes, physically as well as emotionally, over the next months. His job was just to support.

The after-the-baby-came part...a thought would trickle

in occasionally. He'd stopped pushing them away. But didn't search for answers, either.

Sage didn't pressure him to. At all. To the point that on Thursday, one week before Thanksgiving, when they were out on the beach, with Leigh playing with Morgan—who was in Gray's care as Scott had a business-related evening out—Gray said, "Either you've changed a lot, or you're holding back on me."

He didn't like the idea that, with all they were going through, sharing, she wasn't being fully open. "It's not going to work if either of us aren't honest," he told her. Something he'd already learned the hard way.

"I'm not holding back, Gray," she told him. "And I don't feel like I've changed, either, other than, well, my whole life is changing, from the inside out, if you know what I mean."

He did. And grinned. But couldn't let it go. "In the past, you used to have all these scenarios of us as parents, as a family. You built such pretty pictures when you talked about them. You don't do that anymore."

"You thought my scenarios were pretty?"

"Of course I did. Who wouldn't want the happy family cushioned in love who took on all their struggles and challenges together?"

Her head turned toward him, sharply. "You."

He deserved that, he guessed. Shook his head. "I wanted it, Sage. I just knew that if I walked into that with you, I'd be setting you up for failure. But that's no reason for you to quit dreaming your dreams…"

Her sigh hit him deep. Her gaze was turned toward her daughter as Leigh threw out a crooked pitch. Then the little girl ran after the ball, along with Morgan, as it headed toward the water. "Stop!" he called, at the top of his lungs, with no hint of compromise included.

The child stopped immediately. Glanced down. Saw her toes just touching wet sand. As a wave came up and stole her ball.

Morgan dove into the wave, swimming with it, retrieved the ball and swam back.

And Gray turned to see Sage, with tears on her cheeks, looking up at him.

"What?" he asked. He'd yelled too harshly, he knew, but…

"You," she told him. "I just love you so much."

He didn't get it. He screamed at her kid when she was right there. And loving him made her cry. Was she some kind of masochist?

Her gaze turned back to Leigh, who'd moved farther up the beach, toward Scott's cottage, to play ball. And then she looked at him, eyes open wide and shining with emotion.

"You had a tough childhood in many ways, Gray. And it taught you young to go it alone. In your heart. Losing your mom so young. And then watching your grandmother go, with no way to stop it…"

He stiffened beside her. Hands in his pants. He'd asked her to open up. He had to listen. He didn't have to like it.

And couldn't really argue her words, either. Just wished she'd get to the damned point.

"You learned as much about loss as you did about loving," she said. "The two going hand in hand, so to speak. Kind of like…having your things sold."

He'd forgotten he'd told her about that. Being happy to get a new toy. Knowing that it would be sold when it had to be. And he needed her to get to the point. Faster. Didn't much feel like failing so early in their little lifetime project.

"I didn't quit dreaming my dreams, Gray," she said softly. "I just opened my eyes to let them become real."

He frowned. "I don't get it." Not a usual thing with her.

He didn't like it. Dug his toes over the sides of his flip-flops to feel the sand.

"I was so busy building our family, playing my part of mother, that I failed to be a fiancée. And a wife. I didn't think about you, Gray. And your needs. And you, having grown up used to the women in your life being unable to see, or if they saw, attend to your needs, you had to take responsibility for yourself. Feeling as though you didn't have a place in my dreams, you erased yourself from the picture so there'd be room for the guy who did."

Okay. Maybe not so flowery or…whatever…but…there was some truth there.

"There is no other guy, Gray. I've had ten years to find him, and I'll admit to trying. Hard. It didn't work. Because you were the man of my dreams. Just you. And the problem was, I didn't look to know that you needed me to see you."

Oh. Okay. Yeah. Wow. He stared at the ocean. And then the dog and child just yards away from them. Still running. Emitting occasional screams and barks.

And his gut settled.

Dogs and children. They were who and what they were.

And accepted what they were given.

As he had.

"So now…that you…as you say, see me?"

"You're the man of my dreams."

He turned slowly to look at her. Read the truth in her eyes. Felt no surprise. His heart leaped. Soared. And then slid into land.

"So what, you want to get married? Is that what you're telling me?" He tensed at the words. But didn't entirely hate the idea. In some ways, it made sense.

"No." She didn't blink. Didn't hesitate. "That's just it. I want to be with you in whatever capacity you can thrive, being with me. And if that's a cottage down the beach, and you disciplining our child to keep her safe, while we stand together after work exercising my twin brother's dog, then I've got my dream come true."

Gray's throat got tight. So much he couldn't swallow. He had to blink at the prick behind his eyes. As he wondered, if he'd ever dared to dream bigger than a business and a house on a cliff, would his dream be coming true, too?

He knew the answer.

Just wasn't sure how to access the dream.

Sage waited another month before making her doctor's appointment. Her doctor's office had offered the option, as long as she was careful about her diet. And she'd needed the time. Knew that Gray did.

And, in a practical sense, she'd wanted to be able to do the first ultrasound and exam in the same office visit.

For all that was changing in their lives, and the passion that always seemed to be sizzling under the surface between her and Gray, the month had been surprisingly…calm. With all of his buildouts going on, both in the clinics and on the beach, Gray was occupied constantly. And seemingly never alone.

And any off time had been surrounded by neighbors in holiday mode. From the Thanksgiving feast set up on a long table and served buffet style around a bonfire on the beach, to the weekend of light hanging and attaching as a pathway in the sand along the beach, too. Everyone helped everyone, wore smiles and had a few drinks. Everyone but Sage, on the drink part, that was.

No one seemed to realize she'd been without her customary glass of wine.

One night, when Leigh had been with Scott and Iris, Sage

had walked the entire two-mile strip of beach along the pathway of lights, taking in the individual decorations on every single cottage—even the ones that were still deserted—pretending that she was perfectly content alone with her unborn baby. But, in truth, she'd hoped to run into Gray.

It hadn't happened.

The two of them had had a moment, in the courthouse, after the judge had granted her request to detach Gray's income account from the assets frozen in the GB Animal Clinics case. They'd exited the small courtroom into an empty hallway, and he'd grabbed her up and kissed her.

Fully. On the lips.

And in spite of being fully in her professional persona, at work, she'd engaged full throttle. They'd both jumped back as soon as their tongues touched. And neither of them had mentioned the episode since.

They'd both appeared at all the big gatherings with neighbors. Just no more alone time.

She and Leigh had put up their tree without him.

But she'd hung a stocking for him, along with Scott's. She had one for Iris, too, if the photographer chose to join them.

Leigh had asked Gray to come look at her tree. He'd told her he would but hadn't gotten there yet.

Nor had he and Sage entertained in-person private conversations. She'd initially instituted the text message communication plan to get them through the first few days of shock. And there they were, a month later, continuing to hide behind phones.

Thing was, it was working. She was hearing more of Gray's thoughts than she'd have heard in person, at least based on past experience, and was falling more in love with him every day. Something she hadn't thought possible.

If only they could do the doctor visit by text. She'd made

the appointment to take place during her lunch hour, while Leigh was fully occupied in her preschool class at the day care. And Gray was meeting her there. He wanted to be present for the ultrasound. She'd made it very clear he needn't be, but being a doctor, he knew the technology. Had run countless ultrasounds during his career, and when he'd reminded her of that fact, she'd wanted him there. For his sake. Not hers.

They weren't romantic partners. Or even sexually active. And he was going to be standing over her stomach, bared to the top of her hair down there. To manage her stress, she'd insisted that he not be brought back to the room until she was already on the table and ready to go. Thankfully, her doctor was a gem, and the ultrasound technician about as understanding as they came.

Both knew that Gray was the child's father. And that they weren't married. She'd already had her exam and she and Gray would be meeting with the doctor after the completion of the ultrasound.

She'd chosen her clothes accordingly. Leggings—they had an elastic waistband. And a formfitting tunic-type short dress that she could roll up to her breasts. And not care if the bottom of it got a little gel on it.

He'd worn dress pants and had tucked in his button-down shirt. Could be the chosen clothes were for a business meeting that morning. Or might have been for the doctor visit. Didn't much matter to her heart. It lit up the second she saw him come through the door. His longish hair falling around his ears, and those brown eyes locked on hers.

They were about to meet their baby for the first time.

What bit of it would be developed so early in gestation.

She already knew the doctor had heard a heartbeat. Gray didn't.

The technician had already been in the process of spreading the gel on Sage's stomach when Gray walked in. She barely noticed the cold. But was suddenly nervous.

Extremely so.

Would Gray freak out on her? He was the scientist. Seeing the proof of life on the screen would make everything real to him.

And…she was living a dream she'd had so many times. Getting ready for the first glimpse of her baby with the man she loved.

"Okay, ready?"

Sage nodded as the technician looked her way. Took a deep breath. And felt Gray take hold of her hand. She didn't glance away from the screen they'd been told to watch.

But she started to breathe again.

And listened as Gray and the technician threw around some technical terms, talked about fetal fluid balance and aquaporins. Both seemed pleased with what they were seeing.

"There," Gray said first, his tone still sounding doctor-like. Professional. "Right there." He pointed to the peanut-looking shape in the center of the screen, while the technician pushed buttons to record images and continued to move the radar device on Sage's stomach.

When the tattooing sound first started, she'd thought it was some kind of digestive gurgle inside her. Was embarrassed. Until she recognized the evenness of the sound. It was way more rapid than she'd expected before arriving at the office that morning.

"We have a heartbeat!" the technician's voice announced with obvious pleasure.

As enthralled as Sage was, she'd already heard the sound, though at a slightly different pitch, through her doctor's stethoscope.

What she was most of aware in those first seconds of steady beat was Gray's total and complete silence.

Afraid, suddenly, dreading what might be happening to him, preparing for him to walk out on her, she kept a smile on her face and glanced up at him.

The look of utter awe on his face made her heart skip a beat.

But the moisture around the rims of his eyes…that right there…most definitely a dream come true.

She'd seriously imagined, back in the day, that he'd cry when he heard their baby's heartbeat.

And knew, without a doubt, that, as odd a family as they were, they were meant to be.

## *Chapter Twenty-Nine*

Gray was like a man on fire the rest of that day. He went from appointment to appointment, made decisions with precise, on-the-spot thought, and moved on. He knew his stuff.

And somewhere midafternoon, he stopped everything to send a text.

The earrings themselves didn't matter to me any more than the surfboard did. I like them both, by the way. What mattered to me was that they meant something to you. The giving of them, and having the gift valued, meant a great deal.

There was no marriage proposal in the offing.

But a father taught his children by living authentically. It was something he'd heard on television somewhere along the way. That had just popped into his head out of nowhere.

A lot of things were doing that recently.

Like the fact that he hadn't been jumping for joy with relief when Sage had first told him she wasn't pregnant.

If anything…there'd been a tinge of disappointment. He hadn't dwelled on it at the time. But looking back…

More and more, he was growing confident in his ability to fulfill his responsibilities to Sage and the kids.

The kids.

Like he really was some family man.

Try as he might, he still couldn't see himself that way. And couldn't really even say why. He didn't doubt his ability to learn how to be a good father. Or his ability to stick around.

He'd even reached the point where he was certain that he had what it took to be able to hide his resentment of any calls on his time or energy.

And he wasn't suffocating.

On anything.

Except, maybe, an overcharged, overloaded unrequited need for sexual release.

With Sage.

And yet, thinking about suggesting that they just bite the bullet and get married stopped him every time. He still didn't feel like that guy.

He felt more and more like one of Leigh's people, though. If Scott was missing his niece's company as she spent as much or more of the group beach time with Gray now, instead of with Scott, the man didn't say.

Nor did he ask any questions.

About Leigh or Sage.

Or anything that might or might not be going on between the two of them.

Gray knew Scott suspected something. The man was sharp. Was used to reading people. Juries filled with them.

Scott would know soon enough. He and Sage had said all along that after the doctor visit, they'd tell her brother. And Iris. And a few others, as selectively decided by the two of them.

She was waiting until after the first trimester to tell her partners.

And whenever she started to show, Leigh would be clued in.

Gray had been hoping he'd be moved into his place before

Scott found out that he'd impregnated the man's twin sister and wasn't marrying her. Facing his friend, who'd surely see Gray's lack as a second fatal blow to his sister, he wasn't nearly as confident as Sage was that Scott would be fine with it as long as she was. He'd tried to hope for that, too.

Even sent up a little note, asking for it for Christmas.

He'd also learned, probably in the womb, not to expect to get what he hoped for.

But was pleasantly let off the hook for another night when Sage texted late afternoon, the day of her doctor's appointment, to say that telling Scott that night was out. Her brother the prosecutor was going to be out of town for a couple of days, consulting on a case in another county.

He got the same text from Scott, asking him to look after Morgan, right after Sage's message came through.

Gray texted back a thumbs-up, to each, immediately.

Didn't say much about him that his mood lifted noticeably at the reprieve.

He also hadn't worked his mind around how he'd be a father to his own child, treat Leigh equally, but be less than her uncle Scott to her. Because damn straight, Scott wasn't going to give up his father-figure role in the little girl's life for Gray.

Who wasn't marrying Scott's twin sister.

He did get one detail figured out though. The three bedrooms and one of the two bathrooms in his cottage were complete. As were parts of the kitchen and great room. Flooring still had to be laid. Drywall put up in the great room. Stove installed. Dishwasher and garbage disposal put in and hooked up. Some electric to finish up.

But the bedrooms and the one bathroom were done.

He could move in before Scott returned. Hook up a small

refrigerator and a coffee maker in the bathroom. Be no different than living in a hotel room.

He texted Sage when he got home. Letting her know his plan. Had his suitcases thrown together and his stuff out of Scott's place before her car was parked in her space four cottages down. Driving by her place, he smiled. He was on his way home.

And he'd be passing Sage's house every single time he came home. They'd be that close.

He didn't check himself, but felt as though he'd smiled all the way through getting his stuff in the cottage. And toiletries set in the bathroom. It was all just stuff he'd take on an extended vacation. There were many boxes of things to bring in when the time was right.

But for the moment, he was a man who owned a thing he cared about.

And one with visitors, too, he realized as he heard a knock on the front door.

Figuring one of the residents of Ocean Breeze for giving him some kind of housewarming, he'd just gotten to the part where no one but Sage knew he'd just decided to start sleeping there yet, as he pulled open the door.

His gaze locked with Sage's first. Seeing happiness glowing there, he grinned down at her sidekick. To see the little girl holding a tiny puppy.

"We 'cided that you could keep him," Leigh said. "Him's name's Puppy."

Eyes wide, but still, surprisingly, smiling, he glanced up at Sage, who said, "I'm babysitting him for a colleague. Just overnight. And after I told Leigh that you were going to be sleeping in your cottage instead of Uncle Scott's, she thought you needed the company." She kind of grimaced, looking like there was more to the story.

"He pooped on my shoe," Leigh announced, pushing past them to walk around the cottage, still carrying the three-to-four-pound poodle in her arms.

"And I figured, with you…" Sage started in again.

And he interrupted with, "Not having flooring in yet…"

"No, with you moving in, we'd keep Morgan. She was…a little territorial of Leigh…and kept the poor thing cornered in the living room, yapping anytime Puppy tried to move."

Gray frowned. "How long have you been home?" He'd driven by less than an hour before.

"Fifteen minutes," she told him, with another grimace. And a smile. "Seriously, I can keep him. I've already got the laundry room gated off for him."

Gray shrugged. "I don't mind keeping him," he told her. Maybe, at some point, he'd even get a dog of his own. The thought had occurred enough times over the past month that he figured it would happen at some point.

"You don't got a bed!" Leigh called from one of the bedrooms. Gray figured she'd already been in all three. One thing was for certain, from the first time the four-year-old had been inside his cottage, she'd made herself at home there.

And had paid careful attention to his rules, too. No getting near any wires of any kind, for any reason, or close to walls without paper over top of them.

"And you don't got a kissmas tree, either."

Sage looked at him. "You didn't get a mattress out of storage?"

Still in the dress pants he'd worn all day, he shrugged again. Looked first to Leigh, and said, "I still have time to get one. Christmas isn't for another almost two weeks." He'd already opted out of decorating inside the house. But no way he was going to disappoint that little girl.

Deciding he'd pick up some pre-decorated and lighted thing, he turned to Sage.

"I didn't actually decide to stay here until the last minute. And it's not like I haven't slept down here without a bed before."

Both times in the sand. Not on hard floors.

"I've got a blow-up mattress," Sage said then. "I'll run and get it." Looking toward Leigh, she asked, "You okay with her for a couple of minutes?"

The question had come so naturally but stopped them both. Her probably for different reasons than him. "You don't trust me with her?"

"Of course I do. Completely."

"Then you think I might not want to be entrusted with her?"

"No. I just…"

Tilting his head, brow risen, he stared her down. She was the one who'd said if he took on the one, he had to take on the other. Something he'd have figured out on his own, anyway. Just made sense in terms of Leigh's adjustment. And Lord knew he was not going to be responsible for ruining that little girl's childhood.

"You're right," Sage said then. "Though not like you're thinking. I've been doing it alone a long time," she told him. "It's just going to take some time to realize that…I don't have to. All the time."

Her words struck right at the core of him. *Doing it alone a long time. I don't have to.* Almost as though she'd been speaking for him. Trying to get him to see. But she hadn't been. The stark look on her face was proof to him of that.

Gray was still thinking about that look on Sage's face when Leigh came into the great room a minute or so after Sage left. "Why you just standing here?"

He came up blank. "I was deciding what to do next," he shot from the hip. Leigh, with the dog in her arms, seemed satisfied.

"Where's Mommy?"

"She went to get a blow-up mattress for me."

At that, Leigh looked up at him. "You can't jump on it," she said solemnly. "Not ever."

Figuring her for having learned that one out the hard way, wanting to hear the story, he kept his expression as straight-faced as hers and said, "I won't. Thanks for the warning."

She nodded with an air of importance. And then stepped closer. "Are you Mommy's boyfriend?"

Oh, God. Sage. He needed Sage. This wasn't his call. "Why do you ask that?" he prevaricated. As "wait for Mommy" occurred to him too late.

"Jeremiah said that when mommies spend time with grown-ups who aren't their brothers, it means boyfriend."

Ahh. Enlightenment settled his panic a tad. Not a lot, but enough to free up a thought or two. "What else did he tell you?"

"Nothing. But are you?" He wasn't. Not a boyfriend. But they were becoming a family, the three of them. To be four in another seven and a half months give or take. He couldn't start that out on a lie.

Hunching down, he faced the little girl, glanced at the puppy that had fallen asleep in her arms, and then back up at her. "Would you be mad if I was?"

"Uh-uh." She looked him straight in the eye, those big blues of hers wide beneath that swath of blond curly hair. "'Cept I'd have to make you a Christmas present, too, like Mommy, and I don't got forever left to do it, you know." That little brow furrowed and the child continued, "But I color good so it should be fine."

"You sure?"

"Yes, I'm sure. You wanna know why?"

A question he could answer with no doubt. "Yes, I do."

"'Cause then I don't have to worry 'bout being alone?"

Danger. Danger. Life sure turned on a dime. "Why would you worry about being alone? You've got your mommy."

"Sarah told me that when you just have one then if something happens to them, you're all alone and have to go to some services to live. That's what happened to her other friend. That's why a home's called broked, she said. Member? I told you. And I don't want to be alone." For the first time since he'd known her, Leigh's chin started to tremble, then her lips, and tears pooled in those so-sweet eyes.

"Hey," he said, setting the puppy on the floor, to pick her up. Fighting such a huge rush of emotion, he couldn't get any other words past the lump in his throat. He swallowed. Hard. And said, "First, Sarah's not quite right…"

"I told her that and she still won't be my friend no more."

Yeah, they'd get to that. Maybe some other day. When friends were the issue at hand.

"Well, you were right to tell her that. Because she's not right. Even if I wasn't Mommy's boyfriend, you still have your uncle Scott. Which is super special because that's even a whole other house. And I can promise you one thing…"

His face right up close to hers, he looked at her and said, "I'm yours, okay? From now for forever. No more worrying about being alone, okay?"

She nodded.

"You promise?" He asked her a question that usually was rolling off her lips.

"I promise, Mr. Buzzing Bee." Throwing her arms around his neck, she kissed his cheek and then hugged him. Tighter than he'd have figured for four-year-old arms. He closed his eyes to savor the second.

And opened them again to see Sage standing there, staring at him.


Sage couldn't move. Holding the mattress case in one hand, with her other on the front doorknob, she just stood there. Mouth open. Staring.

*I'm yours, okay? From now for forever. No more worrying about being alone, okay?*

She'd been gone no more than seven or eight minutes. Right?

How could the universe have tilted so drastically in less than ten minutes?

Gray's eyes were staring at her. Then not, as Leigh pushed to get down and run after the puppy.

What in the hell had just happened?

Feeling as though she was hallucinating, she was afraid to move. To wake up and find that she'd hit her head and was dreaming.

Gray didn't seem to be suffering the same malady. He walked up to her, holding her gaze the whole time, took the mattress bag out of her hand, dropped it to the floor and held both of her hands. Peering right into her soul.

"It wasn't the resentment," he told her. "Or the responsibility."

She didn't get it. "It wasn't?"

He shook his head. "Truth is, turns out, I'm a coward, Sage. I didn't get it until just now. Leigh told me."

She really had to be losing it. "Leigh told you you're a coward?"

"No, she told me she was afraid of being alone." He spouted some stuff about her daughter taking the few minutes she was gone to ask Gray if he was her boyfriend. Involving Jeremiah.

"She never said a word to me."

He nodded. "It had to do with something Sarah said. The broked home thing. If something happened to you, she'd be all alone and have to go to services."

She was getting further behind. "Okay, since you've managed to make her feel better, good job by the way, I'll deal with her in a second..." She heard her words and stopped. "No, maybe I won't. You already did it just fine," she corrected herself. And continued right on with, "Now, about you being a coward..."

"It hit me smack in the face...when I saw the raw fear on Leigh's usually happy features. Why aren't we getting married? Other than that we'd now own two cottages, that is. But otherwise...why? And yeah, I learned some tough lessons growing up, and clearly wasn't mature enough to get married ten years ago, but why not now?"

She wished she had that answer. Wished every single night.

"Because I'm afraid of loving, Sage. Weird, huh? The idea of being tied to you, and you getting sick, or something happening, and having kids and not being able to be there for them...it scares me to death."

Understanding dawned. Her mouth opened to say the right thing. And she had nothing. There was no cure for life's limitations.

No guarantees of the kind he needed.

"I looked in Leigh's eyes, and I saw something else," he told her.

Pray God it wasn't more unsolvable vagaries of the universe. "What?"

"Trust. You and I both know that there's a chance we could be run off the road and be gone, while she's with a sitter. There aren't ever guarantees. But she trusts that as long as she's loved, she'll be okay. Even if it's just that that love will see her through, give her strength to carry on."

Staring at him, Sage was holding on to a vestige of control with everything she had. And used it to ask, "She knows all that?"

"Well, maybe not in so many words. Not knowingly. But what she showed me is that losing the chance to have that love, the chance to live fully, because of the fear of loss..."

Sage pushed herself up against Gray. Without hesitation. Didn't care that her daughter was present. Kids needed to see their parents hugging sometimes. To be aware of the love not only for them but surrounding them. "You aren't a coward, Gray," she told him, loudly enough for Leigh to hear. If, indeed she was listening.

Which she usually was.

"You had a chance to start up one clinic, or dare to risk more to get back everything you lost," she told him. "You didn't let the fear of a second loss stop you." And then she asked, "Grayson Bartholomew, will you marry me?"

"Who's Grayson Barfew?" Leigh asked, coming up to stand beside the two of them.

"It's Mr. Buzzing Bee's other name," Sage told the little girl, with her arms still wrapped around Gray's waist.

"But, if you want, you can call me Daddy."

With one arm wrapped around Sage's waist, Gray bent down to pick up Leigh in the other, bringing them together in a circle. Seemingly unaware of the tears pouring down Sage's cheeks.

"Yes," he said, looking between the two of them. "I will marry you. Both of you."

"And that means you're my daddy," Leigh said, nodding. "Right."

Reaching over, the little girl wiped her fingers down

Sage's face. "Mommy does this sometimes," she said matter-of-factly. "Sometimes when I give her a present. She calls it happy tears, but that doesn't mean right, does it?" Screwing up her little cheeks and forehead, Leigh giggled.

Then, looking down, squirmed to get away, saying, "Uh-oh, he pooped again!"

If there'd been more than dirt on the ground Sage might have cared more. But she doubted it. "I love you, Grayson Barfew," she said. Seeing the glow of the Christmas lights on the back of his cottage reflected on the side of his face.

"Not nearly as much as I love you, Mrs. Barfew," he said back to her.

Sealing her fate.

And giving her an eternity of dreams to start living.

The two of them sharing life—and a home. Leigh with a mom *and* a dad. The new baby. And stockings hung together.

Her Christmas wish had just come true.

\* \* \* \* \*

close to the edge of the counter. He knew exactly what she was going to do and before he could stop her, she lunged forward in her high chair just enough to grab the cheese off the counter and smash it all over her high chair.

Bruce Wayne, who normally viewed their demonstrations from his red velvet cat tower in the living room, witnessed the mayhem in Gotham and decided the best way to help was to leap onto the counter and lick Bell's hands clean.

Law fell over laughing while Chrysta attempted in vain to shoo Bruce Wayne away from his ill-gotten cheese gains.

Lucas stuck his face in front of the camera, something he never would have imagined himself being so comfortable with one year ago. "Sorry about the chaos, guys. This definitely wasn't what we had planned."

He angled the camera in on Chrysta as she mopped up the baby. Both of them were laughing uncontrollably, and as happy tears streamed down her face, she looked back at Lucas and beamed. "If I've learned anything over the last year, it's that the best things in life can't be planned, my love," she said, affection softening the mirth in her voice. "They happen all on their own."

\* \* \* \* \*

*Be sure to look for Laurie Batzel's
next book in her Crystal Hill series,
available in May 2025!*

## HARLEQUIN
### Reader Service

# Enjoyed your book?

Try the perfect subscription for Romance readers and get more great books like this delivered right to your door.

See why over 10+ million readers have tried Harlequin Reader Service.

**Start with a Free Welcome Collection with free books and a gift—valued over $20.**

Choose any series in print or ebook. See website for details and order today:

# TryReaderService.com/subscriptions